Beneath The Warm Summer Sun

Vaile Feemster

DEDICATION

To My Grandfather

Robert Denzel Feemster

A Man of Southwest Arkansas

A Man of Principles and Faith

Beneath the Warm Summer Sun is not a recount of Island history.

It is a fictional story

FOR MY MOM
WHO PASSED AWAY DURING
THE WRITING OF THIS BOOK
YOU ARE FOREVER IN MY HEART

The cover photo is of Charlie and Ora Lee Mallon, the real Toke and Laura, Circa 1930. Their love and compassion inspired these stories... they are my heroes.

Jake smiled as he waved, a sign to his friend that this was the one. Frantic, yet slow, he began to run in the waist-deep water before taking one last look over his shoulder. Salt water stung his eyes, but he smiled anyway. As he dove forward his arms and legs took over and he began swimming as fast as he could. The wave behind him was no more than a few inches high, a swell rolling across the Gulf's floor, but Jake knew it'd be a nice one.

The wave grew, as did the water surrounding Jake's body, lifting him up and away from the sandy bottom of the Gulf. The wave grew to two-feet... and continued. Jake's smile broadened just as the height of the wave increased...... three, four, now five feet. The wind from the south poked and prodded the Gulf, and on days like this a young-man could glide on his stomach long enough and high enough that it would take his breath away. The wave tapered and thinned as it stretched for the sky, and at six-feet it crested. Jake offered one last smile. Within seconds the wave was in less than a foot of water, curling at the top and slamming Jake to the bottom. Jake pounded into the sand, his body twisting and turning as he struggled to right himself. As Jake popped to the surface the wave had completed its journey and was now retreating. The outgoing surge dragged him sideways before he fell to his knees. He smiled as he looked at Will standing on the beach and Will returned the gesture. "Great wave," Jake yelled to his friend.

Will jogged into the water and helped Jake to his feet. He patted Jake on the back. "Yea," he said, "but I'm gonna get one even bigger." It was Will's turn to take a ride and Jake would stagger to the beach before plopping in the sand.

The power and energy of the Gulf was unlike anything Jake had ever known, and he'd never forget that...... just as he'd never forget those warm summer days with his dearest friend.

Chapter 1

John Canfield's hand moved in rhythm, his near baritone voice leading the entire congregation of Rock Creek Baptist Church. 'Rock of Ages' was always one of John's favorites, and it showed in the rigid and anxious movement of his hand. John stood behind the oak pulpit, his voice towering over all others in the small church, and sang every word on page 236 of the hymnal. As the song came to its end he carried out the last note, holding it a second-longer after everyone else had finished. He then nodded to the Preacher as he took his seat next to his family in the first row of pews.

Brother Elijah was in no hurry to end the one-and-a-half-hour sermon but realized it was nearing noon and that everyone needed to get home and tend to chores and dinner. So, he concluded with a prayer to protect the parishioners of the church and their relatives, to watch over the boys overseas, and to bring an early end to the war. As Brother Elijah finished, he walked down the center aisle of the building, his flock silent and still, their eyes trained upon him. He opened the front door of the church and a rush of cold swept through the building. He smiled as he moved to one side of the vestibule. The line moved slowly as the Reverend shook every hand and said a few kind words to most everyone, paying particular attention to the women whose husbands and sons had already been called upon to serve the country.

John Canfield held the hand of his middle child, five-year-old Melissa, as they walked to their flatbed wagon. His wife Katy carried their two-year-old son while their eldest boy, eighteen-year-old Luther, brought up the rear. Luther took the baby from his mother and while holding the child in one arm, used his free hand to help his mother up and onto the wagon seat. Luther handed the baby back and moved to the rear bed of the wagon where he took his spot. Katy used the extra blankets she'd brought to cover her and the two youngest children while her husband and Luther pulled the brim of their hats down and buttoned their coat collars. It was Sunday, January 4th, 1942 and the winds that blew across the barren fields and open countryside of southwest Arkansas were brutally cold.

About a fourth of the congregation of Rock Creek pulled away in a car or pickup, the noise from the engines causing a stir among the horses and mules. As most of the vehicles disappeared, the men on horseback crept onto dirt roads and through paths that disappeared into the timber line. As for the Canfields and other parishioners with wagons, they were the last to head out. John used the reins to set the horse in motion and the wagon pulled onto the red clay drive and headed north. John glanced to his right where a black Buick, the lone car remaining, idled. As soon as the Canfield's passed, the car eased to a roll.

The trip home was less than two miles but took forty minutes, and today it seemed much longer as the freezing temperatures and constant wind proved miserable. John's head remained tilted, the brim of his hat partially deflecting the wind that gnawed at his face. Only on occasions would he turn to look behind him, to see if he and his family were alone. But with each passing glance his aggravation and worry grew. He had hoped the black Buick would get stuck in the narrow ruts that only a wagon wheel could make, but it never happened. The driver rode the edges of the thin grooves, apparently having done this before.

The Canfields owned one-hundred and forty acres of good farmland, with two creeks passing at cross-angles through the property. And like all the soil in this part of Arkansas, it made for good crops and healthy grass for cattle. John owned thirty-one head of Angus beef that grazed on fifty acres of his land, while the remaining property was plowed under and farmed year after year. John and his family had made an honest living for themselves and were content with being salt of the earth farmers. They were God-fearing and believed in the good book, which John read from every night and made sure his children learned to read and write using the same.

John pulled on the reins and the wagon came to a halt on a bridge that crossed-over one of the creeks on his property. He looked down, more than ten feet, and saw nothing but rocks. Rain had been scarce in the fall and early winter and he hoped the spring would be better. After examining the creek-bed a moment longer, he turned to see if the man in the Buick was still there. John flicked his wrist and the snap of the reins provoked the animal to move forward yet again.

The lane that led to the Canfield home was less than a hundred yards past the creek and John turned right, down a road lined on both sides by barbed wire. As he made the turn he again looked back, noticing that the Buick had stopped at the bridge. He smiled for the first time today. John and Luther had built the bridge themselves, and it was nothing more than railroad ties and rough-cut planks. Whether it could support a vehicle was questionable, and the man in the Buick obviously felt the same. The man stepped from the car and John noticed his heavy-set frame and lack of clothing for such cold weather. Again, John smiled. The man walked back and forth across the bridge, inspecting the planks and ties that supported it while shaking his head on more than one occasion.

The wagon pulled alongside the house and John quickly helped his wife and children from the seat while instructing Luther not to bother with unhitching the horse just yet. He told his boy to fetch a shotgun and head to the sweat box and not to come back until he sent for him. Luther did as told.

From the house on the hill that overlooked John's land, John could see the dry creek bed, the bridge... and the Buick, and none of them had moved in the last fifteen minutes. He looked for the man, struggling to see

6

if he was still at his car or if he was crossing the field and heading for the house by foot. Eventually the car backed up and his question had been answered. Again, he smiled as he settled into a rocking chair on the front porch and tucked his hands into his coat pockets.

The black Buick disappeared behind a thicket of pines and a moment later it raced into sight. John leapt from his chair, a worried expression overtaking his face. The vehicle made it to the bridge and John could hear the distant thump of timbers as they bounced against each other from the weight of the fast-moving car. Like a cowboy breaking a bronco the car bounced and rocked, the rider keeping his nerve and riding it to the end. The car made it across and sped toward the lane that led to the house. As the car turned right, dust... red and thick, billowed from behind before scattering in the wind. John again sat in the rocker and tried to appear unconcerned as the car came to a stop in the front yard.

Chapter 2

It wasn't the first "army hawk" (what those in these parts called men who were assigned by the government to search out and bring in eligible recruits) that John had encountered since the war began. There had been two others, neither of them brave enough to cross the creek in their cars, and both eventually walking across the pasture and to the house. But not this man, this man was different and that made John worry even more. John pushed his fears down deep before making a decision. He decided to handle this like he handled the other Hawks and smiled as the man stepped from the Buick. As the man stretched his back he made a show of force, and again, neither of the others had done the same. The man made sure his coat flew open, almost by accident but not quite, showing that he had a side arm and badge and silver manacles that looped over his belt. John took notice of the intentional display, and his smile disappeared.

The man stepped onto the porch and extended his

right hand, like it were a pistol, and aimed it at John. "John Canfield," he said with self-assurance and a grin. He then pulled the imaginary trigger and made a "click" sound.

Both John and the rocker seemed to be nodding in simultaneous acknowledgement.

The man eased into the porch swing, about five feet from John, and spread his arms across its back, making himself at home. The grey sky cast a shadow over the raw and bitter day, and although John dressed in the heaviest coat he owned, his body shivered from the cold. As for the visitor who wasn't dressed accordingly and should have been freezing, there seemed to be no ill effects. "Natural insulation," the man said as if he could read John's mind. He then patted his large stomach.

John mustered a disingenuous smile.

"You know Mr. Canfield," the man began, "I've seen a lot of farmers. Brought in a lot of eligible boys..." he paused, a thoughtful expression filling his eyes. "Some of those boys didn't make it to the army, some only got as far as the State pen. And one, well let's just say it didn't work out so well."

John nodded, understanding what the man didn't say.

"There was even one time," the man looked around, studying his surroundings, "I was sitting on a porch just like this and the mother of the boy came out of the house and poked a shotgun in my face." The man chuckled while shaking his head. "Well, that didn't end well either."

John's eyes met those of the man and he could see an undeniable seriousness that crept outward. He stood from his chair and walked into the house. The man continued to swing, waiting patiently while listening to the muffled voices coming from within the home. Moments later John was back in the rocking chair and about to say something when the man held up his hand. "No need to say anything... got two boys of my own."

The front door swung open and the man in the swing flinched, reaching to his side where he holstered his pistol. John's wife appeared, and in each hand a cup of coffee steamed in the afternoon cold. She handed each of the men a cup before taking her place, standing next to her husband. She placed a hand on his shoulder.

The man in the swing calmed, grinned, and sipped at the coffee. He gave an appreciative nod. "I came for the boy," he said as if it were no different than a simple hello.

John shook his head as if he didn't understand. "My boy's only two, come back in sixteen years and we'll talk."

It was now the man's turn to smile. "I hear and see different. I hear you got another boy and that he's old enough to be drafted. And on the back of that wagon I saw a boy as big and strong as an ox just a short time ago."

It seemed to John, from conversations with men at the church, that Arkansas, like most other rural agricultural states, was having difficulties in meeting the unrealistic recruitment quotas put in place by the federal government. The sparseness of the state's population, the reluctance of fathers to give up working hands and free labor, and the fact that some boys hadn't gone to school and weren't recorded with birth certificates, made it a difficult task of searching out eligible recruits. And although the majority of the young men in the state had voluntarily enlisted, there was always an ongoing effort to fill the conscription void. John shrugged.

The man nodded admiringly at the cat and mouse game the senior Canfield so expertly played. But what Mr. Canfield didn't know was that he was the mouse. "I'm gonna get the boy!" the man said. "If I gotta walk down the hill to that tin building he went into, then I will." Having decided to up the ante, he looked to the woman with deadly seriousness. "Your boy is awful big and I ain't gonna fight with him. If he don't come peacefully I'm gonna shoot and I aim to kill!"

Katy's hand gripped John's shoulder, her face showing the alarm that ran through her veins. Katy's real name was Kk`ate, and she was full blooded Quapaw Indian born to a tribe near the town of Mena along the Arkansas, Oklahoma border. Throughout her marriage to John she had always obeyed her heritage, customs, and native traditions, and knew her place as all women of her tribe did. She never spoke of things that men were meant to handle. But fear began to strangle her insides as she fully understood what was about to happen. As a mother she had no choice but to speak. "My boy, he is not okay," she said slowly, "he doesn't understand life." Her accent was undeniable, her speech a rough and jagged patchwork.

The man's brows inched closer together as he stopped swinging and leaned forward, draping his arms across his thighs. He kept his eyes trained on the woman, wanting her to know that he understood her concerns. He nodded. "The Draft Board evaluates everyone, physically and mentally. If there's something wrong, if he's not 1-A, they'll send him home for now...... I promise."

Chapter 3

The man sat in his car and looked across the rickety old bridge. On the other side of the bridge John Canfield stood in front of his son, his hand resting on the boy's shoulder, his words, words that all fathers speak in moments like this, forcing Luther's head to bow and take notice of the changing world. The man had witnessed scenes such as this more times than he cared to remember, but this had a different ring to it. As he closed his eyes and took in a deep breath, the man thought about the job he'd been doing, about how he was good at it. He had brought in many young men, many abled bodies that would become fine soldiers, but he didn't like this particular case as it felt all wrong. Perhaps it had been the words of the boy's Mother, about how the boy wasn't "okay". He'd seen it once before, a young man who was unable to function in the real world, who had been unable, for whatever reason, to move from boyhood to adult. And he remembered that it didn't end well. He wished he would have let this one be. He wished he would have just written Luther

13

Canfield off.

A tap against the car window startled the man. His body jerked and his eyes flashed open. As the surprise wore off he motioned for Luther to get in the front seat. Luther climbed in, removed his hat, and looked down at the floorboard. The man said nothing as he turned his body and draped his right arm over the back seat. He began backing the car down the road and soon found a spot to turn around. The two headed for the main highway.

Once the hum of driving on blacktop replaced the sound of gravel, the man glanced over to Luther. Luther continued to glare at the floor, his hat in hand and dangling between his legs. "Your maw's Quapaw," the man asked.

Luther nodded ever so faintly.

The man turned his eyes back to the highway and slowed his speed as he spotted a wagon alongside the road ahead. "And your paw is colored?" The man continued to look ahead, though he cut his eyes to the boy sitting next to him. It was obvious from the first time the man saw John Canfield leaving church that he was black, or at least half black. His skin was the color of dusk and his nose wide and flat. And Luther, well Luther was almost the spitting image of the elder Canfield. He had the same wide nose though his skin looked like most white farmers who'd spent a lifetime in the summer sun. He hoped it would be enough.

Luther offered no reply and the man kept thinking he should have just left this one be.

14

The car came to a stop a few-hundred-feet from the wagon, and the man shifted to neutral. As the engine idled, he turned to Luther. The man rubbed his forehead and then his eyes. He felt tired. "I don't normally do this," the man began, "but I don't want to see you end up somewhere you don't want to be."

For the first time today, Luther turned to look at the man.

"Colored boys have a tough time. They don't get mixed in with everyone else, they get sent to their own camps and you don't want to be there.... it's...... well, at least in the regular army you'll get a decent meal and decent quarters. Those colored boys ain't so lucky."

Luther blinked, though his face remained blank and expressionless.

The man wondered if the boy could even comprehend what he was saying but continued anyway. "When you fill out your forms...." the man's voice calmed and quieted, "when they ask you what your race is, tell them your Quapaw and white." The man paused as he stared at Luther's broad nose and black hair. "You can do this," the man said with encouragement. He pointed to the wagon ahead and Luther followed with his gaze. "We got more boys to pick up, so we won't talk about this again."

By the time the Buick stopped in front of the County Courthouse, there were five recruits crammed inside. The man told the boys to return to the same spot once they were finished and he'd see they got home. He then pointed to an entrance at the side of the building and instructed them to get out and head inside.

Luther didn't want to move at first, seemingly waiting for the rest of the boys to step out.

The man didn't force Luther and waited patiently for the others to leave.

Luther shook his head as he struggled for words.

The man thought it odd that such a large and undoubtedly powerful person could be so timid and unsure of himself. But he let Luther move at his own pace.

A rasping sound came from Luther and he paused to clear his throat. Luther continued with what he had to say, his point separating right from wrong.

The man smiled, ever appreciative of Biblical notations. "The Bible also says that if we confess our sins, he is faithful and just to forgive us our sins, and to cleanse us from all unrighteousness." The man waited for a moment, studying Luther all the while. There was a pitying the man felt and yet again he wished he could undo what he had started. It was clear that the Canfield's weren't draft-dodgers, just a family trying to protect a boy who wasn't ready to face the world. "I don't think the Lord wants you to suffer..." he added. "And I don't think you're meant to suffer. I'm sure this one little lie will be forgiven."

Chapter 4

"Whoooowee!" a clerk yelped as Luther entered the courthouse and stepped into line. "We got us a big one here today!" The Clerk stood behind a counter with a shelf of frosted-glass stretching its length. There were two openings in the frosted glass, about four feet apart, and the Clerk manned one of the openings. A sign hung in front that read, "Recruits, Line Forms Here". The other opening was void of anyone though a sign hanging above it read, "Marriages, Taxes, Court".

Another man appeared from a door directly behind the counter and studied the clerk, who quickly made busy shuffling papers. "That'll be enough," he said with authority before disappearing again.

The Clerk didn't reply, he simply shook his head and handed Luther his stack of forms. He motioned to a row of tables. "If you have trouble with that, you let me know. I know most of you can't read and write."

Luther sat in silence, filling out his forms. Occasionally he'd glance at the others, the ones that

17

rode in the car to the courthouse with him, and some were clearly having trouble. One of the men asked for assistance from the unruly clerk while others whispered amongst themselves. But not Luther, he didn't need help because he had taken his studies seriously, his Paw making sure of that. And his only hesitation came when it was time to list his, and his parents', race.

The physical exam, the shots and drawing of blood were simple. A man only had to stand in line, do what he was told, and keep his mouth shut. And Luther was good at all those things. The boy had learned patience, solitude, and calmness from his days in the sweat box. Being a farmer and having crops meant having animals trying to eat those crops. And ever since Luther had been old enough to tote a shotgun or rifle he'd been doing his best to protect those crops. He and his dad took turns, alternating days, where one would head out before daylight and climb into a small tin building in the middle of their planted fields. Dawn would bring deer and raccoons and such, while mid-morning in southwest Arkansas brought crows and unbearable heat. Luther had spent what seemed like half his life in the middle of those fields, sitting and watching and killing. But mostly, he spent his time sitting quietly and sweating.

Luther was the last in line, and it seemed fitting. As he made his way to his last stop, the last of the other recruits was exiting the courthouse. And now, well now Luther stood before a row of doorways, none of them having actual doors, which opened into tiny, hastily erected offices. Earlier, the line had grinded to a halt hear, each recruit entering a room as directed, speaking with a doctor, and exiting about ten minutes later. The process had repeated itself and it was finally Luther's turn. He stepped through the middle doorway.

The man sitting behind the desk extended a hand, its intent aimed at the papers in the young recruit's hand. But instead, Luther reached out and shook it with a polite gentleness. The man smiled while shaking his head. "No son, I need your papers." He pointed to the stack of papers in Luther's left hand. After instructing Luther to sit, he said "this shouldn't take long". The Doctor sifted through the papers, his lips moving as he read, before turning to the hulking figure on the opposite side of his desk. He began the questioning.

The clerk at the counter smiled as Luther, the lone remaining recruit in the building, handed him his papers. The clerk flipped through the stack, his eyes scanning only what was important.

Luther never looked directly at the clerk, perhaps he should have as it might have made his lie more convincing. Instead, he turned away and headed for the exit.

"You must think your one of those smart ones," the clerk said.

Luther stopped and stared at the exit a few feet away. Like the days in the sweat-box in the middle of the planted fields, he began to sweat.

"Indian my ass?" The Clerk said to himself. As he flipped through more pages and finished reading the psychiatric assessment, he fixed his glare on Luther. "Who you trying to fool," he asked.

The doctor had declined Luther for entry into the Army, though Luther wasn't aware. The Doctor had scribbled, "Not suited for military duty at this time; further evaluation required." And at the bottom of Luther's psychiatric evaluation he stamped it, "4 F - Declined".

Luther was more scared than he'd ever been and the last thing he wanted was to turn and face the Clerk. He lied on his enlistment forms and could only imagine that he'd be imprisoned for doing so. A confession crossed his mind, and he was about to spill the beans when the Clerk spoke. "Don't worry boy, I'll take care of it. You can go."

Relief washed over Luther, almost to the point of thanking the man, as he headed out the door.

The clerk had processed many recruits and seen it all. And he knew how the government machine worked. There was nothing he could do about Luther Canfield's blatant attempt to hide his race as he knew it unlikely the boy was born in a hospital or had any kind of birth certificate to verify otherwise. But clerical errors in the Army, well that was a different story. Errors occurred all the time, and besides, no one ever looked closely at a recruit's enlistment forms. The government only wanted to see "Approved" or "Declined" stamped in red ink across the front page. So he switched Luther's psychiatric evaluation with one from another recruit's pile and slammed an ink soaked stamp against the cover page and right below the name, "Luther Enos Canfield".

Chapter 5

Toke Cullen leaned against a cedar tree and watched as two boats rounded the point and entered Dauphin Island Bay. There was a light chop on the water and the lead boat, a skiff like all other wooden skiffs along the coast, buoyed and rocked as it made its way towards the Shell Banks. As for the other boat, it wasn't like anything Toke had ever seen. Twice the size of a skiff, it was squared across the front, but not like a barge or having a deck that one could stand on for tonging oysters. Deep-sided and grey, a lone navigator positioned himself up high and near the stern. But what seemed truly odd about the boat were all the greyish-blue kettles turned upside down, their shiny facades glistening in the morning sun. "About time," Toke thought, "we been needing some new pots." The two boats nosed their bows onto shore and Jim Cowl, the Sherriff from Bayou La Batre (the Bayou), jumped off the skiff, a satchel in his left hand. As for the other boat, as soon as it touched shore the front end opened, the entire bow releasing from its hinges and slamming onto the sand and oyster shells that made up the beach. Toke jumped, startled by the sudden motion. Once the door hit the beach, Toke could see men stuffed inside, all of them wearing blue kettles, along with a huge bulk of supplies stowed beneath a khaki colored tarp.

Jim walked to Toke and shook his hand. Both men turned to appraise the landing vessel.

"Which one's McArthur," Toke asked wryly.

Jim smiled and the two watched as men began to offload. But more importantly, they watched as the war officially came to Dauphin Island. There was no fighting or machinegun fire, no large naval fleet, and no tanks or artillery, but the war came all the same. It came in the form of a squad of US Airmen, twelve to be exact, and more than likely it wouldn't be the last group of soldiers to arrive. It was now official, Dauphin Island had become a frontline observation and submarine reconnaissance base, and the Island would never be the same.

One of the soldiers approached Toke and Jim as the others fell into rank. He introduced himself as 2nd Lieutenant Robert Brantley, the senior officer. However green the twenty-two-year-old may have been, he appeared to be the oldest man in the squad. "Could you direct me to Fort Gaines," Brantley asked with a stringent military dialect. Fort Gaines is a brick and mortar fort built on the east end of the island in the mid-1800's. It had played a part in the Civil War as it watched over and protected the entrance to Mobile Bay, and remained well fortified to this day. It would be an ideal place from which to garrison troops and scan the open gulf.

Toke squinted, the morning sun shimmering off the water and those shiny-blue kettles. He then described the paths the men needed to take to get there, using his hands to show all the curves and forks along the way. It became a rather lengthy account and the officer tired of the details. He needed to get his men to the fort and settle in before dark. Even without Toke's drawn-out directions, it'd take the entire day to transport the supplies and set up camp. "Now, when you get to the large magnolia tree..." Toke said as he began the second leg of the journey.

Brantley grimaced and held up a hand. He abruptly thanked Toke before turning to his men. He barked orders and the group began emptying the transport, working as a team by tossing boxes from one man to the next to the next, in a line that stretched well onto the beach. As the offloading concluded, a good twenty minutes of hard work, Toke waved the Lieutenant back over. Brantley sighed but did as requested. He'd been given orders to interact with the locals, and he wanted to get off on the right foot.

"If it were me," Toke said as soon as the officer drew near, "I'd load that thing back up and head outta here."

"Load it back up?" Brantley shook his head. His first thoughts were to call the Islander crazy, but he decided on a different response. "I'm sorry but I've got to get these supplies moving. I've got my orders."

Toke shrugged and the man turned away. Toke looked

to Jim. "Billy Goat Hole sure is a lot closer to the fort than here," he said as the two of them started inland.

Having overheard what Toke said, the soldier stopped in his tracks and grimaced. Feeling like an idiot for unloading the boat at a point so far from his destination, he muttered "Son of a bitch." He spun on his heel and yelled for Toke to stop. He needed directions once again.

Chapter 6

Jim and Toke walked toward the Catholic Church and word spread like some sort of cowboy movie where the sheriff had finally arrived to face the villains and save the day. But there were no villains nor was he here to save the day. Everyone knew why Jim had come and it caused quite a stir.

Most everyone on the island was close kin, and they either had a son or grandson or husband about to be signed up for the draft and likely head off to war. And Jim's presence on this day would be the source of a lot of pain for years to come.

In the midst of its own struggles, the community was still coming to terms with their own tragedy, the recent deaths of Will Burton Jr and Mary Gorman. Less than two weeks ago, during the Christmas holidays, Will had been killed for no other reason than being in love with Mary. The girl's father and brother had seen to that. As for Mary, well she disappeared a week later, an apparent drowning, though her body was never found.

And it seemed, with what the Islanders had been through, that they should be left alone, at least long enough to properly mourn. But that wasn't going to happen as it didn't matter to Jim or the US government. It seemed both wanted even more blood.

Thirty-two, that's how many men aged 18 to 65 there are on the Island, and twenty-nine of them gathered inside the church. The only exceptions were Julius Carter and his son Pate, and Willy Burton. Pate Carter had already enlisted in the Marine Corp and would be heading to basic training in North Carolina in four days, and that had clearly taken care of his draft requirements. As for his dad Julius, he served as a Marine in WWI, which made him exempt. And Willy, well Willy was also a veteran of the first war though there's much more to his story.

Inside the church men stood expectantly. They mumbled to themselves as Jim walked up and found a spot just behind a small table that had been set up for this occasion. Jim set his bag down and looked to the quieting crowd. "Glad to see all of you again," Jim said. "I just wish it were under better circumstances... like the annual brawl." A smattering of laughter spread through the church. Last October, like every October, families from the Island ventured to the Bayou to play the annual-rivalry baseball game. And though most everyone from the two communities are kinfolk, the game is always high spirited and always interrupted with a brawl. As for Jim, well he's the umpire of the annual game and has the delightful job of keeping order.

Well versed in all the forms, Jim understood the requirements and exemptions the draft afforded. After all, he'd been doing this all over the south part of Mobile County for weeks. He knew who was eligible and who wasn't, and which forms men of differing ages needed to fill out. Orderly and patient, he also went to considerable lengths to help anyone who couldn't read or write or didn't understand the questions.

Ralph Cullen, the youngest of the Cullen boys, stood across the table from Jim. He and four other men huddled alongside the wooden table, staring at the Sheriff. The five decided to enlist in the Army, as they weren't going to wait to be drafted. Ralph and two of his nephews, Kermit and James Cullen, and brothers Paul and Lester Clark had made a pact. They wanted to serve their country and hoped the Sheriff would help them end up in the same unit. Besides being kin, all of them were in their mid-twenties and single. These men had grown up as friends, and when Japan attacked Pearl Harbor they knew they needed to do something. The attack had stoked a firestorm of national pride, and these men, along with millions of others, were determined to make them pay. After hearing what they had to say, Jim Cowl promised he would do his best to help but stopped short of guaranteeing they'd end up together.

Toke Cullen stood in line and peered over Jake's shoulder as Jim handed his son varying forms and explained what each represented. Jake moved aside as Toke stepped up and grabbed one of the pencils that lay in a pile on the table.

28

"You can't sign up," Jim said without hesitation.

"Why can't I? I don't think I hit sixty-five yet." Animated as he spoke, Toke drew the attention of everyone around him. They all laughed.

"You're a government employee and that makes you exempt."

"I'm a government what?" Toke said loudly. His job as a mailman had been more of an enjoyment than a job, and he'd forgotten all about the two days a week that he worked.

"Mailman," Jim said affirmatively.

"Then I'll quit! I don't have to deliver the mail. I want to do what's best for the country."

Everyone gathered in close and listened.

"You can't quit. If you were to quit I'd have to arrest you. Its wartime and things have to go on, like the mail and policing and such. It's vital that things stay as normal as possible during these times. Besides, you are serving your country and you'll keep serving it by delivering the mail. Now step aside!" Loud and forceful with his words, Jim wanted everyone to know that Toke had no options. There had been cases where men were beaten by their own community for taking the easy way out, and he wasn't going to leave any doubt that this was a governmental decision.

Toke turned from Jim and stared at his son. He shook his head before studying the surrounding faces. When he looked into their eyes he saw kindness and understanding... and that aggravated him even more.

"Are there any other options," he asked Jim as he turned back to the table.

Jim shook his head. "Nope. Now step aside!"

Toke threw the pencil onto the table before turning and heading out the door.

Jake set his paperwork down and ran to catch up with his Dad. "You ok?" He asked.

"I'm fine," Toke replied with disgust.

"It'll be ok. There was nothing you could do. The Sheriff said so."

Toke stopped walking and faced his son, the bright sun beaming down and warming the chilly day. "Son, what I do with delivering mail ain't no job. It's barely anything. I've always made it out to be more than it is... you know what I mean. You know how I sometimes stop and fish, or swim, or layover at Little Dauphin and take a nap. I'd hardly call that a job."

Jake listened to his Dad and knew he was wrong. "I was young but I remember when you took the job. Old man Lander asked people all over the Island if they wanted his job and not a single one piped up. They all knew how dangerous it was and that you were the only one bold enough to do it."

"You mean crazy enough," Toke said.

"Bold, crazy... they're both the same," Jake said as the two laughed.

Chapter 7

A party! Everyone from the Island decided to show their boys how much they loved them and the bash called for something special, something like stuffed flounder. Besides the flounders, they needed blue crabs, which are hard to come by in the winter months, but they held out hope that they'd scrape up enough. Besides, there was no better place in this world to find the delicacy than on the north side of the Island, in and around marshes and sandbars. It was three days past a full moon and the men of the village scattered out along the shorelines, bayous, and sandy beaches as dusk fell. Besides gigs and croaker sacks in hand, men were armed with flashlights and fat-lighter, the center sections of aged pine trees that had hardened over time and created a resin that easily burned.

Lit up like a Christmas tree, sparkling lights trimmed the edges of the Island while voices echoed in the clear night sky. With everyone out in full force it didn't take long, and in just a few hours the main course had been gathered. Further adding to the celebration, the wives and daughters baked cakes and pies while Saul Clark butchered a large hog and put it on a spit for overnight cooking. As for Toke, well he helped gather crabs and fish as well, but it wouldn't be until tomorrow before he carried out his main duty. Tomorrow he would visit the ghost.

Julius Carter greeted the cool bright morning with a smile, happy to see that almost no wind existed. He wanted to get an early start as he had a lot to do before tonight's party, and the conditions were perfect. He decided to head into Mobile, to take care of the remaining details, and he needed things to go smoothly if wanted to be back by mid-afternoon. Julius was the only Islander with a motor boat as well as a car that he kept on the mainland at Cedar Point. And these luxuries made a trip into town, or anywhere for that matter, not nearly as burdensome for him as for the other Islanders. If things went as planned he could make the roundtrip in less than six hours. As Julius headed out, other men did the same but with different destinations in mind. These men headed to the reefs to tong a few oysters. A staple of life if there ever was one, this was the perfect time of year for oysters. With little to no rain during the winter months, and near frigid waters, they'd be cold and salty.

At just past two in the afternoon, Julius' boat puttered around the point that led to the Shell Banks. He eased the bow up to shore and threw his anchor onto the beach. Pleased with himself for getting every last thing he'd set out for, he smiled a broad smile and breathed in the cool crisp air of home. Only God could understand how much he loved this place. Besides the box of items he purchased at Aster's Department store, he wasn't alone. His son Pate had only talked about two things over the past month, the Marines and Sherry Larson. And now, well now Sherry Larson and Mira Lea stepped off the skiff. Sherry was an incredibly pretty girl and best friend of Mira Lea, a local girl who attended college. The girls had met at school and instantly bonded. The two became such good friends that even Sherry's dad, Ted, had come to the Island on several occasions. The Larson's quickly became a part of the Island family, spending their days with the locals while sleeping over at the Lea's. Julius smiled yet again, believing he had made an important and sound decision. He hoped Sherry would give his son a reason to return home safely. It never mattered if the girl actually liked Pate in a romantic way... it was the hope that counted. He himself had fought in the First World War and there were plenty of times that "his girl" gave him the strength to fight on. While overseas he would lie awake at night and think about Alice, remembering the delicate lines of her face and the grace of her lips when she spoke. She was beautiful and he imagined her love to be real, which proved to be correct as he ended up marrying her when he returned home. Yea... if there's anything a young man would fight for, it'd be a girl.

On a moment's notice, Sherry had agreed to go along with what Julius requested. It wasn't such a big deal since she only had to take an interest in Pate, nothing more. Plenty of other girls from college were doing the same, their part of the war effort, and Sherry even brought a picture of herself to give the young Marine. She'd do her best to play the role.

As Julius and Mira and Sherry entered the church, the sweet smell of calico-g's (a pan-fried bread that beignets resemble) invited them into the sanctum. Julius took in a deep breath and let it out. Man, those things smelled good.

Sherry had never smelled anything so heavenly and could hardly contain herself. "What's that smell?"

Mira smiled. She loved the damn things too, but hated what they did to you. One look at her momma's hips and you knew exactly what calico-g's could do to a woman. Mira told Sherry what they were and the two made a beeline for the table they rested on. Big hips or not, the calico-g's were calling and the girls were gonna eat their share.

"You could at least give your momma a hug before diving into the food," Bess said. Mira and Sherry turned and smiled. Bess put her arms around Mira before letting go with her left and bringing Sherry in close. Sherry returned the gesture by squeezing as tight as she could. Sherry's mom had passed away several years back and though no one could ever substitute your mom, Bess had a lot of love to give and Sherry needed it.

Julius set the box from the department store in a corner and headed out back. Some of the men were picking the meat from freshly boiled crabs while others were cleaning fish and shucking oysters. Eventually the women would gather the crabmeat and fish and take them home to season and bake, while the oysters would be eaten on half shells or fried.

"Quick trip," Toke said.

Julius nodded as he rolled up his sleeves and began opening oysters.

Toke helped the men finish with the oysters, washed up, and headed east. It was time to see the ghost. He walked the two-mile path towards Fort Gaines and found himself at the entrance to the fort, no ghost in sight. With a locked gate staring him in the face, he wasn't sure what to do. He tried knocking on the iron bars, but that produced almost no sound. He then whistled, but still no movement from within. He was about to yell when the barrel of a rifle, with a bayonet attached to it, jutted outward. Suddenly, he felt that yelling may not be his best option. Toke took off his cap and scratched his head while glaring at the tip of the blade. "You sure know how to make a fella feel welcomed," he said to the guard.

The guard, just beyond the locked gate remained obscure in one of the many dark crevices the fort offered. But his bayonet wasn't obscure as it protruded between the bars and in the direction of Toke's throat. The caution was palpable. "Sir, what can I help you with?"

Toke smiled, trying to lighten the moment. "I'd like to see the head ghost." The Islanders had labeled the garrison of airmen as the blue-helmet ghost. And like ghost, the blue-helmets would only appear for brief moments along the top of Fort Gaines' wall, or briefly at the gate to the fort, and occasionally at night while on patrol along the beaches or in the woods that skirted the village. The apparitions were eerie and silent and always ducking for cover when spotted. And this made the locals skittish. People felt like they were being watched, as if they were the enemy about to be ambushed.

The guard looked puzzled, but figured the man was talking about the Lieutenant. "Why?"

Toke rubbed his palm into his right eye-socket. He could feel the stress of this job rising to the top but handled it in usual Toke fashion. "The Germans just landed on the beach," he said with a half-smile.

The bayonet disappeared and within seconds a hand-cranked siren began to wail from behind the fort's walls. The high pitch whirling sound increased with each passing second, as did Toke's alarm. Unsure of what he'd started, Toke froze. "Son of a bitch," he said. His instincts told him to run but decided otherwise as he figured he might get shot in the back if someone thought he was a traitor, or a spy, or a German! So he did the only thing he could, he dove into the embankment, an earthen-wall that encircled the west side of the fort, forming its outer perimeter. He hunkered down, behind a small shrub, doing his best to camouflage himself by the plucking at the sparse leaves and throwing them atop his head and back. The siren continued its cry just as the chain that held the gate closed, rattled. The gate swung open and men streamed from the fort.

"Son of a bitch," Toke said again, his worry growing. Toke looked on as the men fanned out, one of them stumbling and nearly impaling himself with his own bayonet. "Son of a bitch!" he said again and as he watched the nearly impaled soldier pat his stomach, searching for blood.

"How many are there?" Lieutenant Brantley shouted.

Toke looked back, and Brantley was exiting the fort. The man raced towards him, his long legs propelling him at a fast clip. At this moment Toke took notice of two things. First, the pistol in Brantley's hand, which Toke was certain the Lieutenant would use on him once he discovered the truth, and secondly, the large caliber machinegun now straddling the top of the fort's wall, its barrel pointing westward.

Brantley dove into the embankment, a grunting sound escaping his lips as his shoulder met earth. His helmet was tightly fastened, but still spun sideways from the impact. "Where are they," he asked in a panic and as he shoved the helmet to the left.

Before Toke could reply, gun shots sounded. The men to the left of them opened fire...... on something, somebody. "Jesus Christ," Toke thought.

Toke panicked and tried to get to his feet so he could run away but Brantley grabbed him by the seat of the pants and yanked him back to the ground. "Don't be a hero," the Lieutenant yelled. Brantley lifted his head, looked over the edge of the hill, and squeezed off two rounds. One of the shells that ejected from the pistol landed on Toke's back and scorched his skin. Toke yelped, but realized he deserved whatever he got. "Well" the Lieutenant demanded, "How many?"

The machinegun now joined the imaginary fracas. For what seemed like forever, the deep thump of the gun rattled hundreds of shots. Toke could only shake his head and pray that no one was actually out there for half the village could be dead by now.

As the gunfire ceased, a soldier to the right of them shouted. "I think we got one!"

"Oh my God!" Toke thought. Toke and Brantley looked at the soldier, the man now pointing in the direction that all the gunfire had been directed.

"Over there," the soldier added. "He's down! I think we got one!"

Toke became nauseous and swooned. If he'd been standing he'd have crumpled to the ground. Of all things in this world he didn't want to do, looking over that embankment headed the list. He even thought about saying a prayer but couldn't muster the spit to do so.

Men moved in evasive measures, ducking and hiding behind whatever the landscape offered, all the while moving forward and covering one another. No more shots were fired as they made their way to the slain enemy. As the men moved covertly, including Lieutenant Brantley, Toke paced along at full height. "Get down you idiot," Brantley hissed. "There may be more of them." Toke shrugged his shoulders and continued on, passing a crouching Brantley. Brantley yelled for his men to move at double time, he didn't want the idiot Islander to get to the enemy before they did and take all the credit.

As Toke reached the gathering of soldiers, who encircled whatever they'd shot, he took a deep breath and squeezed between the men. "Thank God," he thought as he eyed the victim. His body finally relaxed as he looked at a dead Blue Heron.

"What the hell's going on?" Brantley screamed at his men... spit flying from his mouth with each syllable. He then turned to Toke, a vein across his forehead bulging to the point of bursting.

"Well," Toke began, "I just came to see if ya'll wanted to come to a party tonight."

Brantley looked at the men that had gathered, at the dead bird, and back to Toke. "Son of a bitch!"

Chapter 8

Toke never bothered knocking, no one on the island ever did, and he walked inside. His best friend, Willy Burton, sat at the kitchen table, a two-week beard on his face and a coffee cup next to his hand. "Willy," Toke said.

Willy showed no expression, his face as solemn as the day he buried his eldest son. "Toke," he replied with a gruff whisper.

Toke poured himself a cup of coffee before joining Willy at the table. "Where's Rache," he asked. Rache, was Rachael, Toke's sister and Willy's wife.

Willy nodded to the hallway and Toke nodded in understanding.

Toke set the cup on the table and leaned to his left, scrounging around in his right pant pocket. He produced a wad of money and set $9.71 and a button on the table next to Willy's hand. "The button's from Saul's shirt. He couldn't pay up so I took the last thing he owned." Toke waited, hoping this would produce a smile from his friend. But Willy never smiled and Toke moved on. "That's what's left over for the month."

Willy huffed, stared at the money for a moment, and pushed it away. He knew it was his money, what the bar had taken in since Toke began running it for him, but he also knew that Toke hadn't taken a single penny for compensation. "It's yours," Willy said. "In fact, you can have bar and all."

Toke rubbed the inside of his left ear. "You know I ain't gonna take it. And as far as the bar goes... well it ain't the same. It won't ever be the same until you come back."

Willy shrugged as if it made no difference to him.

Toke had been coming by to see Willy most every day, and every day appeared blacker than the one before. It never seemed like Willy's slide would end. But Toke prayed it would, it just had to because it was Willy, his best friend, the man he'd walk through fire to help. Toke looked around the dull and drab room. The curtains were drawn and with it being late afternoon, a colorless existence strangled the surroundings. He did his best to smile as he turned back to Willy. "You coming to the shindig?"

Willy shook his head.

"It's not just Pate you know. There's some other boys headed out as well and they'd all like to see you before they leave. Hell, most of 'em growed up in your bar." At the mention of those boys growing up in Willy's bar,

Toke watched the anguish swell in Willy's eyes. He tried to imagine the demons his friend fought, the man that was like his brother, but he couldn't. So, yet again, Toke put on his best face and steered the conversation elsewhere. "Tell you what," he added. "You come out this evening and me and you'll head to West Point (the western tip of Dauphin Island) tomorrow and catch us some reds (redfish). I'll bet some bulls are running. And when we get back we'll drink some beers and cook 'em over a fire. Whatcha say?"

The evening sky and closed curtains cast shadows, making Willy's eyes look as if they had sunken inward... or maybe it wasn't the shadows. Willy peered upwards, his eyes bloodshot along the bottoms, and shrugged.

Toke sighed, and before taking one last sip of coffee he added, "I hope you make it". Toke set the cup down and pushed his chair away from the table. As he stood he paused for a moment, as if he wanted to say something more. But he never said anything before disappearing through the door and into the approaching dark.

Chapter 9

Uncle Paul, one of the twelve Cullen kids, though many years past being a kid, plucked at his fiddle while tightening the keys at the end. He soon struck a chord and other men joined in with guitars and a harmonica. The party began as dusk settled over the island. Everyone greeted the frigid night air, a suitable companion to what this moment represented, as there was plenty to worry about and even more to lose.

Mira surprised Jake with the trip over and now held his hand. Jake's smile beamed like Sand Island Lighthouse, a hopeful glow that couldn't be doused. As for Sherry, she made sure Pate was given the attention he deserved, touching his arm and smiling pretty and such. When Mr. Carter first approached her about coming to the island and doting over Pate, she saw it as yet another act on the stage of life and was soon lost in her imaginary role. And as for Pate, well he'd never be the wiser.

Outside, a group of men stood around a fire and

talked about the war while music drifted into the lonesome night. The music and talk of war seemed to be at odds with each other, engaged in some kind of struggle that grounded the celebration long before it ever took off. As proof, only a handful of people drank wine and even fewer danced. The younger generation seemed to be the only ones braving the dance floor, and Sherry made sure Pate had the opportunity to stretch his legs to a couple of songs. Pate wasn't a good dancer, stiff and rigid in his movements, but Sherry stroked his ego by telling him otherwise. It would become one of the sweetest nights of Pate's young life.

It must have been like the star that guided the Wise Men to baby Jesus, because as soon as the oysters were through cooking and placed on the table, two ghosts appeared from out of the dark. "Better late than never," Brantley said as he walked up and gave a hesitant nod to Toke.

"Right on time," Toke said. The circle of men parted like the Red Sea and welcomed their guest.

The men shook hands and introduced themselves. "What's that smell," Terry Franks, one of the soldiers, asked.

Saul looked over his shoulder, back towards the church, and although he couldn't actually see them inside the building, he knew the women were setting the table with the stuffed fish and oysters and everything else. "Fried Blue Heron," he said with a smile.

Brantley gave Toke a serious glance, but Toke just shrugged as the Islanders laughed.

"I had an itchy trigger-finger and decided to take some revenge on those pesky birds we got," another Islander added.

The ribbing continued for a few more minutes before settling into a normal conversation. "So where you boys from," Saul asked.

"Long Island," Terry Franks said. Saul shrugged and Franks took exception. "What's wrong with Long Island," Franks asked.

"I'm sure it's fine," Saul said.

"Damn right it is..." Franks said with a bit of ire.

"Okay, Corporal," Brantley interjected. "Settle down."

Franks glared at his Lieutenant, expecting an apology for speaking down to him in front of the locals. But he never received one and Franks stormed off in the direction of the church.

"Where's Long Island," Saul asked as soon as Franks walked away.

Brantley smiled at the question as he watched his Corporal vanish through the church doors.

"So what about you," Toke asked Brantley.

"Georgia," Brantley replied. He paused before telling them that he attended college at a school in Alabama near the Georgia line.

The men shrugged, never having heard of the place. "Sooo... what'd you study," someone asked.

"Agriculture," Brantley responded.

"Like growing crops and stuff," Saul questioned.

"Yea, sort of," Brantley replied.

Everyone burst into laughter. "You mean to tell me that you went to college to do something that people been doing since the beginning of time," someone said. The laughter continued.

Brantley tried to talk over the group of laughing men. "It's not like that," he yelled.

It was no use though as the men kept jeering.

"Maybe we need to change the subject," Toke said. "He has a gun you know."

"Yea," Brantley agreed. "Let's change the subject before I regret what I'm about to do,"

Eventually the laughter died and the conversation turned more serious, and it would be the distant knock of Julius Carter's diesel generator, the only source of electricity on the Island, which would spur the most contentious question of the night. "When we getting electricity," Peter Lea asked. With the beginning of the war the government had set out placing power poles across the bay, a slow process but a process all the same. The electricity was coming and most of the Islanders were ecstatic over the prospect, but not all.

Brantley looked skyward, the clear crisp night beckoning every star in the heavens, before looking back at the group. "No time soon," he said. "They're putting a halt to it next week. They'll be sending a generator about then as well, and only our base will have power." He then pointed to the church and the glow of light streaming out its windows. "And whoever owns that generator."

The locals stared at that same glow and collectively shook their heads, except for Toke. Toke never wanted the electricity anyway and relief filled his heart. "Tell you what," Toke said, "you keep the electricity away and I'll make sure you get all the seafood you can eat."

By the smell of things, Brantley wished he could make such a deal.

Chapter 10

Piles of food stretched nearly twenty feet across a row of tables. The boys heading off to war were allowed to go through the food-line first, followed by the women and children, and then the men. A single wooden table rested near the altar and the six, soon to be soldiers, were seated with the respect they deserved. As for everyone else there weren't enough tables to go around and most would have to eat while sitting in a pew or standing against a wall.

Sherry dug through a platter of half-shells and picked out the smallest oyster she could find. She didn't like the looks of them though everyone else appeared to love them. Mira wasn't nearly as bashful, and both oysters and stuffed-fish and pulled pork topped her plate. As the girls made their way to the end of the food line, Sherry stopped while reaching for a fork. She wasn't looking at the tray of silverware, but across the room instead. Terry Franks stood against the wall and stared at the two girls. "Well hello," Sherry muttered to herself.

"We have got to talk to that cute boy in uniform."

Having heard Sherry's comments, Mira glanced up from her pile of food and then back down to her pile of food. She picked up a calico-g, as if she hadn't eaten enough of them already, and tried to figure out where to put the dessert. "I don't think so," she said to Sherry. She then placed the crowning jewel on top of everything else.

"Come on," Sherry whined. "I want to have some fun." She lowered her voice and rolled her eyes. "And we both know what a cad that Pate is." She suppressed a laugh as she added an extra layer of sarcasm. "He's the original lady killer."

Mira frowned at the comment, and shook her head no.

Sherry was about to reply when another soldier walked through the door. She studied the soldier and then turned to find Jake. Having spotted Mira's beau, she grabbed Mira's arm. "Don't shake your head no because another one just walked in." Sherry glanced around the room, making sure all the players were in place, before turning back to Mira. "We have got to do this," she said.

Mira looked up and noticed the tall Lieutenant speaking with a group of men at the door.

"He's gorgeous. Tell you what, I'll leave that one for you," Sherry said.

Mira said nothing as she took her pile of food and headed for the opposite side of the room.

Sherry followed, close on her heals. "You owe me!" she

said. "I agreed to come here, and if I hadn't then you'd be in the Bayou at your Aunt's. You'd probably be sewing or something, like an old maid."

Mira scanned the room and found Jake, who stood next to the table where the six soldiers sat. He was leaning over and saying something to Pate, who laughed. His distraction would be Mira's only salvation because he'd have seen right through her. "I don't think this is a good idea," she said to Sherry, though realizing the outcome.

"You owe me!"

"No," Mira said again, though less resolute.

Sherry stared at her friend, tapping her foot with impatience.

Mira stared back while devouring an oyster, slurping the liquid off the shell in the process. And yet again she shook her head.

Sherry never touched her food, holding her plate with both hands while waiting for Mira to finish. But she didn't wait very long and took the plate from Mira as a teenage boy walked by. "Would you please take these?"

The boy blushed, and gladly accepted the plates and cups.

"Now," Sherry said as she placed her hands atop Mira's shoulders and turned her to face the soldiers. "Let's go," she added as she pushed Mira forward.

Mira protested at first, digging in like the dead weight of an anchor, but finally surrendered to the wave that washed her towards the door. "Fine," Mira relented. "But only for a minute. And we're even after this."

"No problem," Sherry agreed.

As everyone ate and talked amongst themselves, Julius retrieved the box he had placed against the wall earlier in the day. He walked next to the table where the boys sat and gathered everyone's attention. "I just wanted to thank these young men," he began. "I understand the pride of defending our country and doing the things no one else wants to do. It's something that's hard to put into words, but it's a gift of sorts...."

As Julius continued and the entire gathering clung to every word, Sherry pushed Mira past the soldiers. Mira continued her protest with a series of moans, but the fight in her had vanished. As the girls passed the soldiers Sherry motioned for them to follow, which they obliged.

"...and I can't believe that my boy, and all these boys for that matter, have grown up so quickly," Julius continued. "And I guess I shouldn't use the word, 'boys', anymore. All of them are men and... well, I just wanted to say how proud I am of each and everyone one of you." Julius reached into the box and produced six items. He shook the hand of each recruit as he handed them the finest shaving kits made, the leather carrying case for each kit engraved with their initials.

The crowd clapped and hooted and whistled. As everyone paid tribute to their boys, Jake searched for Mira who had vanished from her spot. He peered out and across the room, looking past the smiling faces. If someone had walked up and punched him in the stomach as hard as they could, it'd have felt better than the pain caused by what he saw. Jake watched haplessly as Mira and Sherry neared the exit, two soldiers close behind. And so help him God, Jake would never forget the moment when Sherry stopped just inside the church and turned to look at him. As her eyes met his she smiled that damn smile that everyone thought was so pretty. But Jake didn't see what everyone else saw, he saw the truth and the disdain and selfishness that hid behind that smile. He hated that smile just as he hated the rest of the girl. And truth be told, right at this moment, he wasn't too fond of Mira either. Jake shook his head, his face reddening with anger and disappointment. Normally he'd have gone after them and done his best to stomp a mud-hole in those airmen, but he didn't want to cause a commotion and have Pate find out what Sherry really thought of him. So instead, he again leaned over and patted his friend on the back while adding more words of encouragement. Pate turned in his seat and put an arm around Jake's waist, his face expressing an unbelievably broad smile and rosy cheeks.

Chapter 11

Julius squeezed the primer bulb on the gas line before wrapping a cord around the flywheel and pulling. After repeating the process several more times, the air-cooled engine sputtered before gaining its normal rhythm. Julius moved to the bow and helped his Wife onto the skiff, and both settled in as they awaited the rest of their crew.

Like a rising tide, the beach at the Shell Banks swelled with people. Pate was the only one heading out today, the other five wouldn't say their goodbyes for three more days, but that didn't matter. Pate took these precious moments, seemingly the most valuable thing God ever created, and hugged everyone in the crowd. As he finished, he waived a half-hearted waive before walking to the edge of the water where Jimmy and Jake waited. The three shook hands as the rest of the Islanders closed in, making a crescent-shaped arc around them.

"Guess it's time I go beat up on someone else," Pate

said to Jake.

Jake smiled, though he didn't feel much like smiling. Last night had robbed him of something, nearly the same thing he'd been robbed of when his best friend died. Will's death took a toll, and he truly believed he'd never recover from it, but the stinging blow that Mira inflicted was proving nearly as insurmountable. He was no longer an innocent boy who only daydreamed about life and fishing. The world was changing, he was changing, and he was scared beyond his wits that Mira had already changed. "Yea, take it easy on 'em. They ain't never seen how nasty an Islander can fight," Jake said with a fake smile and uninspiring passion.

"You take care of the place and go see Mom and Dad every once in a while," Pate said to Jimmy. "You've always been like a son to them and with me gone they may need someone to hug every now and then."

Jimmy nodded. "I won't let you down," he said.

Pate made one last gesture of goodbye before heading for the skiff. He took two steps, paused, and then turned and walked back to his friends. The Shell Banks was just a small strip of beach on a tiny island, and Pate was just one of millions of men who would leave home and serve during this war, but life forever changed on this chilly morning. It would mark the last time the three would ever be together.

"Pull yourself together," Jake said after a lengthy time had passed, "you're a Marine!"

Pate proudly lifted his head and gave a broad smile.

Pate helped Sherry onboard and climbed in behind her. The girls needed to get back to class and Pate and Sherry would say their final goodbyes when the girls were dropped off in the Bayou.

Jake stepped to the side and Mira made her way to him. She put her arms around his waist and squeezed, but Jake never reacted. She looked into his eyes and his expression caused her lovely smile to disappear behind a haze of acceptance. He obviously knew, hell you couldn't fix a cup of coffee on the island without someone knowing, and it made her sick to her stomach.

"I love you," Mira said. She placed a gentle hand on Jake's cheek, hoping he'd acknowledge her.

Jake continued to gaze past Mira, his eyes focused on the small island across the bay known as Little Dauphin. He never replied.

Mira let her hand slide down Jake's chest and fall to her side just as Julius yelled after her, telling her they needed to get going.

The boat backed away from the beach and Julius swung the bow to the north, the boat now parallel with the shoreline. Pate stood on the center seat so everyone on the beach could see him. As the boat jerked forward he nearly fell but managed to keep his balance. He waved both hands vigorously as the boat headed away from shore and around the spit of land that protected the launch.

The ride over was smooth, a beautiful day to be on the water, and the group safely made it to Cedar Point and

Julius' car. Pate loaded his bag into the trunk and everyone piled into the vehicle. They drove the nine miles to Coden and the house of Mira's Aunt. Mira headed inside while Pate and Sherry walked away from the car and stood beneath a large oak, the limbs draped with dangling moss, the ever-green leaves a sharp contrast to the barren landscape of a cold winter. "Are you over Will," Pate asked.

Sherry smiled. "I think so," she genuinely stated. The girlhood crush Sherry experienced with Will was apparently just a crush. At one time she wanted to believe that she loved him, trying her best to convince herself, but could now see that she never did and never would have. As tragic as Will's death may have been she never felt the loss to be overwhelming.

"Will you be my girl," Pate asked.

Sherry again smiled, but never answered the question. Instead, she gave him a hug, and a kiss on the lips, and then a picture of herself. "Keep this with you and think of me. I promise to be thinking about you."

Pate smiled, took advantage of the situation and stole another kiss before heading back to the car and his parents.

The Carter's drove to the bus station in downtown Mobile, a twenty-mile drive that took more than an hour. Alice cried the entire way while Julius sat quietly, his mind struggling with the courage needed to send his only child off to war. He reflected on the day that he went overseas, and how his Dad had handled it. "Be brave" his father said, "and make us proud." His father then patted him on the back and sent him on his way. Looking back, Julius hated that day because he hated the things his father didn't do and didn't say. His father only wanted his son to be 'brave,' and to 'make em proud'. It now seemed petty, those days when he believed he was invincible and hungry for a fight, but that goodbye had left a mark on him. He was young and anxious back then and could have chewed barbed wire and spit it out, but what he really wanted was for his father to hug him, to say that he loved him, and that things would be alright. Even now, he could never recall a time when his father had told him that he loved him. He vowed that his son would not have the same regrets.

"Mom, don't worry," Pate said as they stood outside the bus station's glass doors. Pate had turned into a man, tall and strong and fearless, but today he was just a son, a child whose love swelled in his eyes as he spoke. "I'll be back before you know it. You'll see."

Alice tried to smile while wiping away tears that streamed down her cheeks before angling to the corners of her mouth. "I know you will. You know I love you... and come home safely. And I'll write... please do the same." Alice said the rest of her goodbyes just outside that old bus station's doors before heading to the car so Julius and Pate could talk. She sat in the front seat and watched as the two hugged for a long time and then hugged again. She couldn't hear what they were saying, she didn't want to. It was between father and son, one soldier to the other, and man to man.

Chapter 12

Sweat glistened on Luther's forehead as he loaded a dozen bales of hay onto the wagon before climbing up and onto the seat. It was the first week of February, and though temperatures only warmed into the mid-thirties by early afternoon, Luther sweated. Luther snapped the reins and the horse trudged forward a few steps. A second later Luther tugged on the leather straps and the animal stopped. Luther glared out, across his family's property and the two creeks that crossed it, and watched as a wagon turned up the long dusty road that led to their house. He knew the wagon and that it belonged to their closest neighbor who lived the better part of a mile away.

Mr. Harrell and his daughter Ruth rode the wagon up the hill and stopped in the Canfield's front yard. Ruth remained in the wagon as her father climbed down one side and moved toward the house with a purpose, a degree of knowing.

Luther stood from the wooden bench of the wagon and

jumped off the side, his heavy frame causing a thump as his feet met earth. He walked in the direction of the house and the wagon, stopping just beyond a barbed-wire fence. Leaning on a post, he watched as his Paw walked out of the house and met Mr. Harrell at the bottom step. The two men shook hands before walking away from the front steps and to the furthest side of the house.

Bending at the waist, Luther took one strand of barbed wire in his left hand and lifted. While stretching the wire skyward he used his boot to push down on the one just below. He ducked his body between the openings and strode in the direction of the Harrell's wagon. Ruth had kept her eyes on Luther the entire time and slid sideways in her seat. Her dressed bunched upwards a few inches and she pulled at the hem, bringing it back down so that it covered her ankles. She now faced Luther and smiled. "Luther," she said amiably.

Luther paused. Other than Sunday school he'd never spoken to the girl, and even then he didn't actually speak to her as it was more of a question and answer and prayer session. But boy, he wanted nothing more in this world. Among the many prayers he said in Sunday school, he always had one extra one, a silent prayer, where he'd ask the Lord to have Ruth picked to read from the Bible. He so loved hearing her read as every word she spoke carried his dreams, her soft and delicate voice taking him on a journey that soothed his soul. To Luther, Ruth was lovely and beautiful and sweet, like a fence row of honeysuckles in early May. And as for today, well today the sound of her voice made his mind take that journey yet again.

"Luther!"

Luther shook his head, snapping from his daydream. Just having her at his house and hearing her say his name made his insides flutter and his mouth go as dry as a creek-bed in late summer.

"Nice day I said."

Luther was doing his best to muster some spit and moisten his mouth, and actually felt as if he may say something, but before he could utter a sound his Dad called after him. "Luther!"

Luther lifted his head and sighted his father.

"Get that hay off the wagon and put some wire and posts on it." John Canfield walked steadily towards the house as he spoke before disappearing inside. He soon returned and handed Mr. Harrell a handful of money, likely all the money he had. Mr. Harrell counted the money and then counted off some of the bills that he handed back to Mr. Canfield. John gave an appreciative and neighborly nod.

Mr. Harrell's entire crop of early cabbage and greens had been demolished by Canfield's cows when they broke through the fence in the middle of the night, and what the cows didn't eat they had trampled, along with most all of his strawberry plants.

"Bye Luther," Ruth called out as her father climbed onto the seat next to her and the wagon began to roll forward. "I'll see you on Sunday."

Luther somehow found a grain of courage and lifted a hand so as to say goodbye.

Chapter 13

Pate left for the Marine Corp and three days later Ralph and the others departed for the Army, and yet, no word had come from any of them in the three-weeks since. The not knowing was the worse, and even Toke, who rarely appeared ruffled, struggled in this unchartered world. All of the enlisted boys weighed heavy on his mind, but the departure of Ralph took an exceptional toll. It wasn't that he didn't care about the other boys, two of them were his nephews and all of them kin, but Ralph was his baby brother and that made a difference. And especially difficult on Toke was the days he visited Mom and Dad, which now ventured near every day. Ralph had never lived anywhere but at home, and the old house, now void of the last of the Cullen children, seemed to call out like a song you once knew but could no longer remember the words. Even Nellie and Jim (Mom and Dad) sat cooped up in the straggly old house that had somehow lost its purpose, both of them outwardly waiting for that familiar glow to return.

Chapter 14

Toke looked into the black sky, the stars quietly
sparkling, the breeze soft and crisp as it drifted from the
north. Toke closed his jacket and pulled up his pant
legs before turning to Jake. It was time to begin their
day as they shoved the skiff into the water, waded out
behind it and climbed aboard. The early hours would
prove uneventful, and with the slight breeze in their
faces it was only a mild struggle to Cedar Point. As Toke
eased the skiff onto the shell-laden beach, Jake lassoed
one of the pilings that guarded the shoreline. After
securing the boat, the two milled about for nearly an
hour, taking turns at seeing who could throw an oyster
shell the furthest. By the time the mail-truck arrived,
Toke's arm ached and he was happy to be getting back
to business. After exchanging mailbags, the two focused
on the Bayou. Nellie, the Cullen matriarch, hadn't been
out of the house not once since Ralph left for the Army,
and the damp house had given her the croup. So
instead of getting outside and sitting in the sun when
the croup first set in, it progressed to the point that she

needed medicine. And Doc Meyer was the man to see.

When Toke and Jake left the Island this morning, Jake knew they'd be heading to the Bayou. He'd been anxious and jittery the entire trip over and as soon as the skiff was untied from the piling and the bow turned westward, Toke stepped off the stern and into the center of the boat. "Here," Toke said as he handed Jake the pole. "That nervousness is gonna eat you alive if you don't do something about it."

Jake smiled. "Thanks Dad," he said. Jake was glad he had a Dad like Toke, someone who understood him. Jake needed to calm himself and do some thinking, and poling the skiff was the best way to do it. The repetitive motion, the feel of the sandy bottom of the bay, and the accomplishment of being good at something, relaxed a man's thoughts and put him at ease. Jake had been stewing in his own self-pity ever since Mira and Sherry walked out of the church with those soldiers, and he needed to set a few things straight. Mira never should have done what she done, Jake was certain of that, but not talking to her, not giving her the chance to explain had made it worse. On the beach on the morning when Pate left the Island Mira told Jake that she 'loved him' and he never returned the gesture, believing he could inflict some sort of revenge. But it didn't feel like revenge, and the weeks since had left him hopeless and miserable. If he didn't speak to her soon he just knew he'd explode.

Jake eased the skiff next to a wooden dock along the bayou's banks, allowing the bow to touch first. Toke quickly tied the bow of the skiff to a piling while Jake did the same with the stern. Both jumped off and Toke headed north along Shell Belt Road, in the direction of Doc Meyer's office. Noticing his son wasn't tagging along, Toke stopped in the middle of the road and watched as Jake jogged along a lane that would take him south and into the community of Coden. "Where you going," Toke yelled.

Jake stopped running and spun around. He continued his backwards trek as he spoke. "Gotta go see if Mira's home. I'll be back before you, I promise."

Toke held up a hand, as if to say okay, and then went on his way.

Jake ran all the way to the large house that belonged to Mira's Aunt. He stood in the drive, catching his breath while surveying the yard. A car rested alongside the building and he was certain that at least someone was home. He hoped more than anything that Mira would answer the door. Having gained his composure he walked up the short walkway and stepped between two enormous porch columns that could have swallowed his house. He knocked at the door.

Mira's Aunt, Rebecca, had an air about her. Lovely and stunning, even in her fifties, she walked with a graceful elegance and spoke with a gentle southern drawl. On top of that she always appeared as if she'd just dressed for a picture, not a strand of hair out of place and her clothing impeccable. And if one didn't know her very well they'd probably say she was highfalutin, and since Jake only knew her a little bit, that's what he believed. But he could say one thing about the lady, she'd always been nice to him and that was worth something. Jake waited a considerable amount of time before knocking again. As someone fidgeted with the doorknob, he prayed it was Mira.

Rebecca opened the door and Jake's smile vanished. "Jake," Rebecca said as a question. She looked over the boy's shoulder, expecting someone to be with him. "You alone?"

"Yes Ma'am," Jake replied. "My Dad's gone to see Doc Meyer."

"Yes... Toke," Rebecca said. Her reply balanced somewhere between disdain and dread, not to mention that she didn't seem worried if Toke needed to see a doctor.

Jake didn't understand the reply, but also didn't have much time. He pressed on and it may have been viewed as rude in nature. "Is Mira home, I really need to speak with her."

Rebecca stiffened her back before disappearing from sight. Jake grinned with relief. A few minutes passed and Jake figured Mira may not have been presentable. If she wasn't presentable and needed more time, then he'd wait, which meant his Dad would also wait. Rebecca, not Mira, returned to the open door and instead of asking him inside, she handed him a ledger. "Mira isn't here. This is her schedule."

Jake ran a finger along the page, studying the dates and times. He finally found today's date, February 10th, and ran his finger sideways, across the page. He let out a long breath as he discovered that Mira's last class of the day wouldn't end for another three hours.

Rebecca studied the young man and tried not to hold his Father's lifestyle against him. She was all for socializing, had done it many times since her husband passed more than twenty years ago, but Toke, well...... the way he celebrated 'was a sin against God and society!' Rebecca smiled, realizing this wasn't Toke, and softened to the sympathetic plea of a young man in love. "Come in and I'll fix some tea."

It was a generous and heartfelt offer but Jake didn't have time. "I'm sorry, but I gotta go. Will you tell Mira I stopped in?"

Rebecca nodded and gave a warm smile. As Jake turned to walk away she called after him. "Don't worry, things will work out." Jake glanced back and thanked her with a genuine smile.

The day slowly disappeared, drifting into early evening by the time Toke and Jake made it to the Island, and they still needed to drop off the mail and take Nellie her medicine before heading home. On top of that, the two never even had time to fish or tong oysters or catch anything for dinner. But as Toke stepped off the skiff he smiled anyway, realizing that dinner would consist of scrambled eggs, biscuits, and grits. Not too shabby all in all.

No more than a rundown wooden building, the Island's post office stood as a testament to life on the barrier island. Ever short of supplies and money, the exterior boards on the building had dried and splintered over the years, and it appeared as if the structure would blow over in the slightest wind. The sturdiest part of the entire building was a hand painted sign hanging from one corner that read "Post Office". The sign had recently been added, and this seemed odd since everyone knew where the post office was and that newcomers rarely visited the Island and never visited the post office.

Inside the little building sat a little old lady, who'd been sitting the entire afternoon. The lady lifted her head with a weariness of an old hound as Toke and Jake walked in. It took a few minutes for her to stand, her back, ankles, and probably everything else stiff, but she finally made it to her feet and extended a hand for the bag.

Doree, the post lady, wasn't around, apparently having headed home to cook dinner because of Toke's delay, and Bell, her mother, substituted. Bell, or in Toke and Jake's case, Aunt Bell, may have been slow as a blue heron fishing the shallows, but deceptively strong as she snatched the bag from Toke's grip. She'd had enough waiting, and Toke and the late arriving mail irked her to no end. Jake laughed as Toke stepped out of her way. Bell put the bag on the only table in the room and turned it upside down. She shuffled through the letters, seemingly sorting them by size, or color, or something that didn't make sense.

"For God's sake," Toke thought. His stomach growled and he could hear Jake's doing the same. "Might want to hurry," he said to Bell, "your eggs are boiling."

Bell did her best to eyeball Toke through glasses as

thick as the bottoms of coke bottles, while muttering something under her breath that sounded a lot like curse words.

***

Last summer, Toke and Jake fished along the rocks near the fort and caught enough sheepshead to feed most everyone on the island. So the two cleaned the fish and began passing them around, including a visit to Aunt Bell's. When Toke and Jake walked into Bell's home, an inviting aroma stirred the air. Bell sat at her kitchen table, a pot of boiling water on the stove next to her. "Smells good," Toke offered. Jake set the plate of fish on the table and Bell thanked him while Toke inspected what was on the stove.

"Whatcha cooking," Toke asked as he lifted the lid on the pot.

"Boiling some eggs," Bell replied.

Toke stared into the pot and at the five lemons that boiled inside. "I think they're done," he said with mocking assurance.

When Bell found out what she'd done and that Toke had been making fun of her, she took a broomstick and chased him out the door.

***

Bell picked up a letter and drew it close to the end of her nose. Her lips moved as she read the name.

Toke tilted his head and watched as the crooked-backed lady stared at the address for what seemed like forever. She then walked to the general area of the appropriate box, a group of small wooden covey holes along the east wall, and leaned forward. It took a while, but she eventually found the right box and slid the letter in. She returned to the table and the process repeated itself. Eventually, and with considerable mercy I might add, Bell handed Toke a single letter before waddling to the front door and exiting.

Toke stared at the letter before handing it to Jake. Jake now glared at the envelope and after reading his name on it, looked to see who had sent it. A stamp in the corner read, "Draft Board of Mobile County." Jake glanced at his Dad and sighed. Toke showed no emotions though his insides churned like a hurricane in the open gulf.

Jake read the letter, as brief as it was, and read it yet again. "It says I have to report to Brookely Field on Friday." Jake handed his Dad the letter and Toke read it in turn. And it wasn't clear who was more disheartened.

Toke put on his best smile as he put an arm around his son's shoulder and squeezed. "Let's go home and eat some grits, and tomorrow we'll go fishing."

Chapter 15

Toke's skiff rested in the crystal-clear water along the Island's south side, rarely bobbing in the smooth gulf. The sun beamed brightly and with the exception of a few seagulls calling out, the slow roll of waves on the nearby shore was all that could be heard. Dauphin Island was a tranquil paradise wrapped in the arms of a beautiful afternoon.

"Dad," Jake began, "would you mind if I go to the Bayou tomorrow and see Mira?" Jake's eyes wandered past the tip of his fishing pole and to the horizon, his thoughts meandering along that hazy-point where ocean and heaven meet.

Toke smiled as he cast his line. "I think it'd be good for ya," he replied.

Jake reeled his line in and set the pole down. He gave his Dad his full attention. "Would you mind if I go alone?"

Toke's eyes continued to glare at the spot where his

fishing line entered the water, the water glimmering in the midday sun. At the mention of heading to the Bayou alone, fear ran through Toke's body. Now Toke knew Jake could cross the bay and channel, his son could pole a skiff as well as him, but he was scared. Toke's eyes wandered to the afternoon sky, his worry as vast as the waters that surrounded the Island. The time had come, something every father dreads. He had to let Jake go, to allow him to venture past childhood. His son was no longer his little boy. Toke took a deep breath and let it out. He turned to face his son. "If you go," he said, "you'll need to stay the night so you don't have to cross back in the dark. And you can bring the mail back when you come."

"Maybe I could stay with Uncle Nolan," Jake asked with measured excitement.

Toke shuttered at the thought of Laura's brother, but this wasn't the time for jokes. "Yea that sounds like a good idea."

"I'll leave in the morning if it's ok?"

"Yea," Toke agreed, his eyes drifting away from his son and to his fishing line that had become taut. He yanked on the rod but his heart wasn't in it and the fish got away.

"What about Mom," Jake asked, his excitement now tempering. Last night he could hear his Mom and Dad whispering, just as he could hear the muffled cries that his father desperately tried to soothe. The last thing Jake wanted was to hurt his Mom, but he hoped she'd understand. He hoped she could see that he had to do this and that he had to live his life.

Toke reeled the line in but didn't put a new piece of bait on the hook. His day of fishing was over. "Don't worry about Mom." His eyes met Jake's. "I'll take care of it." Toke wasn't sure how he'd take care of it, he just knew he would.

After cleaning the fish and giving most away, Toke and Jake took a large flounder filet to the house. Jake held the door open for his Dad, who carried the fish in his hands. Laura looked at the two, their expressions, and immediately decided there was more to worry about than Jake's draft notice. But instead of asking a bunch of questions she forged a sweet smile and took the fish from her husband. Jake washed his hands in a basin before heading to his room to pack. He needed a change of clothes and a few other items for his trip, and his excitement was palpable. His dreams of seeing Mira would stir his spirit throughout the night.

As Jake disappeared into his room, Toke washed his hands and moved next to Laura. He put both arms around her and pulled her close. Laura had cried herself to sleep the night before and appeared on the verge of bursting into tears yet again. "It'll be okay," Toke whispered.

Laura didn't want to cry, not again, and swallowed hard, pushing her emotions down deep. She wanted to be strong for her husband and son... but mostly for herself. "There's more bad news," she said. By saying the words, a new round of tears emerged that she struggled to control. Toke held her ever tighter, but never said a word.

The conversation during dinner was softer and quieter than usual although the stuffed flounder tasted better than usual. The conversation became trivial and seemed to purposely steer clear of the draft. Instead, they told stories of the past. Some stories were about Jake, when he was a baby or young boy, while others were just stories that had circulated the island for generations. But of most importance, all of the stories were filled with love.

The bedroom window had been open most of the day, and the retreating sun allowed the cool night air to enter. It was cold enough that Laura placed an extra blanket on the bed before climbing beneath the covers. She snuggled against her husband, her body aching for his warmth. "This war is crazy," she whispered. "It's crazy that our boys have to go fight because a handful of people on the other side of the world think they can rule us all."

Toke scanned the room, his eyes taking in the shadows. A faint glow from the stars faded across the furniture and into the dark corners, a lifetime of belongings becoming nothing more than shadows. "I agree," Toke replied.

Laura shook her head as she thought about everything going on. "Does Mira know?"

"No... I don't see how." Toke paused, letting out a long breath. "She might, because Jimmy Clark and John Gardner have also been selected... Papa told me when I took him some fish." Toke hated this. Everything of late had been bad news, and he hated having to tell the woman he loved such things. He had always liked to laugh and joke and kid, but the world seemed to have been robbed of such things.

"It doesn't seem right." Laura replied. "We've gone through so much with Will... it just ain't right."

"I don't think the Army cares about any of those things. They need men," Toke said candidly.

"They need boys, you mean," Laura corrected with a stern disposition. "They need a bunch of boys who ain't scared and who think they'll live forever. That's the only reason they take the young. They need boys who haven't yet realized they can die!"

"They're men Laura. Jake isn't a little boy anymore. He's a man in every respect and he's been a man for some time now."

Laura pulled Toke's arm across her stomach as tears crept from the corners of her eyes and slid silently down her face. "He's my little boy," she said between sobs.

"I reckon he is," Toke offered as comfort.

Laura sniffled and wiped at her eyes. "What about Mira? He needs to tell her. They love each other and she needs to know." Laura paled, unsure of her words. "I'd want to know," she added as her words faded into the night. She lifted her head to look at Tokes face. She couldn't believe it was time to let her child go. "Take him over tomorrow. Do whatever it takes." Toke's eyes sparkled in the faint light and Laura studied them, searching for answers. She lay her head back down on the pillow.

Toke lay silent for a moment. "No, I won't take him. He needs to do this alone. Like I said, he's not a little boy anymore."

Laura knew Toke would take care of everything for Jake's trip, so she did the only thing she could and cried.

Chapter 16

Jake awoke two hours before daylight and spent both of them in the bathroom. The night before, his Dad had told him that he needed to leave just after daylight so he'd arrive at the channel with the tide dead low. It would make for the safest time to row across. By the time Jake walked into the kitchen, Laura had biscuits and grits on the table and he gobbled down his breakfast. The morning meal was quiet, as was Laura. As much as it pained her, she understood youth and the freedom they sought. So she did her best to hide her emotions, choosing to focus on her morning coffee and the daily chores that lay ahead. As the meal ended she stood and gave her son a kiss on the cheek. "You do what you have to," she said. "I only want you to be happy." She meant what she said but began to cry.

"It's okay," Jake said. "I love you and I'll be back before you know it."

Laura wiped her tears with her apron and smiled. Her son had grown into a decent young man, and for that she was truly happy. "I love you too."

Jake picked up his bag, which lay against the wall by the front door, and opened the door. "Is Dad at the boat," he asked.

Laura nodded.

Jake smiled and closed the door as he left.

Water seeps into the bottom of all wooden skiffs, and Toke's skiff seeped more than most. As he finished bailing-out the last of the water, he looked up. Jake walked towards him, his smile bright and his footsteps light upon the sand. "Pretty day," Jake said as he made it to the edge of the water and threw his bag onto the middle bench of the skiff.

"It's a good day," Toke replied.

"You know I can do this," Jake added. "I've watched you a thousand-times Dad."

Toke smiled a broad smile. He liked that his son had confidence, just as much as he liked his son. "You know I'm proud of ya," Toke said. "And you may just be the best kid there ever was."

Jake climbed into the skiff and walked to the stern. He stood on the very back edge so as to lighten the bow as much as possible, which rested onshore. Toke pushed the skiff off the beach and waded into the water a few feet. Once the boat was fully buoyant, Jake picked up the poling rod that lay in the bottom. Jake waved before digging the pole into the sand and heaving. The boat turned while moving forward.

A spot beneath a cedar tree on the northern most point of the Island was the best spot, and Toke sat down beneath it and relaxed. He could see Jake making his way north, across the bay, stroke after stroke, and watched as both the skiff and his son became smaller and smaller, eventually vanishing in the morning glow. Toke would sit beneath the tree for two more hours...he needed time to think.

The skiff glided across the glistening water, a million points of sunlight dotting the bay. Jake poled like his Dad had taught him, the bow of the boat acting as a compass, always pointing toward the Bayou. With a breeze at his back and no waves or chop on the water, the shimmering blue water of the bay cradled the boat, accepting it as a part of itself. It was a gorgeous day, the southerly flow of wind bringing gulf moisture back into the air and helping him along. Gulf moisture usually meant unstable weather and thunderstorms this time of year, but no clouds had gathered as of yet and the sun shone unabated. In the warmth of the day Jake's mind drifted, relaxing as he repeated the long strokes. It seemed he had a lot more to think about these days and the solace of the water became his shelter, clearing his mind and thoughts. Ever at peace on the water, today would be no exception.

It neared noon by the time Jake arrived in the Bayou and from what he could remember of Mira's school-ledger, he figured she wasn't home just yet. So he walked north along Shell Belt Road, which led to the center of town and more importantly to Mitcham's Drug Store. He had some serious business to take care of, and when he stepped through the entrance he knew exactly where to head.

"Have a seat," the man behind the counter said with a smile. "What can I do you for?"

Jake eased himself onto one of the padded stools that rested in a neat row across the front of the counter, and set his bag on the stool next to him. He spun on the seat, taking in the room and how white and clean everything appeared. He smiled a big smile before turning his focus to the soda jerk. "Strawberry malt," he said exuberantly.

The man smiled and gave an approving wink.

Treats like a strawberry malt didn't come often for people from the Island, and Jake wasn't about to pass up the opportunity. In fact, he had thought an awful lot about Mira on his trip over with the malt coming in at a close second.

Amazed by the soda jerk's affable ability to throw scoops of ice cream, three to be precise, into the air and then catch them in the mixing tin, Jake cooed over the spectacle as if he were a child at a circus. It seemed a dazzling feat and Jake thought it might be something he'd like giving a shot. Besides the money, he believed there had to be a lot of perks when it came to being a soda jerk. But the novelty soon wore off as the man sat the tin down and began wiping away the flecks of ice cream and syrup on the counter. Having cleaned the mess, he moved to a machine and the whirling sound peaked Jake's anticipation. Moments later the soda jerk returned and set the concoction on the counter. Jake snatched the glass up and took a long swig, struggling to suck the thick slurry through the straw.

This wasn't your typical jerk, much older and wiser looking, though experienced and talented. Jake reckoned all the young applicants had taken up the war cause, leaving a void in the work force.

The man was quick to converse and having noticed Jake's bag lying on the stool next to the boy, struck up a conversation. "Being called up," the man asked.

Jake spun once on the stool and stopped as soon as he faced the man. He took the straw out of his mouth long enough to answer. "Not just yet, gotta go to Brookely later this week."

"Yep, that's the way it begins," the man said as he continued wiping the counter. The man finished, threw the rag in the sink behind him and leaned on the counter. "If you're not headed out, what's with the bag?"

Jake glanced to the chair and then back at the man. "Staying the night. I just came over from the Island a little while ago."

The man furled his brow but didn't say anything. He did, however, end the conversation as he retreated to the sink and began to wash dishes.

Jake never paid the man any mind, knowing all too well how it worked between the Bayou and the Islanders. He'd seen it many times, and truth be told, if it weren't for the temptation of the malt, he'd be nowhere near this place. But it was an awfully good malt, and he'd be back if given the chance.

With the malt being everything Jake remembered, and the people-watching not overly exciting, he bored just about the time he sucked the last drops of ice cream from the bottom of the glass. He paid the man, thanked him, and exited the pharmacy. As he stood on the sidewalk, people pushing past, he decided to walk to Rebecca's house and pop in for a minute. Perhaps it was wishful thinking, or wishful forgetfulness, but he remembered the ledger and that some of Mira's classes ended by mid-afternoon. And maybe, just maybe, Mira would be home. So he made up his mind to visit Rebecca's first before heading to his Uncle's house to nail down plans for the night.

The walk through town was nice, the same gentle breeze that greeted him earlier in the morning now guiding his way as he headed south, the taste of strawberry ice cream lingering in his mouth. It didn't take long and Jake soon glared at Ms. Rebecca's house from the street corner. He never noticed how immaculate the yard was, clean cut and filled with crepe myrtles, magnolias, large oaks, and dormant azaleas. A white picket fence surrounded the yard and just inside the gate a large magnolia stood guard over the sidewalk that led to the front door. Jake stepped through the gate and put his bag on the ground next to the tree. He didn't want to give the wrong impression. He didn't want Ms. Rebecca thinking he had come by with the notion that he needed a place to stay.

Jake knocked at the door with his knuckles, and like the first time he visited he only glared at the large brass seashell in the center of the wooden door. Unfamiliar with the purpose of a doorknocker, he shrugged his shoulders as he studied its beautiful design. But still, Ms. Rebecca took only a few seconds before answering.

"You again," Rebecca said. She caught herself, her lapse in etiquette, and smiled casually as she looked at his glowing face. "What a nice surprise." Her voice had a calming effect, a southern drawl that would have made Scarlett O'Hara envious. She exemplified all the beauty and splendor of southern culture, and she never tried to disguise it.

"Good afternoon," Jake said with exuberance as he stood on a porch that stretched the full width of the house before disappearing around both ends.

After a few seconds of awkward staring, Rebecca said, "Will you please come in?"

Having refused on his previous visit, he happily obliged the current request. Jake was led through the house and soon found himself at the kitchen table with a glass of tea resting before him. The large kitchen was painted all white, a separate room from the rest of the house. It was almost like it had been an afterthought and built many years later. "Good tea," Jake said as he lifted his glass and took another sip.

Ms. Rebecca smiled. "Is Toke back at the doctor? I do hope it's nothing serious."

"No. I mean no Ma'am, Toke's not... I mean Dad's not with me. I came alone."

Rebecca raised her brows. "That's quite a feat."

Jake smiled with content. It was quite a feat and he

was rightfully proud of himself. He nodded agreeably before his smile vanished. Jake tensed in his chair, on the verge of asking a question but not really wanting to.

"She isn't here," Rebecca replied intuitively.

Jake shook his head, his face now straining to relax, the rich ice cream in his stomach now curdling.

"Then speak up child!"

"I'm sorry," Jake said, "but I really must use the bathroom."

Like everything else in Rebecca's home, the bathroom was also very nice. She had running water, a toilet that flushed, an array of hand towels neatly folded and resting on a shelf, and perfumed bath soaps that dotted the edge of a tub. "It's like a movie," Jake thought.

When Jake returned to the dinner table, the fragrant aroma of chamomile and roses followed in his wake. Rebecca cut her eyes and smiled. "Let's get to the reason for this visit," she said. "Is there something wrong or are you just calling on Mira?"

Jake squinted with his right eye, as if he were avoiding the sun. "Well.... kinda both I guess. I've been selected for the draft and I wanted to talk to Mira. I didn't want her to hear it from someone else." Jake paused as he stared at the glass of tea. "I report to Brookely on Friday and I really need to see her."

Rebecca nodded... a regretful expression upon her face. She understood love, having recently fallen for a man after more than twenty years as a widow, just as she understood the pain of losing such love. "I'm sure that whatever happens, things will be fine. Being selected doesn't mean you'll be sent overseas."

Jake liked Rebecca's assuredness, her strength as a woman, and he nodded with appreciation.

"Are you staying over until Friday or are you going home," Rebecca asked.

"I'm going home, my Dad's gonna take me."

Rebecca smiled at the thought of Toke taking Jake to Brookely. She knew Toke didn't own a car and imagined him poling his skiff up Mobile Bay and dropping Jake off on the beach at Brookely Field. She could envision the guards rushing out as if they were under attack from the sea as no one ever figured a draft inductee would show up by boat. She didn't say what she was thinking and did her best to suppress a laugh. "I'm sure Toke will do his best," she finally said

Jake frowned, not understanding the comment.

The two sat and talked for the rest of the afternoon, both waiting patiently for Mira. To Jake's astonishment he enjoyed the conversation as they laughed at each other's stories. Jake came to realize that people from the Bayou weren't so different, and that their lives and their stories were just as entertaining and colorful as the Islander's. The afternoon became a haze of laughter, until Jake began the story of the manger scene. At the mention of Will, Rebecca's expression turned sour and the mood in the room changed. "What a shame," Rebecca interrupted, "A boy so young with his whole life ahead of him. I just don't understand how someone could take another person's life, it's beyond me." She spoke a little more about the tragedy and added a few thoughts on how much she had liked the boy and how much she hated it for his parents. "Those poor souls," she said.

Jake listened and realized it was backwards. Everything Rebecca said was backwards. Will shouldn't be remembered for what had been forced upon him, he should be remembered for everything he'd ever done and what he meant to people. Jake fell silent, he had wanted to talk about his friend, to show Rebecca how much he loved him and what a good person he was, but he no longer had the desire. In all fairness it wasn't just Rebecca who didn't understand, there had been plenty of others that passed along the same sentiments. He figured Mira might just be the only one that understood, the only one he could confide in when it came to Will. Rebecca soon got the message and changed subjects.

The conversation once again meandered, like a small stream through the countryside, and Jake smiled and laughed at a story Rebecca told about a man from the Bayou who needed a haircut. It seemed the man hadn't been in a barber's chair since childhood, cutting his own hair when the time arose. Well the man needed to look good, his son had proposed to a young lady and was about to be married, so he headed for the barbershop. After waiting his turn, the barber called on him and he climbed into the chair. Twenty minutes later the barber spun the chair around and the man looked at himself in the mirror. The man stared in disbelief, it was such a good haircut that he turned to the barber and said, "Do it again, I wanna look twice as good."

Jake was in tears by the time Mira walked in the side door of the kitchen. Mira stood there, books in hand and a dumbfounded expression on her face. Jake rose from his chair, a smile on his face and tears in his eyes. He wiped his eyes as he walked to Mira and kissed her on the cheek. It was as if they had been married for years and they did this every afternoon. But they weren't married and a problem sat a few feet away. Rebecca had always made sure that Mira presented herself as a young lady, and after the short kiss she intervened and made sure daylight separated the two.

Jake stepped back, conscious of the moment, of his surroundings, and of Rebecca. On top of that, the hurt and humiliation he endured when Mira exited the church with the soldiers lingered.

"God I've missed you," Mira said as her expression changed to a huge smile. "I'm so glad you came."

Jake shook his head... it was the only words he needed to hear. "I don't care what happened," he blurted. He couldn't believe he said those words under any circumstance, but especially with Rebecca sitting so close by. After grimacing and rolling his eyes to the ceiling, he added, "I've missed you too."

The two stared at each other and Rebecca could see that this wasn't a passing fancy. She saw the love that a man and woman rarely share and she was happy for both, as long as it remained respectful.

Jake and Mira sat across from each other at the table,

and the euphoria of the encounter began to subside as comfort settled in. "Not that I'm not happy to see you, but why are you here," Mira asked.

Jake knew no other way than to just tell her. "First of all I wanted to see you. I wanted that more than anything. And secondly...."

Mira waited for what Jake needed to say, knowing it must be important for him to come all this way.

"Secondly...," Jake struggled with the words as he looked into Mira's beautiful green eyes. He loved those eyes, the way they had somehow captured the sun. "I've been selected for the draft."

Mira lost her breath and put a hand to her mouth. "No," was all she could utter.

A slight shaking of Jake's head told Mira that that wasn't the only bad news. "That's not everything," Jake added with a softer voice. "I report in two days and I'm not sure what's going to happen. I don't know how it works or if I'll have another chance to say goodbye." Jake felt self-conscious with Rebecca so close by, listening to every word.

"So you may be called up, right then and there," Mira asked.

Jake shrugged his shoulders. "I don't know. I don't know anything and that's why I needed to come here. I couldn't take the chance of not seeing you."

Rebecca fixed a pot of coffee and the three talked about the changing times. Hours raced by, and through a side window the sight of the sun passing just beyond the bayou's bank caught Jake's eye. It was pretty, not quite like the Island pretty, but pretty enough that a smile crossed his face. "Gosh!" Jake said in a startled tone just as the last rays of the sun disappeared. He jumped from his chair, realizing he hadn't yet made plans with his Uncle. "I need to get going," he added. "I need to see my Uncle about a place to stay for the night." Jake didn't say it as if he was angling for an invitation, but if Rebecca extended one... well, he'd graciously accept.

"Can he stay?" Mira pleaded to her Aunt.

Rebecca thought for a while, thinking mostly about the neighbors and the rumors that may arise from such a decision. She waivered back and forth without saying a word, and a genuine struggle seemed to be teetering within. Finally, she nodded and both Jake and Mira smiled. "There will be rules," Rebecca said sternly. "Your homework will be first priority young lady. And when I go to bed, we all go to bed. And Jake must stay in the downstairs room. I can't have the neighbors or your parents thinking that I haven't done my best to make sure you've remained a respected lady." Rebecca was clear in her demands and neither Jake nor Mira argued the points.

For Jake, the entire evening became a treat. Rebecca broiled steaks, which she thawed from a deep-freezer, and Jake thought she must have been the only person in the world with such an appliance. They also had homemade dinner rolls and turnip greens. And following dinner they had coffee and pound cake in the living room. The night was orderly, ceremonial, and regal to an extent. The coffee, served on a tray and poured from a silver urn was inviting, just as the warm and upbeat conversation had become. And Rebecca did a good job of steering the conversation in an amiable direction, a testament to her fluency in dinner-party etiquette. The evening moved at an even keel and Jake wished it would never end. But it did as Rebecca mentioned Mira's studies, followed by a subtle movement of the hand that directed Jake towards the guest bedroom.

Jake nodded in understanding before excusing himself and stepping outside. He hurried to the magnolia tree, picked up his bag and quickly dropped it. Jake swiped at fire-ants that had covered his hand. The poison from the insects burned, and it would eventually cause small bumps to rise in every spot he'd been stung. Jake kicked the bag over and it was covered with the potent critters. And he couldn't understand why until he unsnapped the fasteners and popped it open. On top of his best shirt, his mom had packed galettes with fig preserves. She had wrapped them in parchment paper and they swarmed with ants. He smiled at her concern before dumping the contents onto the ground. He beat the bag against the tree, followed by his clothes and toiletries, before repacking everything and heading back inside. As for the galettes and preserves, they were left on the ground for the ants and squirrels and birds.

Chapter 17

The kerosene lamp in the center of the table flickered, the room strangely quiet. A bowl of oyster gumbo cooled while Laura finished cooking the cornbread. Toke, sitting in his usual spot at the table, never went out tonight, deciding the bar could wait for one day. Jake's departure had left a void, and it made Toke ache. He shook his head, his thoughts carrying him to his last visit with Willy. Willy had lost a son for the rest of his life and Toke only had to endure one night. "God bless Willy," he thought. Toke managed his best smile, for Laura's sake, but truth-be-told he was also tired. He didn't like work, everyone knew that, and now he had more jobs than he could count. Besides ferrying mail and people and whatever anybody needed to the mainland, he also opened and closed Willy's bar most every night and then fished or crabbed or tonged oysters on what seemed to be every other waking hour. But not tonight, having endured the toughest day of his life he needed a break more than ever.

Laura finished the cornbread and set it on the table

before taking her place across from Toke. The usual glow of the lamp failed to brighten the room, a rare moment in the Cullen household.

"It's good," Toke said of the gumbo.

Laura smiled but never replied. The lines along the corners of her eyes stretched further and deeper than ever as the strain of the world aged her features while quieting her spirit. She had cried for the past two days and even now she felt as if the weeping would start at any moment.

Toke lifted his head. "He's okay," he said.

Laura nodded in understanding though her expression said otherwise.

"He's a good kid, a smart kid." Toke grinned. "Like his Dad."

This brought a smile from Laura. "You mean smartass."

Toke shrugged. "Oh," he said as an afterthought, "he's also handsome like his Dad, and charming."

Laura's smile brightened even further. "I guess he is," she agreed.

Toke stood from his chair and picked up his bowl.

Laura raised a brow. "Finished," she asked.

Toke didn't say anything as he set his bowl next to Laura's and pulled his chair alongside hers. Ever since Jake was old enough to sit at the table the two had been separated.

"Thanks," Laura said, and she nearly cried yet again.

"Tell you what," Toke said, "when we're done we'll go for a walk. I ain't seen the beach at night in a hundred years. We'll bring a blanket and a bottle of schnapps and make a night of it. What ya say?"

Laura perked up just a bit and began eating her stew a little faster.

Chapter 18

He turned the cold water on before turning it off. He then did the same with the hot until he couldn't stand to make it any hotter, before sliding his entire body below the soapy surface. Jake bathed in the guest bath and thought, "this running water thing is quite handy." The soap Ms. Rebecca had set out for him was nice, and Jake noticed he smelled quite flowery. After bathing he shaved with a fresh razor, something he hadn't done in months, and then splashed a little aftershave on his face. He smelled good... and felt even better. This was definitely something he could get used to.

The bed he nestled into was large and comfortable, with white linens and a thick wool-blanket. But he quickly decided he wouldn't need the blanket as his bedroom rested along the west wall of the house and had warmed in the late afternoon. So he lay beneath the sheet as the night closed in, his mind and body restless. To the far west the sound of thunder rumbled, and outside his window the night came to life with distant flashes that awoke the sky. Jake sat up in bed and stared out the window for the longest time, admiring the beauty of such a storm. He listened and watched as the sounds and lights moved closer, his mind rarely stirring from a state of dreaminess.

The last month, and even this last day, had been a struggle. Jake tired, his mind tired, and his life, well his life seemed to be teetering on the edge. The only thing he had was Mira, and the thought of her made him take a deep breath and lie back down. He eventually fell asleep as rain began to pat against his window.

Jake dreamed of a car speeding recklessly down a dirt road. He didn't know where the car was going but did notice that it was the same color as the dust cloud that stirred from its tires, the dust trailing and circling the vehicle like a long-bloated snake that had just dined on a din of rats. The vehicle sped along, out of control, and nearly crashed as it made one hairpin turn after another.

Thunder...... perhaps... or maybe a door slamming, Jake didn't know which had startled him from his sleep. In that moment, not asleep but not yet awake, Jake couldn't focus or react as the sheet that covered him pulled away and someone climbed in bed beside him. Mira took in several deep breaths as she laid her head on Jake's chest. With a nervous hand she touched his face, feeling the curves and shapes of his features.

Jake prayed this wasn't a dream. "I love you," he whispered. He hoped for a reply......the softness of her voice proving to be real.

"I love you too." Mira's body trembled as tears began to surface. "And I don't want you to go. I'll be finished with school before long and I want us to start our lives." Mira shook her head, struggling with what had been thrust upon her. "I can't live without you."

"It'll be ok," Jake said. Jake's words seemed hollow, like they themselves had drifted into a dream that no one would ever remember. "We'll be together soon enough. I promise."

"I'm scared," Mira whispered. She moved her arm so that it lay across Jake's stomach and squeezed tightly, as if it were some last-ditch effort to save them both. "Aren't you?"

Jake looked to the ceiling, his soft brown eyes taking in the lightning flashes that drove the night from the room. "I'm not scared of the war, if that's what you mean," he said. The rain increased and it could now be heard tapping on the tin-roof of the house. "I think I'm scared of not knowing, or not having control over my life." Jake shrugged his shoulders, answering his own question. "The thing that really scares me is losing you," he said as tears formed in the corners of his eyes. He found it hard to swallow, his emotions slowly choking him. As Jake said the words he sensed a change in Mira and wrapped both his arms around her. His instincts were to protect her, to make all the pain go away, but instead, all he could think about was how great her skin felt and how beautiful this night had become. He wanted nothing more than to hold her for the rest of his life.

"Nothing happened," Mira said.

Jake slid his body sideways and peered at the top of her head. Lightning continued to stoke momentary flashes about the room, snapshots that quickly vanished into the dark.

"It was Sherry's idea. I didn't want to go and I shouldn't have let her to talk me into it. But nothing happened... and nothing ever will. I love you Jake Cullen."

The storm moved closer, an attempt to unnerve the world, the night ablaze with lightning and a chorus of thunder. Like an enemy storming a castle, wind and rain beat against the window. But it was okay as the large house felt safe and perfect, like nothing could ever harm you as long as you stayed within.

As Jake and Mira lay next to each other, the softness of a touch and the gentle whispers of hope filled the room. What they shared on this night, the lifetime of dreams and emotions, the heartaches and joys, for all the moments that seemed to mean so little but somehow became memories they'd never forget, for all the brief glimpses of love that they'd fought to hold onto, this night became everything God intended. As the sound of thunder and rain eased to the east, the shadows of night held their breaths as the beauty of their souls became one.

Chapter 19

Jake fell asleep with Mira in his arms, and he dreamed it would last forever. But truth be told it never even survived the night as he awoke alone, the bright morning shining through the window and into his eyes. Jake stretched his back before rolling over in bed and running his hand across the spot where Mira had lay. He could smell the mesmerizing scent of her body as he allowed his mind to drift back to the night before. Mira had been heavenly and beautiful, and he couldn't have envisioned a more perfect night. And he thought...... no, he knew... that whatever lay before him, whatever this insane world threw at him, that everything would be okay and that he and Mira would someday be together. He couldn't imagine it any other way.

By the time Jake made it to the kitchen, Mira had finished her breakfast and now had her nose stuck in a book which obscured her face. She only glanced at Jake as she read on. Ms. Rebecca finished washing the dishes before placing a plate of eggs and ham on the table. Jake thanked her and ate with the appetite of a lion. Mira didn't say a word as Jake stared at the book that shielded her face.

"Big test," Jake eventually asked.

"What?" Mira replied without moving the book.

"Big test, I asked?"

Mira broke from her studies and lowered the book, which revealed a pleasant smile. "Jake looks good this morning," she thought. She cut her eyes to her Aunt, whose back was to them both, and smiled devilishly.

Jake cocked an eye as Mira plunged back into the book. Ms. Rebecca finished wiping the counter and stove, before removing her apron. She asked Jake to be sure and wash his dishes when he was done. He nodded assuredly and again thanked her for breakfast and allowing him to stay the night. She left the room to tend to chores.

Mira leaned to one side, peeking through the open door, and watched as her Aunt disappeared into Jake's bedroom down the hall. "Last night was great!" she said as soon as the coast was clear.

Jake thought so too, his amazement soaring as the normally shy and reserved Mira had become so audacious. As for a reply, he didn't have to say a word as his huge smile said it all.

Mira glanced down the hallway yet again before leaning into the table. "You were great and I loved every second of it." She paused, her face taking on a sad expression. "And I hated to leave you. Making myself get out of bed this morning was the hardest thing I ever had to do."

Jake smiled even broader, glad that it was such a struggle. "I love you," he said.

Ms. Rebecca strolled back in before Mira could reply and looked at the two. Both were grinning sheepishly. "Is there something I need to know," Rebecca asked.

"No Ma'am, everything's fine," Mira said respectfully.

Rebecca had plenty of natural-born suspicion, and her instincts told her that everything wasn't fine. "Well then, finish up so you can get to school. I have errands to run."

Jake understood this to be a polite invitation to leave. Jake washed his dishes and thanked Ms. Rebecca one last time. He walked Mira to her car and set the books he'd been toting on the back seat. Mira held Jake's pinky finger with her fingers, the distance between the two as vast as an ocean. Mira knew Rebecca would be watching, and she made sure she demonstrated a lady-like etiquette. "I love you," she said.

Jake said the same, his heart aching as if it were about to beat for the last time. Leaving Mira was unbearable, and he didn't know if he could do it if called upon to fight. There had been rumors that soldiers could be gone for more than two or three years at a time, and that mail, which often took months to deliver, was the only way to talk with loved ones.

Rebecca stepped from the side door of the house and cleared her throat. The gesture effectively ended the goodbye. Mira kissed Jake on the cheek and Jake hugged her tight. As Mira drove away, Jake watched until the car disappeared. Jake stood in the drive a few more minutes before picking up his bag and throwing it over his shoulder. With the wide lane stretched out before him like a royal carpet he started his trek toward the bayou, a north breeze chasing fallen leaves across the street.

Jake poled his way to Cedar Point, where he waited on the mailman, before heading south on his final leg. The afternoon sun tempered the cool breeze, unmasking a laziness that greeted these afternoons. And it became apparent why his Dad loved this job and why he often took liberties on days such as this. The trip was slow as his lack of focus had him inching along in a haze of memories and indiscriminate smiles. He even stopped over at Little Dauphin and sat beneath a pine tree and took a nap... his Dad had taught him well. Jake eventually made it to the Island and pulled the nose of the boat ashore and threw the anchor onto the beach. After dropping off the mail he walked towards home. As Jake stood in the front yard, looking at the old house, he noticed the crooked front steps that rose to meet a crooked front door, and a roof line that sagged in the middle. Rebecca's house had been immaculate and well-kept, and here, standing in the front yard, he could see a thousand things wrong with his home. "Why would Mira ever come back to a place like this," he said to himself.

Laura and Toke were sitting at the kitchen table drinking coffee when Jake opened the front door and walked in. He halfway expected a triumphant homecoming, the long-lost son who'd finally made good on his promise to return home. But instead, his parents just sat there drinking their coffee. Jake set his bag on the floor and studied them both. His mother looked older and tired, extremely tired, and if he didn't know better he'd swear she looked hungover. And then there was his Dad, who looked like he always looked. "What the hell," Jake thought. "What the hell," he said as he threw his arms in the air. "Is anyone glad to see me?"

Toke looked at Laura and gave her a wink. Laura smiled flirtatiously and Jake's stomach sank. Up until this morning, when he and Mira sat at the breakfast table, he'd been oblivious to those types of gestures. But today, well today he knew what that passing glance meant. "Oh God," he muttered. He shook a chill and threw his hands in the air, as if he were asking them to halt. He didn't want to know anything more. His parents were too old for such things, and well... well it was just plain disgusting.

Laura stood, placed a hand on the back of the chair to steady herself, before walking around the table and hugging her son. "I'm so glad you're home," she whispered. "I'll get you some coffee."

"Thanks Mom."

"Drop the mail off," Toke asked.

"Yea," Jake replied as he took his spot at the table.

"You made good time," Toke added. He smiled at the efficiency of his son.

"Yea, it was a good day to be on the water."

Toke nodded in agreement.

"Did you see Mira?" Laura asked, her voice rising a bit louder, as she placed the coffee cup on the table.

Jake did his best to hide his emotions, taking a sip of coffee in an effort to calm himself. If he weren't careful his parents would see right through him. "Yea," he said coolly. "She's good, doing really good in school too."

"That's nice. And how is your Uncle," Laura continued.

Jake knew the question would come, the test his Mom would give. He hesitated before telling the truth. "I never made it there. It got late and Ms. Rebecca said I could stay for the night." Jake held his hands up again, like it wasn't his fault.

Laura's face showed only minor shock.

"Don't worry Mom, she had rules," he added, his hands still in the air.

"Well," Laura asked.

Jake sighed at the fact he was being treated like a child, but answered anyway. "When Ms. Rebecca went to bed, we all went to bed. And I wasn't allowed to leave my room." And with his best lady like southern drawl he added, "Because the Lord knows I can't have the neighbors or Mira's parents thinking I ain't raising her to be a lady."

Toke laughed though Laura's bloodshot eyes failed to see the humor.

"Well did you?" Laura questioned.

"Ma'am," Jake said as his laughter subsided.

"Did you stay in your room?"

"Yes Ma'am. I did as I was told."

Laura drank more coffee and smiled at the good son she had raised.

Chapter 20

"Pop."

Colonel Edward Webster, Commander of Camp Parker and home to the 9th Signal Corp, bristled. He could hear the men outside his second-floor window, and the sound of gunfire wasn't expected or permitted.

"Pop."

"What the devil," the Colonel said to himself. Men weren't allowed to discharge firearms anywhere but the rifle-range, more than a mile away, and his irritation grew.

"Pop."

After throwing his pen on the desk, the Colonel stood and walked to the window that faced the twenty-acre plot of land that made up the common ground. Three sides of the encampment consisted of a mixture of two story buildings, barracks, mess halls, two movie theaters and three social clubs, while a row of radio towers to the north dotted the hill of the remaining side.

Webster scanned the grounds just below his perch and studied the soldiers that had taken up residence. Mess call neared and most guys were letting off a little steam from the long day. Some men gathered in corners and smoked, complaining about their sergeants and the Army the entire time, while others played craps with the little money they had or did calisthenics. And closest to the window and directly below the Colonel, a group of men played baseball.

"Pop."

Webster stared, his eyes taking in the sight of the left-handed pitcher who struck-out every man he faced while going through three catchers who walked away with sore hands. The Colonel nodded as each man stepped away in defeat. "Corporal," the Colonel shouted. He never turned from the window as a soldier entered the room and stood at attention. "Bring me that pitcher!"

***

Toke wiped the bar with a rag, the room a silent shelter for the sparse rays of sunlight that streaked across the floor. His only two customers, Peter and Bess Lea had taken up residence on the outside deck, the two enjoying an ever-pleasant sunset. Only when needing a refill would Peter venture back in, say a few words as Toke filled his glass, and then exit yet again. Now everyone knew how much Toke liked to talk, after all it was the bulk of what he did, and these long stretches of silence were driving him nuts. He was aggravated, like all men get aggravated when they don't get the things they want. "Damn I'm aggravated," Toke muttered to himself. He was to the point that he didn't care if anyone ever spoke to him again. He paused, thinking about whether he really wanted to be left alone. His spirit quieted. "Maybe not," he said to himself. And so began a lively conversation between Toke and himself. "After all, I am the best company a person could keep!" Toke chuckled at the comment but kept wiping and talking. Apparently he'd be going fishing tomorrow, or so he just found out from a reliable source. He stopped wiping the counter and looked at one of the fishing rods Willy had mounted on the opposite wall. "Now where do I want to go," he asked. "Anybody got any ideas? Don't be shy now!" He was loud as he spoke, looking around the room that had dried up like a ghost town. He waited for some tumbleweed to roll through, paused a bit longer when that didn't happen, and started talking again. "Anybody know a good fishing spot? Come on now, speak up." Toke held his arms open, as if he were a preacher at a pulpit awaiting the congregations' amen.

"I got an idea," someone said.

Toke jumped like a cat. The sound came from directly behind him and it scared the hell out of him.

"You need to act like you got a little sense......how about that for an answer!" Willy closed the door as he entered the room and shuffled to the bar.

"Dang it," Toke said without missing a beat. "Why would anyone interrupt a good conversation?" Toke had made light of the situation, he had no choice if he wanted to keep from crying.

The laminated cedar wood that made up the bar sparkled, Toke had been spit-shining it for weeks, but all the same Willy picked up another rag and began to wipe. "I got this," Willy said.

Toke smiled an inner smile as he threw his rag into the air and watched as it floated to the counter. He then righted the cap on his head and marched to his favorite spot and took a seat. He nudged the chair close to the bar. "How about a beer," he asked wishfully.

"Forget how to serve a beer already?" Willy replied. Toke was about to get out of his chair when Willy held up a hand. "It's on me," Willy said. Willy retrieved a beer, opened it, and set it down in front of his best friend. "Thanks," he said. "I...." 'I," was the only word Willy could muster but it must have been the right one, because Toke really let the tears flow. Toke reached across the bar for the towel he'd just thrown down and cleared his eyes and then his throat, followed by a full-blown batch of sniffles. It was no use though as he started crying like a baby yet again.

Willy gave Toke time to compose himself while needing a moment for himself. So he retrieved another beer and opened it. It'd be his first drink in months.

"So where do you think I should go tomorrow," Toke asked through sobs.

Willy, who was also crying, scratched the side of his face, thinking of an answer. "I reckon," he sniffled, "bull-reds are running across the Half-Moon reef."

Toke smiled and wiped his eyes for what he hoped

would be the last time. "Yea," he said, "I think some fish-balls are in order."

Willy nodded in agreement.

Peter stuck his head in the backdoor, his intention another round of drinks, but having seen Willy he stepped back and quietly closed the door. He gathered his wife and slipped away, along the narrow strip of sand that ran along both sides of the back deck.

Willy and Toke spoke for hours that night, their only interruption coming when Saul Clark ventured in, smiled, and tipped his hat as he turned around. Saul did, however, walk away while whistling an upbeat tune. As for the two old friends they had each other once again. Perhaps it would be enough.

***

Ralph sat in a chair, opposite the Colonel's desk, the formalities of standing at attention since dispensed. The Colonel looked thoughtfully at the man before him, a young recruit by all accounts though not a young or innocent looking man by any stretch.

"You know why you're here," the Colonel asked.

"No Sir," Ralph replied.

The Colonel smiled and it eased Ralph's mind. "You, my boy," the Colonel began, "have a great opportunity before you. Here at Camp Parker we take a lot of pride in being the 9th Signal Corp, the best Signal Corp in the military, and it's not just about watching over our boys." The Colonel paused as a bugler played a short tune, indicating dinner. The officer waited until the nightly

109

ritual was complete before continuing. "We have a great responsibility to morale and the utilization of young men to their fullest potential. Why, morale alone can win or lose an entire war. And what we need is to have every man's potential uncovered and refined, and for that man to be accountable for his actions in winning this war. I believe that's something we can both agree on."

The last sentence wasn't a question, but the way the Colonel nodded his head suggested that Ralph needed to reply. Ralph remained completely still during the Colonel's dissertation but understood the request. "Yes Sir," he replied.

The Colonel smiled as he eased further into his high-back leather chair. "Fine then," he said. "I can expect you to do your part, to be one of the many fine soldiers that have made the 9th Signal Corp proud?"

Ralph raised a curious brow. "What exactly is my part, Sir?"

A shriveled smile crossed the Colonel's face. "First off, I need you to be a leader. Your name was run up the ladder and landed on my desk, and by tomorrow's end you'll be a corporal. After that, sergeant stripes may be in order. And who knows, if you play ball you may even make captain before this war is over."

"Play ball," Ralph asked.

"Play ball," the Colonel confirmed. "We have a long history of producing a winning team here, and we compete with other outfits, to boost morale like we just spoke of. And from what I've seen, you have what it takes to make sure Camp Parker's morale stays high for a long time."

The air in Ralph's chest escaped him, his posture drooped and his face lost a measure of respect. "Sir, with all due respect, I want to go over with my unit when the time comes. I came here to fight a war, to help our country."

Colonel Webster looked at Ralph with a measured glare, giving a long pause. The Colonel had been in the Army for thirty-plus years and knew that every man had a weakness, a vulnerable flank that could be exploited. He pressed on. "Don't you believe that using the gifts God gave you, that making sure your men take pride in your accomplishments is important? You have the opportunity, the ability to inspire the men of this Corp. To have soldiers, no matter what difficulties they face, to raise their heads and fight on. Isn't that important to you?"

Ralph didn't know what to say. The only thing that mattered to him was heading out with the guys he came in with.

"Tell you what," the Colonel replied, realizing the moment was slipping away. "Give it a few days and talk to your unit. Ask them if you have a gift and see what they say. Get back to me by Friday and if you still want to go overseas, I'll make sure it happens. Give it some serious thought and whatever your decision... I'll still make you corporal for standing up for what you believe. Can I count on you to do that?"

Ralph nodded as the Colonel dismissed him. He then stood and walked to the door.

"Soldier," the Colonel said. "I want you to know that being overseas isn't easy, but I have no doubt you'll make a fine soldier just like the thousands of others that have come through here." The Colonel ran a hand through his thin grey hair. "You have a lot of pride and I respect that, that's what this country was built on. But this war isn't just about you. There are millions of other men doing the same, fighting for what they believe in, and if only one of them can stand up and make a difference, if only one can inspire so that others may live, then he is a true hero."

Ralph took in a deep breath and nodded appreciatively before disappearing from the room.

Chapter 21

Jake may have slept an hour... maybe, as anxiety and fear slugged it out like two prize fighters. The fight in Jake's mind went the distance, lasting the entire night. It also kept everyone else awake as he brushed his teeth and washed his face at two in the morning, then went outside for wood and God knows what else at about two-thirty before heading back in and into the kitchen where he started a fire in the stove. Thirty minutes later he cracked some eggs and scrambled them in a bowl with a fork. He then combed his hair for the ninth time and fidgeted with his clothes, changing his shirt four times. He only owned three shirts but it didn't slow him down as he eventually ended up with the one he'd started with. The early morning hours waned, painfully I might add, and by the time the fire warmed the room a pot of coffee perked on top of the cast-iron pot-belly stove. As for his parents they never had a chance, lying in bed and listening to the unspoken struggles of their son. They soon joined him in the kitchen. Laura cooked the eggs, since Jake had no idea what to do after scrambling them, along with a pot of grits that no one ate. "Please eat something," Laura said to Jake and Toke. "It might be a long day?" Father and son smiled as they quietly dabbled at their food.

Jake finished his coffee and left the plate on the table before retreating to his room once more. Toke did the same with his plate before stepping outside and sitting on the porch steps. He lit a cigarette. Toke had quit smoking eleven years ago but sure needed one today. He took a puff and stared at the sky that begin to brighten. All he could do was shake his head.

Once Jake finished his final assessment of himself, he passed through the kitchen and stopped just before the door. He couldn't help but feel for his Mom who was doing her best not to cry. "Don't worry," Jake said.

Laura forced a smile. "I'll see you for dinner," she said with certainty.

"Yea, we'll be home for dinner," Jake promised, though he no idea if he was telling the truth.

Laura openly braved a smile as Jake headed out the door. Laura listened as her husband and son spoke for a few minutes, only about the trip over, and then they were gone. With the exception of the pine logs crackling in the stove, the room became silent. Laura rubbed at the aching pain in her temples. "Please God," she prayed, "take care of my child."

By the time Toke pushed his skiff into the water, Jimmy Clark, John Gardner and their Dads had all made it to the beach. And it was like their Mothers had spoken the night before as none of them showed up, each of them saying their goodbyes at home. Perhaps the moms had the right approach, hoping this wasn't goodbye and just another long day. The six men climbed into two skiffs and headed north to Cedar Point. The mostly quiet ride seemed to define the morning, separating good friends, fathers......sons. But all the same the sun rose about halfway across and it was spectacular, the hues of red and orange blanketing the sparse clouds, making them appear as if they were on fire.

As Jake tied his Dad's skiff to a piling, Saul, who had spoken to Julius the night before, jumped off his skiff and headed for Toke. He handed Toke the key to Julius' car, which Toke instantly tossed to Alvin Gardner. Alvin shook his head and threw the key back. Toke never even tried to catch the key and it landed in the sand, nearly burying from sight.

"I vote you drive," Alvin said to Toke. "You come over here more than anybody so I figure you got the best idea of where to go."

"I agree," Saul added.

"Yea, I come over more than ya'll," Toke acknowledged, "but my finger works just fine. So if one of you drive then I can point the way."

Both men stepped back and Toke nodded in understanding. The truth was none of them had ever driven a car or been to Brookely Field, unless you count Brookely's waterfront along Mobile Bay. "What if we pole our way up and drop 'em off on the beach," Saul asked.

"It'd take half a day," Toke said. "We'd never make it in time."

Saul and Alvin nodded in agreement. "It's settled then. You drive and me and Alvin will figure the rest out," Saul said.

"Figure out the rest of what?" Toke asked. "Sounds to me like you're through for the day!"

The men crammed themselves into Julius' car with Toke taking the wheel. "If I crash this thing we all take the blame," Toke said as he studied the dashboard and gear column. Julius was a hard man and his wrath would be monumental if someone smashed up his beloved car. The others moaned in agreement even though Toke doubted he'd ever get a dime out of any of them. But Toke shrugged anyway as he started the engine. The car, nosed in and pointed towards the water, needed to be backed out and across the oyster shell drive. Toke ground the transmission into reverse and looked over his shoulder, making Jake lean to one side so he could see out the back window. Everyone else turned in their seats as well, their eyes wide and their minds and hearts filled with dread... and excitement... and fear. The engine revved as Toke eased off the clutch. The engine continued to whine, higher and higher, until the car jerked into motion, but it wasn't in reverse. Toke panicked! He began pressing every pedal beneath his feet as they raced onto the beach and towards the bay. Luckily, the front tires bogged in the sand and everyone fell forward from momentum as the car stalled. Toke chuckled and grinned. "Wrong gear," he said. After grinding some more, he finally had it in reverse. He revved the engine yet again, though not quite as high as before, while easing off the clutch. The car spun its wheels while trying to climb the slope of the beach. Eventually, the passengers had to get out and push.

Saul stood against the front bumper of the car along with everyone else. "I'm only pushing if you promise you got it in reverse," he shouted at Toke. "I ain't gonna take kindly to being run over."

"I got it," Toke yelled back. And he did have it and the car was soon positioned on the road and all its occupants back inside. God must have blessed Toke this morning because for the first several miles there weren't any other cars or people or anything to contend with as the blue Pontiac careened and jerked down the road with a heavy-footed driver who had trouble shifting gears and keeping it in one lane.

"Did you hear about the others," Saul asked, his voice rising to a high pitch and squeaking as he stomped the imaginary brake pedal on the passenger-side floorboard. Saul, referring to the original six enlistees that had already left for basic training, put up a defensive hand as a street sign tried to kill itself by jumping in front of the car. The suicidal road sign was dodged and the car load of passengers let out a collective sigh.

Toke acted like the near miss meant nothing. "Nope, haven't heard a thing," he said. "And it makes me worry about Ralph."

Everyone nodded, each one reflecting on the possibilities. After a moment of silence Saul continued. "When I talked to Julius yesterday he said Pate was in the Carolinas but didn't know exactly where."

"I hear Lester's in Mississippi and Paul and James are together in Texas," Alvin said.

"And Kermit's in Alabama, over by Georgia somewhere," Jimmy added.

A pause, as sad as losing one's best terrapin dog, spread throughout the car. "So much for them ending up together," Saul whispered.

By the time the group made it to Mobile, Toke had a pretty good handle on this driving thing. And with help from the others he only ran one stop light and two stop signs. He thought he'd done rather well and made sure they all knew it, crowing like a morning rooster, bragging that he didn't kill anything or hurt anyone, other than Saul's right leg.

The car stopped just beyond a barricaded gate and everyone stepped out. After a moment of stretching and getting the blood flowing to their legs again, the boys were escorted away, to a two-story building at the rear of the compound. The Dads watched, each man studying their sons, as they disappeared from sight. Toke shook his head, fighting back tears, as the others did the same.

Once inside the boys were herded into a line with more than two hundred other men. An officer gave a brief talk of what would be required on this day and as soon as he finished another man started yelling names and instructing draftees to "Line up, single file!" Everyone moved in alarm, pushing men aside and racing to their spots, just before everything screeched to a crawl. They moved like a stubborn mule, starting and stopping and digging-in with their heels. It was monotonous, as they stammered into different rooms and around tables where doctors and nurses took varying samples of blood and performed tests normally associated with a routine physical. And modesty, well modesty was out the window as every draftee had to quickly rid himself of the notion. Jake would eventually refer to it as the 'Great Turkey Shoot' as groups of men, twenty-five or so at a time, found themselves' with their boxers around their ankles and staring at the backside of another boxer-less man who bent over in front of them. "What I wouldn't give to be at the head of the line," Jake thought as he closed his eyes tight. After all the embarrassment and poking and prodding, each man sat with a psychiatrist who asked mostly meaningless questions, though there was one about whether or not they liked girls, which seemed to be a requirement of the military.

"I wonder if Pate had to deal with this kind of stuff," Jake asked himself. He didn't speak out loud because they had been instructed not to speak out loud. Above that, and earlier in the day, several men had been rudely admonished for talking and giggling and he wanted none of that. In fact, if today was any indication, he wasn't too sure he'd fit into the Army way of life.

***

Pate Carter endured the things all recruits endure and considerably more. He had since finished basic training at a naval base in South Carolina and was on the verge

119

of completing boot camp in North Carolina. The strains and hardships, the physical and mental drills, what it took to become a Marine, had pushed Pate to the brink. The Marines never allowed a man to get comfortable as they didn't want the norm to become normal. Nights blurred into days and days into months as the war machine forced men to yield to their strengths or die trying. Recruits were taught to fight each other with different weapons, with their hands and knives and rifle-butts, the outcome determined more by mental toughness rather than physical attributes. Every man looked the same, acted and ate and spoke with the same coarseness, and wore the mark of 'Marine Boots' with pride. A cookie-cutter machine, the Marine Corp took the best and molded them into warriors.

Pate's transformation had begun the very first day he stepped off the bus, and unimaginably his body became leaner as muscles rippled in his arms and back and legs. Chiseled and reformed, his mind endured the biggest change, creeping inward and leaving his exterior void of humanity. His mind and body fought for survival of the Pate they once knew, though the war raged half a world away. Life quickly become more serious and it wouldn't be long before he no longer recognized who he used to be. There were things he did during his training that he never believed possible. He could charge down a man with a knife or bayonet, or shoot any rifle or machinegun with fluency. And if his commanding officer told him to, he would take the world and turn it on its ear...... and do so with punishing cruelty. The Corp was in charge, no mistaking that, and his naivety of the world vanished. Pate Carter would never be the same.

***

Luther acknowledged the good Lord, softly concluding a prayer. As Luther exited Rock Creek Baptist he received pats on the back, plenty of handshakes, and an occasional hug. This amounted to more than he had received in his entire lifetime. As some of the parishioners said 'take care of yourself', and others said 'God Bless', he made his way out the door and onto the stepping stones that formed the entrance to the sanctum. As he made his way across the stones he noticed Ruth standing no more than twenty feet away, her Daddy close at hand.

The distance between the Harrell's and Luther vanished, and Mr. Harrell reached out and shook Luther's hand. He then gave him and appreciative nod before turning to his daughter. "Let's go," the elder Harrell said to Ruth.

Ruth stared past her father. "Be careful," she said to Luther.

Luther smiled.

Ruth sighed as she stepped past her father. She placed her arms around Luther's waist. She could barely bring her hands together, clinging by her fingertips. "Come home safe," she whispered.

Luther smiled again......the dumb smile that he hated, the stupid expression that somehow held him back and kept him from uttering the words he longed to say.

121

"Come along," Mr. Harrell added.

Ruth stepped back and looked Luther in the eyes. She waited for the smile to vanish and words to appear.

Luther glanced to Ruth's right, taking a second to look Mr. Harrell in the eye.

Mr. Harrell responded to the glare. "Come along," he said again, this time with more force.

"Luther," Ruth softly begged.

Luther's smile disappeared and he spoke. Times had become desperate, and if he wanted any chance at a life with Ruth then it was now or never. Luther said the words, a lifetime of dreams and hopes escaping into the morning air, and now he felt as if he may faint. His face flushed and he swooned. And truth be told, the words were so beautiful that Ruth swooned as well.

Mr. Harrell didn't swoon, and he didn't appreciate Luther's words. He snatched his daughter's arm and spun her around. "I said come along!"

Luther reached out and placed his rather large hand around Mr. Harrell's wrist. The two stared at each other. Mr. Harrell was a man to be reckoned with, and when it came to his family you'd better be serious.

"This is not the place," John Canfield said to his son. "This is God's land and we aim to keep it that way."

A strain appeared on Mr. Harrell's face. He couldn't pull away and Luther was hurting him.

Luther had been fixated on the elder Harrell, his teeth clinching together like a vise, his anger, something he

122

knew little about, driving him to hurt another person. But the sound of his Father's voice calmed him, as it always had, and he released the man's arm.

Mr. Harrell had been silently tugging at his arm in an effort to get away and stumbled backwards once Luther let go. "Keep that boy away from me and my family," he said to John.

"You better hope I do," John replied.

Mr. Harrell stared at the Canfields', waiting for something more to happen, maybe an apology. But an apology never came and he eventually dragged his daughter in the direction of their wagon and his waiting wife.

"I'll wait," Ruth yelled. "And I love you too."

Mr. Harrell stopped in his tracks and took a deep breath. He glared at his daughter, unable to comprehend the words she'd just spoken. He shook his head as he turned and looked at the gathering of parishioners. His face reddened even more as he imagined what each of them was thinking. A second later he continued to the wagon.

"Horace," Mrs. Harrell scolded. "Let those children be."

Mr. Harrell, red eyed and flush in the face, fixed his glare on his wife. "Move over and help Ruth up," he stammered.

Mrs. Harrell knew he meant business and slid over in the wagon seat while reaching a hand for her daughter.

Luther stood beneath the old oak in the front yard

and stared across the pasture. Cows grazed in the valley, along a creek bed, and Luther took comfort in the earth and what it offered. The episode at church was over and he held no resentment toward Mr. Harrell. In fact, if given the chance, he'd apologize. He understood some things about the world, the things that no self-respecting parent could allow.

"Keep your faith," John said to his son.

Luther wasn't startled by his Father... he had heard him coming from the moment he stepped from the house.

John looked out across the field, just as Luther did, and smiled. He loved this piece of land, something he hoped to pass on to his children one day. "God has a purpose for us all, including you and Ruth. It's his decision, where we go in life and who we love, not Horace's."

Luther turned, smiled, and hugged his father as if he were still a six-year old boy.

The train made its usual stop in Nashville, taking on water while offloading grain into silos. There were plenty of chickens and cattle in this part of the country and grain was a necessity. There was no bus service to Nashville and the engineer agreed to allow Luther to 'hop a ride', as it wasn't an uncommon practice. Luther had to make his way to Texarkana to catch a bus where he could use his Army pass for the ride south. Luther stared at the railcars which wasn't passenger cars unless you count the cattle and chickens as passengers. But some of them were empty and Luther would manage. Like everyone else, Luther and his family and struggled throughout the Great Depression, and if God could afford a little food and a place to lay his head down at night, then he'd be fine.

With two dollars in his pocket, his bag of cloths, a sack of biscuits, two jars of preserves, and a pound of salt-cured ham, he'd take the train ride northeast to Hot Springs before doubling back to De Queen and heading south to Texarkana. It would be a two-day ride, followed by another two days on a bus to Corpus Christi, Texas.

Luther hugged his family, said his goodbyes, and climbed aboard just as the train's engine gained steam. His family watched as the train pulled away and moved along the tracks at an increasing speed, the black smoke billowing from the stack and flowing outward and into the blue sky. And just like Luther, both he and the smoke seemed to vanish into thin air.

**

For Jake, Jimmy and John, the morning turned into afternoon and the day dragged on as they stood in what amounted to a lifeless conga-line. All the men, aligned in alphabetical order according to their last names, endured the drudgery of a draftee. Jimmy Clark was the first of the Island boys, followed by three men, then Jake, followed by eight more men, then John. Baby steps were made, the men getting closer to the end an inch at a time. Jimmy listened as the men ahead of him were told which branch of the military they'd be entering. Jimmy turned to the other two, his mind trying to calculate where he and his friends would end up. An officer administered undisputable decisions that alternated; "Army, Navy, Army, Navy" … and so it would go until the last man was processed.

"I hope I get to see the water," Jimmy said to himself.

"I have to be on the water," Jake thought.

"Navy, Navy, Navy," John repeated in his mind.

Now enlisted servicemen, the three boys from the Island met their Dads at the same gate they'd been dropped off. The dads had spent the day visiting downtown Mobile by foot, not in Julius' car, as Saul believed it best on the busy streets of downtown Mobile. Besides, it wasn't a very far walk anyway. The Dads and sons quietly climbed into the car and headed towards Cedar Point as the sun vanished over the Mississippi Sound.

"What happened," Saul asked from the back seat. He sat next to his son and leaned sideways so he could get a look at him.

Jimmy told his Dad about the physical and all the times he'd been plugged by a needle. He also talked about the questions the psychiatrist asked, including the one about liking girls, as well as the silver tags that now hung from each boy's neck.

"Did any of you say you didn't like girls?" Toke asked.

The boys laughed and John said he honestly thought about answering "no," just to see if they'd kick him out. John finally told his Dad, Alvin, that he had been selected for the Army and that he'd have to report back to the complex in six days. He would be shipped off to a training base at that time, although he wasn't told where.

"What about you," Toke asked his son. Toke's hands would have been shaking had he not had a stranglehold on the steering wheel. Until the end of his life he would never forget the fear of this moment and having to ask that question.

"The Navy," Jake said. "I'll be on the water."

"A small victory," Toke thought, but at least his son was happy with the selection.

"And what about you," Saul asked Jimmy.

"According to these tags around my neck," Jimmy replied. "I joined the Navy and I'm a Catholic with negative-O blood. Jake and I spoke to an officer and he said we may be heading to the same base." Jimmy quieted for a few seconds, the car filling with a blackness that a disappearing sun never tried to abate. "Dad... me and Jake head out on Monday."

Toke bit his bottom lip.

The car load of men drove on as silence gripped them with an unbreakable force. Saul thought about his son having to go away in just two days and looked over at Toke, whose face showed the same worry. They drove for several more miles without a word. Toke eventually spoke up. "Water, land, Army, Navy... it don't matter. We're proud of each of you. And you're gonna make fine soldiers."

The men poled their skiffs homeward, and Toke and Jake, along with the others, made a few quick throws with their nets. Toke hoped it wouldn't be the last time. Catching fish with his son was one of the joys of his life, something he never wanted to end. They caught a few silver-mullet and the boys cleaned the fish before each family took some home for dinner.

Toke, Laura and Jake finished a late dinner, deciding another pot of coffee was needed. As they drank the coffee they talked, and it was a conversation that no family should ever have to share. But here it was and they had to deal with it. For the most part Jake assured his Mom that everything would be ok and she did her best to pretend that she believed what he said. It did, however, bring to a close the longest day they'd ever known.

Chapter 22

Peter and Bess spent Sunday afternoon with their daughter in the Bayou, and Rebecca, Bess' sister, invited them to stay the night. Typically, Peter wouldn't be a party to such things as he had his own family in the Bayou, including his Mother. But he obliged the request anyway and Mira thought it odd as both her parents had never stayed before. Mira loved her parents and even enjoyed their company, but she didn't like this. Jake had recently been selected for the draft and required to report to Brookely, she knew that much, but everyone had become tight-lipped ever since. "You'd tell me if there was bad news," Mira asked her Mom. Mira stared her Mom in the eyes, looking for a sign.

Bess wasn't very good at lying, to anyone, and could only muster a slight shrug of the shoulders. Mira's eyes welled with tears, the chair she sat in fighting to keep her upright. Bess pushed her chair back from the kitchen table, stood, and walked over to her daughter. All she could do was put her arms around Mira's shoulders and cry with her.

Rebecca prepared a good meal that only Peter ate, while everyone else picked at their food, waiting for the moment when they could call it a night. And Mira would be the first to head off to her room. As Mira readied for bed, Bess tapped at her door. "You have a hug for your Mom," Bess asked. Mira's eyes were red and swollen with more tears on the horizon. She needed a hug more than anything.

Mira and Bess sat on the edge of the bed, a wall sconce prodding shadows into the far corners. "Do you know when," Mira asked.

Bess was hesitant but decided that her daughter needed to hear the truth... she deserved that much. "Soon I guess. It seems everyone on the Island is on pins and needles."

"I figured as much. Daddy wouldn't be here if it wasn't serious."

Bess nodded. "Try not to worry. You have school to think about and Jake will be alright. You'll see."

Mira couldn't see anything her Mom was telling her... her pain had risen too fast and swelled too big to be overcome in one night. "I want to go back with you and Daddy tomorrow. I need to see Jake."

Bess placed a soft hand on Mira's leg and did her best to raise her daughter's spirits. "Whatever it takes I'll make sure you see him before he leaves." As for tonight though, Bess could do little to quell her daughter's tears.

Chapter 23

Mira kissed her Mom on the cheek and Bess smiled. A gooey concoction of flour and milk coated Bess' hands and she was unable to return the gesture, so she pursed her lips and gave an imaginary kiss to the air in front of her. A pan of biscuits would soon be in the oven and she'd then have time for her daughter. Mira turned to her Dad, who sat at the kitchen table, a cup of black coffee resting in front of him. Mira eyed him and he could feel her attention that bare down on him. He raised a brow while picking up his cup and taking a long sip. Mira pulled a kitchen chair away from the table and slid it next to him. "Did Momma tell you," she questioned.

Peter nodded. "She told me," he said. "But you have class and you know what going to the Island means."

I don't care if it takes a week," Mira responded sharply. It may have come off as anger, but it was only hurt that manifested itself. "I'm sorry," she whispered.

Peter smiled. He understood his daughter and her

passion for those in her life. "Okay," he said. "But you have to promise one thing."

Mira nodded.

"The day after you see him you'll be back in class. You've come too far to let your grades slip."

Again, Mira nodded.

Mira tried to help with the morning chores but Mother and Aunt sent her away. They said it would be a long day and she needed to bathe and dress. As Mira returned to the kitchen, the smell of biscuits and skillet-fried pork filled the room. Bess looked at her child and smiled. Her daughter had put on a dress, a delicate white bow along the neckline in beautiful contrast to the dark blue material. And it was just as pretty as Mira. "Where'd the dress come from," Bess asked. She knew Mira had no money and figured Rebecca must have bought it.

"It's one of Sherry's," Mira replied. "She has more than she can shake a stick at. And she's good about letting me borrow them."

Bess was about to respond when a car horn sounded in the front yard. Everyone in the kitchen looked at each other as the horn further disrupted the morning. Mira immediately fought back tears. This entire morning, her Mom and Dad being here, her Mother and Aunt insisting she bathe instead of helping with chores, her Dad agreeing so easily to allow her to go to the Island to see Jake, had been leading up to one thing. She struggled to breathe as tears now came in earnest. Bess wrapped her arms around her daughter and tried to ease her emotions. She hung on for dear life, longing for her daughter's pain to end.

As happy as Mira was to see Jake standing alongside Julius' Pontiac, she cried with every step she took. When Jake finally put his arms around her, she shook uncontrollably. "Shhh," Jake whispered in her ear. He kissed her cheek, and his warmth and affection made her cry even more. "It's gonna be okay."

Mira shook her head.

"Come with me," Jake added.

Jake and Mira sat on a bench that rested beneath a magnolia tree, its evergreen-waxy leaves defying the winter's chill. As Mira calmed she could finally look at Jake without bawling. "Where they sending you," she asked.

"I don't know. Jimmy and I are both reporting this morning and hopefully we'll end up together. But I don't know."

Mira took a deep breath, again struggling with the tears. "I love you," was all she could muster.

Jake had been nervous, but Mira's words allowed him to relax as it was all he longed to hear. Jake smiled as genuinely as ever and kissed her lips. "I know this isn't the way it should be. It's not how I thought it would be. But Mira," Jake said softly and as he slid off the bench and knelt before her. He took her hand with the kindness of a dear friend. "Will you marry me?"

Mira blinked, taking in the small creases that spread

outward from the corners of Jake's eyes, his face, just as tan in the winter as the summer. Her head spun in dizzying circles and she believed she may faint.

A quick beep of the horn from the waiting car disrupted Mira's trance. She caught her breath as she looked to the vehicle and the smiling faces that pressed against the glass windows. A huge smile crossed her lips and she threw her arms around Jake's neck and began kissing every inch of his face. "Yes," she whispered in his ear. "Yes! Yes!" she said more loudly. Everyone could hear Mira's answer as she continued to deliver the sweet kisses. Those in the house found themselves racing out to congratulate the couple just as the car emptied and did the same. Within seconds, everyone joined in the celebration, patting Jake on the back and hugging Mira's neck. And the moment was joyous and beautiful...... and solemn and heartbreaking. It did, however, offer a glimpse of happiness and hope in an otherwise terrifying time. Jake held close to Mira with what precious moments he had and never took his eyes from her. "She's gorgeous," he thought, "and she's going to be my wife!"

The morning was brief, too brief for a celebration, but Jake and Jimmy could no longer delay their trip. So Jake kissed his fiancé once more and hugged her until the very last second. And he prayed, he prayed with all he had they'd have at least one more sunrise together.

Peter held true to his words and allowed Mira to stay home from school. She needed time to gather herself. The morning had turned her into a wreck, and everyone doting over her engagement only made things worse. "I think I'll go for a walk," Mira eventually said. Mira put on her sweater and stepped out of the house and into the warming day.

The day turned out to be cloudless and bright, and it only added to the eerie silence of the ballfield. Mira sat in the bleachers, looking out and across the dormant grass. She could just about picture Jake in the outfield, his bare feet sticking out from beneath his long pants, his white tee-shirt emblazoned with a number 'three' painted on the back. Jake was the only one whose number was painted in cast-net green, undoubtedly something Toke had a hand in. She almost smiled, the memory becoming a precious gift, but the sound of car tires on crushed oyster-shells made her turn away from the afternoon's game. Mira watched as Sherry stepped from Rebecca's car, leaned back in to say something to Mira's Aunt, before closing the door. Rebecca drove away.

"I wish I looked that good in that dress," Sherry said as she climbed the bleachers and plopped down next to Mira.

Mira studied the hem of the dress that had risen just above her knees and couldn't disagree.

"So I hear you're engaged to some boy," Sherry said. Sherry had always been quick with the sarcasm, and this seemed no different.

"As opposed to a girl," Mira questioned with equal cynicism. A moment as peculiar as a three-legged dog danced between the girls, becoming a terribly awkward four-minutes. "I didn't know I could feel so alone," Mira finally said.

Sherry turned sideways and studied her friend. "But you're not," she said. "You have me." Sherry watched as Mira tried to smile but it only turned to tears.

"I miss him so much," Mira sobbed. Mira doubled over, wrapping her arms around her stomach and leaning forward.

"It's okay," Sherry said. Sherry put an arm around Mira's shoulders and leaned into her. "Please don't cry," she whispered. "It just kills me." Sherry kissed Mira's cheek but Mira never paid her any attention. "Please don't cry," Sherry said again. She kissed Mira's cheek yet again, more tender, gentler......softer.

Mira pulled away, leaning sideways and staring at Sherry.

Mira's eyes were red and swollen and puffy and Sherry believed her to be an angel, the most beautiful creature she'd ever seen. "I love you," Sherry said in earnest. Sherry waited for a reply, but Mira's shaking head spelled out the answer.

"What," Mira questioned. Mira's face contorted and reddened as she strained to understand. The day had been unexpected and beautiful and dreadful, but it now ventured toward insanity. "You love me," she asked.

Sherry took in a long breath, a gentle breeze carrying her hopes and dreams into the afternoon sky. "Of course I do," she replied. "You're my best friend."

Chapter 24

A mile-long train ushered Marines to their destination, and Pate Carter sat in one of the railcars with the rest of his unit. The days of basic training were only a short breath behind as the moment of deployment had arrived. Pate was headed to the west coast, and from there who knows. The men had been quickly ordered-up, given just a few hours' notice and three simple orders. They were told to pack, write to their parents, and board. They had been instructed to write nice letters that said they were in good health, good spirits, and about to be deployed... nothing more. It seems the Marine Corp has a great big heart, allowing boys to let loved ones know they were okay and not much more.

For two days the locomotive crossed the United States, eventually offloading in southern California. As for Pate, well he ultimately stood on a dock with six-thousand other Marines, his eyes wide as he gawked at the enormity of an ocean-going transport. Pate shook his head before turning away from the ship. His stomach gurgled and he placed a hand against it and grimaced. He needed some water and craned his neck as he searched for a cooler. There were no coolers, only men that bunched around him like a swarm of bees. His stomach sank further as he studied the faces, expressions of merciless grief. Every man feared what lay ahead, just as Pate feared it, and the anxiety of stepping onto the ship made his stomach churn even more. He wanted to go home, wishing he could see Mom and Dad and everyone else once more. As he walked the gangplank he found it hard to breathe, so he thought about everyone who had ever been a part of his life and it allowed him to smile. It amounted to the one thing that kept him from passing out.

***

Corpus Christi Texas is a lot like south Mobile County, Jake thought. The water was nice, somewhat clear, and daytime temps were only slightly warmer than back home. And with an abundance of humidity Jake took notice. Not just anyone could dismiss the high humidity, but for Jake a tiny sliver of Dauphin Island presented itself.

When Jake and Jimmy arrived at the naval base, the speed of the Navy ratcheted-up, and within hours they had settled into a barrack, been issued uniforms and equipment, and marveled over shaven heads. Jake had walked in, sat in a chair, and fifteen seconds later he stood outside, removing clippings from inside his ears and from around his neck. He then waited on Jimmy who showed up about twenty seconds later. The barber, if the man could be labeled such, ripped through hair like he hated the stuff.

"Boy, I wish Will could have been here for this," Jimmy said with amusement. Jimmy studied the stubble on Jake's head and the snow-white scalp. It looked odd with his face and neck tanned a golden bronze.

"Yea, he may have already deserted," Jake replied. Jake laughed as he ran his hand across his near baldness. But the laughter quickly ended as Jake wasn't quite ready to discuss his loss.

"Sorry," Jimmy said.

Jake forced a smile but there was nothing to say.

Military life, it seemed, entailed doing your best to remain out of the lime-light. Being screamed at was never pleasant, and there was always, and I do mean always, someone around to do plenty of screaming. So Jake and Jimmy made a pact to keep out of trouble and keep to themselves. Jake figured the Navy would be simple, after all he liked boats and the water, and physically and mentally he could take anything they threw at him. He had his wits and could think fast on his feet. Not yet twenty, he was sharp minded, physically fit, and all knowing... not like some of the other draftees who ventured past twenty-five.

Jake and Jimmy listened to the bugler and like a herd of sheep everyone walked in the same direction, all of them searching for a field to graze in. As the two neared the mess hall Jimmy stopped, placing a hand on Jake's forearm. Jake paused as well, then followed Jimmy's gaze to three men. Donnie Everson, his cousin John Carl Everson, known as JC, and Luther Canfield stood about fifty-feet away and in close quarters to each other. Donnie and JC, being the asses they were, were both in Luther's face, the asses standing side by side and making themselves into one big ass. The big ass stepped into Luther and Luther retreated while turning his face to his right. Luther starred at the manicured yard below his feet. Emboldened, one cheek of the ass, known as Donnie, grabbed Luther by the collar just as the other cheek poked a finger into his chest.

"You okay," Jimmy asked, his eyes square on Luther. Jimmy and Jake had quietly made their way to the scene.

"Beat it!" The head ass said, his hand pulling hard enough to rip Luther's shirt. Donnie and JC were from upper Michigan, and why these two didn't end up at the Great Lakes Enlistment Camp is anyone's guess. But here they were in south Texas and trying to force their asses on everyone else.

Collectively, the five men in this deranged play were in the same unit. They'd be sharing the same barracks, drilling together, showering in the same showers and eating in the same mess. Yea, they'd be a swell unit. Well it seems Donnie spoke with a high feverous pitch, an assault that came so fast that the words blurred into what sounded like "bait-it." "Bait it?" Jimmy asked.

"Scram," Donnie said as clarification.

Jimmy nodded in understanding. "No," he responded, "I'm good."

"You looking for a knuckle sandwich," Donnie asked.

"What," Jimmy said, again not understanding the man. Donnie held up a fist and shook it at him.

Perhaps Jimmy was looking for a fight, or perhaps he just felt sorry for Luther. Either way, he nodded. "Let's do this," he said.

Jake stepped back but kept a close eye on Donnie and JC. Jake had never known Jimmy to be in a fight and didn't know if he even knew how to fight. But Jake knew plenty, he knew that men were sneaky by nature and if one of them could clock Jimmy from the side or from behind, they would. So he watched, and if Jimmy wanted to fight Donnie then he'd make sure it was a fair fight.

"Hey JC," Donnie said as he let go of Luther's shirt and looked to his buddy. "This guy's a wise ass." He turned back to Jimmy. "You a wise ass?"

Jimmy didn't like Donnie's tone, whatever he was saying. "What," Jimmy said with honesty.

JC stepped close to Jimmy, too close, and Jimmy pushed back. JC stumbled in the opposite direction.

"Nope," Jake thought, "he don't know how to fight." If Jimmy really knew what he was doing he'd have used that moment to lay into JC, but he didn't because he was too nice. Jimmy had always been the nice guy.

As he halted his backward momentum, JC's face reddened. After that he did the same, using his opportunity to push Jimmy.

"Oh my God," Jake thought, "neither have ever been in a fight."

Donnie looked past everyone and at Jake. When their eyes met both men realized the other could fight. "What's this," Donnie said incredulously. "This is not a fair fight."

Jake stared back at Donnie, his glare hardened by years of dealing with Pate Carter. "What," Jake asked.

Jimmy intervened. "I think he said 'What's his night of light'?" He then shrugged his shoulders.

Donnie shook his head. "Their idiots," he said to JC.

Jake understood that and moved toward Donnie. Donnie stepped back from Luther as Jake pressed on.

"Hold it," Donnie said as he put his hands in the air, the palms facing Jake. Donnie's eyes moved from Jake and locked on an officer standing near the mess hall. The officer lingered, watching the five men, appraising the situation. "Another time," Donnie added with a sneer. He motioned for JC to follow and the men walked away.

Jake looked at Jimmy and the two broke into a laugh. They laughed for a bit longer before turning away and heading for the mess. After a few steps they stopped, turned back and waved a hand for Luther to join them. As the three of them devoured lunch, in a loud and cavernous room, Jimmy must have asked Luther fifty questions. But Luther never answered, not once. Luther was busy eating, struggling with shaking hands and a trembling body.

Jake lifted a brow, wondering why such a large man was so scared. "You should have taken one of those big hands you got and slapped the smartass across the face," Jake said. "He'd leave you alone after that."

Luther's eyes remained focused on his plate, his trembling hand delivering spoonful after spoonful to his mouth.

"Look," Jake added, "he's just a bully. Don't be scared of him."

Luther finally lifted his head and stared Jake in the eyes. He motioned for more food, his teeth now chattering.

Jake and Jimmy heaped their remaining food onto Luther's plate and watched as he wolfed down every morsel. As Luther finished the meal his body regained its normal rhythm and the shaking stopped.

Jimmy nodded in understanding. "I have an Aunt like that," he said, "something to do with her sugar".

Luther ended his meal with a long drink of water before officially introducing himself. Soft spoken and articulate, Luther extended an odd thank you to Jake and Jimmy. He didn't thank them for coming to his aid, but instead he thanked them for the compassion they showed. He said it was the virtue he and his Dad most admired.

The gesture wasn't lost on Jimmy, who smiled. He liked that. "Why were they picking on you," Jimmy asked.

Luther replied just above a whisper.

"Well why wouldn't they want you in the Navy," Jimmy

asked.

Luther paused, but never answered.

Jake realized what the men likely said to Luther, or at least he had a good suspicion as he studied Luther's features and skin color. He couldn't tell if Luther was black or what. He seemed like a mutt, and that wasn't a bad thing. Hell, Jake himself was a mixture of Irish and Sicilian and nearly as dark skinned as Luther.

"It don't really matter," Jimmy said dismissively and as he waved a hand through the air. "I'll tell you what. You stay close to us and we'll watch each other's backs. And whatever Donnie or anyone else says they'll have to deal with all three of us." He turned to Jake. "Right Jake?"

And with that, Jake gave an approving shrug.

Chapter 25

Like water from an open cistern, sweat ran down the side of Ralph's beaming face. He just completed his second game as starting pitcher for the Camp Parker Falcons, a near flawless effort, and he smiled as he shook hands with the opposing team. His pitching had been improving with each outing, and this one hitter was a real jewel. The smile widened as he said "good game" over and over while reflecting on the recent news of scouts wanting to see him pitch. He hoped there would be a life in baseball after the Army, a dream he'd had since he first picked up a ball. Now it goes without saying that his decision to stay stateside wasn't an easy one, his regrets keeping him awake at night, but everyone said he needed to do it for his squad and pride of the 9th Signal Corp. So, on the day he told the guys he'd stay here and pitch, for them, he had an unsettling in his bones because deep down he knew the truth. He knew exactly why he decided to stay.

***

Luther paid little attention though Jimmy had had all he could stand. Jake bragged for a full week, ever since he found out that Gunnery School was open. Over the next two-weeks men would find out if they had what it took to be a Gunnery Mate, and Jake, well he knew he'd land one of the coveted spots. He'd shot guns, led ducks across the sky before pulling the trigger and bringing them to the ground. Also, he was the smartest guy in his squad and quick to calculate and solve problems. He possessed everything needed to be the best, so he'd see it through with dreams of being topside when the fighting started. Yes sir, he'd be a Gunnery Mate alright... 1st Class.

There must have been a million shots fired on the rifle range. White targets fronted an earthen embankment, the crisp blue sky providing a distant curtain that unfurled and brought the targets into focus. Jake and the rest of his unit marched onto the range, a clod of red clay that formed a long ridge, as another unit exited. Jake scanned the range, noticing the distance to the targets, his stomach rousing with excitement. "Damn that's a long way," he thought...... "for some people," he concluded with a chuckle.

The smell of gunpowder lingered in the morning air and Jake smiled a secretive smile as he marched forward along a line of tables. Midway through the line of tables a man tossed him a rifle. The damn thing landed across his extended arms, the heavy ass thing slamming against both biceps. He'd never shot a rifle, nothing big enough on the Island that you needed a rifle to kill it. "Excuse me," Jake said to the man, "you got a shotgun?" Of course they yelled at him, so he accepted the rifle and after a few minutes of handling the gun, looking it over and sighting the sights, he didn't foresee any issues. "A gun is a gun, after all."

Yelled at by a Marine Corp Staff Sergeant, it seemed the Navy neglected to tell Jake that Marines were in charge when it came to the rifle range, a stiff jawed Sergeant ordered the sailors to lie on their stomachs and take aim at a hundred-yard target. The men did as requested. Jake stared down the barrel of the rifle, aligning the rear and front sights with the target. He smiled as he squeezed the trigger. The rifle kicked as hard as pulling both triggers on a double barrel shotgun. "Son of a bitch," he shrieked in pain. Men on both sides of him laughed, but not the Sergeant. On top of Jake like a gasoline fire, the Marine screamed directly into his ear. "You stupid son of a bitch, who told you to fire that rifle?"

Jake shrugged his shoulders and the Sergeant put a knee into the middle of his back. Jake deflated, gasped for air...... and, well...... squeezed the trigger yet again. The shot was errant and everyone dove to the ground. "Holy Shit," the Sergeant yelled even louder. "You are God damned stupid!"

Jake was finding it hard to breath and if he could have shrugged, he would have.

By the end of the day, all Jake had to show for his efforts was a sore shoulder and deafness in his left ear. He had been average at best and careless at worst. But as he trudged into the barracks he remained surprisingly upbeat. In two days anti-aircraft simulation would take place, and that's when he'd really shine.

Chapter 26

Man those guns had power...... thump, thump... thump thump, followed by four explosions along a hillside. And with that, another man finished his simulation and stepped out of the anti-aircraft gunnery seat. The man moved to the right of the seat, to be a munitions loader and the next recruit sat down. Jake couldn't wait, the line ahead of him shrinking at a rapid pace.

"Baker, forty-eight," a Staff Sergeant yelled.

"Pitiful," Jake thought. There had been scores as high as seventy-one and only one lower than forty-eight. "Pitiful," he said again.

"Breeland, fifty-seven."

"Bukowski, sixty-two."

"Caffey, forty-seven."

Caffey stepped into the loader position as Luther Canfield worked his large frame into the seat. There were four large targets on the hillside and they spanned

149

about forty-feet apart and at differing heights. The Sergeant would yell, 'one' or 'four', meaning you fired left to right or right to left. Luther used his allotted time to maneuver the reels, gaining an understanding of how to lower and raise and sweep the guns from side to side. It was real work, spinning the turret with the hand crank while maintaining proper elevation. Luther took a deep breath and waited. "Four," the Sergeant yelled. The loader slid a four-shell rack into the chamber and Luther did the rest. The thumps were well timed, a nice rhythm that anyone standing nearby had to appreciate. The smoke from the barrel drifted to the north, not quite escaping the muzzle as explosions rocked the hillside.

Within seconds the Sergeant calculated and yelled Luther's score. "Canfield, ninety-one." It was a near perfect showing.

Jake had been watching Luther closely, and counted by patting his foot as the cannon barrel moved gracefully across the horizon. Jimmy stood to be next and Jake grew more anxious.

Luther gave Jimmy a reassuring nod and waited to load the guns. Jimmy smiled back. "Four," the Sergeant yelled. A short time later the Sergeant added, "Clark, 58."

"Respectable," Jake thought as he moved to Jimmy's spot. "Good job," he said to Jimmy as he studied the wheels.

"You got this," Jimmy said.

Concentrating on what he needed to do, Jake paid

Jimmy no mind. Jimmy held the ammo up high and waited. "Four," the Sergeant yelled once more.

Jake rolled the wheels forward, then backwards, he looked through the sight, he ticked the seconds off with his foot, he spun the turret to the left, no... he needed to go to the right to begin. "Focus Jake, focus," he said to himself. Jake focused more than he ever had, spun the cylinders... the turret responded, spinning on a dime. "Thump," he measured his pace. "Thump, thump," ...... a long pause and "thump". Jake peaked out from behind the cannon barrel and watched as the first shell missed high. Then the second, even higher and the third near the summit! "Jesus Christ," he said. "Where the hell's the fourth explosion!" Terror stalked Jake's mind. "Explode! Explode!" he yelled. It exploded...... nearly two miles on the other side of the mountain. "Oh my God," Jake thought. Sweat and panic became real enemies as Jake feared he may faint. Now Jake never fainted, never had time, nor did he hear any yelling, though later on he'd be reminded daily that there had been plenty. What he did remember was a rather stout and hairy arm, attached to a rather stout officer, grab him by the shirt and yank him out of the turret. The man threw Jake sideways and Jake stumbled a few steps before skidding face first. He spit dirt and blood from a busted lip as he rolled over and looked upwards to the man standing over him. He just knew the man was going to stomp him to death.

"Cullen, four," the Sergeant yelled.

***

Toke flung open the back door and a soft breeze waded in, flooding Willy's bar with the scent of the Gulf. Toke's chest heaved a deep breath, taking a moment to enjoy the pleasures of living on an island. A light chop stirred the bay, setting off a dazzling display of flickering lights, and Toke smiled. As soon as the room had its fill of salt-air, Toke turned his attention to the bar. He needed to get started, seeing how he was more than three hours late. He had promised Willy that he'd be here by noon, and should have already swept up and swabbed the tables and counters, but last night had taken him fishing... a beautiful night for floundering. And judging by the twelve fish he cleaned early this morning, it was all worth it.

"About time," Peter Lea said as he ventured in and sat at a table. "I didn't think you'd ever get here."

Toke smiled, he was happy to have someone to talk to. "How 'bout I make it up to ya," he said. "First one's on me."

"I'll second that," Saul Clark added while trudging through the front door.

Toke grimaced, knowing he'd now have to pay for two drinks.

"Where's Willy," Peter asked.

"Yea, we been wanting to see him," Saul added, as soon as he was seated.

Toke shook his head, a solemn grimace upon his face. "He and Rache went to the Bayou," he said.

"Something wrong," Saul asked.

152

"Had to finish one last bit of business with Will," Toke replied.

"Gracious," Saul added.

"A headstone for your child," Peter muttered.

Toke ventured to the bar and retrieved the two beers. He lingered, allowing time for the air to clear. Toke eventually returned and set the beers on the table. He pulled a chair in backwards, straddling the seat and draping his arms over the chair's back while facing the men.

"Thanks for the flounder," Saul said. "Nice fish."

"What," Peter asked. "I didn't get any... and with us practically in-laws." Peter glared at Toke.

"Yea, and that's why you didn't get any. I'll be too old to fish soon enough and that boy of mine will be catching plenty and bringing 'em to his paw-in-law instead of his dear old Dad." Toke smiled as Peter eased into his beer. "Next time I'll make up for it," Toke added.

Peter nodded, knowing he would.

The front door opened, the bright sun racing in and unfurling a long golden carpet. Lieutenant Brantley and his first officer Terry Franks entered, each step unraveling the rug that lay before them. The men hovered around the room, inspecting the fishing gear and pictures that hung on the walls. As they finished their tour the two mumbled something amongst themselves before heading to the table where the three sat.

Toke looked up to Brantley. "Thirsty," he asked.

"You have a glass of water?"

Toke looked at Peter and Saul then back to Brantley. He shrugged his shoulders. "Nope," he said. "Just beer and whiskey."

"No thanks," Brantley said. "It's nothing but rotgut."

Toke leaned away from the back of the chair and shrugged his shoulders again. He stood, walked away and soon returned with a bottle of whiskey. Toke pulled the bottle close and mumbled, "Rotgut, rotgut, rotgut," as he read the words on its side. "Sorry, but all I see is Old Forrester. But the next time I go to the Bayou I'll see if they have any rotgut. They have a pretty good selection!"

Brantley's face soured, even more. "Look," he said, "rotgut is any old swine that's whiskey, not a brand!"

Toke frowned and began reading the label once more.

Brantley snatched the bottle from Toke's hands. "Damn it to hell!" he raged. "Look here, I don't care about no rotgut, the reason I'm here is because you've been breaking curfew...... you've had a light on after nine. You and everyone else need to obey the rules!"

Toke shrugged. "I ain't done nothing," he said.

Brantley turned to Franks and snorted. He turned back to Toke. "Last night, on this entire island, there was only one light burning. The enemy could have seen that from ten miles away!"

Toke looked at Peter and Saul, and both of them

shrugged. Toke spoke slowly. "Well, the enemy's been here before so I don't think we're a secret?" He paused. "And besides, I wasn't on the island. I was across the bay on Little Dauphin."

"I know where you were, I saw you!" Brantley's frustration boiled over and Franks took the lead.

"Secret or no secret, on the Island or not, if they were to bomb us then it'd be your fault. Do you want that on your head," Franks' asked?

Toke thought about the question, shrugging his shoulders as he thought through the possibilities. "I reckon I don't," he finally said. "And that's why you should be thanking me instead of being ugly."

"You're nuts," Brantley said. "Can't you see we're trying to protect you?" Brantley pointed a finger at Toke. "And if you shrug one more time I swear I'm gonna lock your ass up!"

Toke's face contorted as he carefully relaxed his shoulders. "In case you were wondering," Toke said softly. "I was using that light to draw the enemy away from the island." Toke used his hands in a sideways hula motion, demonstrating far away. "Now wouldn't you rather those bombs fall into the water instead of homes?"

Brantley wasn't amused. "Okay," he said with aggravation. "But if you're out there again I'm gonna arrest you. It's that simple."

Peter intervened. "Toke don't care," he said. "He's gotta get me some fish and you ain't gonna stop him.

Tell 'em Toke."

"Shut up Peter," Toke hissed.

"Yea," Saul added. "And if you don't leave right now, Toke will light this island up like a Christmas tree. Ain't that right Toke."

"I'm warning you," Brantley said to Toke.

Toke did a good job of fighting the urge to shrug and instead he lifted his hands in a begging motion, palms up.

Peter slapped Toke on the back. "Go ahead and arrest him," he said to Brantley. "We dare you!"

"Yea," Saul added. "You just try."

"Toke, this is your last warning. You keep that big-mouth of yours shut or I'm going to haul your ass away!" Brantley was adamant.

Toke now pleaded for mercy with his eyes.

"We've had enough," Saul said. "Either take him away or get the hell out!"

"That's it," Brantley said to Toke. "You've gone too far now." Brantley motioned for Franks to arrest Toke.

"Damn it fellas," Toke whined, finally breaking his silence. "I thought ya'll were on my side?"

"We are," Peter replied. "But it's gonna take some of that rotgut we been hearing about to keep it that way.

Chapter 27

The weather turned hotter just as the days and rigors of Navy life became longer. Regimental and disciplined, the military was neither glamorous nor anything like the movies. Hot and tired, men were grumpier than usual, quicker to pick a fight than usual, and just plain aggravated with the Navy. Hell, and Hell may be a good word to describe south Texas, half the men said they were thinking about going AWOL...... to Alaska.

Besides the heat, Jake had his own problems as he meandered in from kitchen patrol, mumbling to himself. "Potatoes peeled, check; pots washed, check; counters cleaned, check; floors mopped, check; yelled at twice by a man with a meat cleaver, check...check." It seemed KP duty would be the extent of his Navy accolades, the firing range had seen to that. His blurry eyeballs ached, his dishpan hands remained shriveled beyond recognition, and his potato-peeling-wrists hurt like a bastard. "Damn," he said as he struggled to climb up and onto his bunk. It was only two in the afternoon but he'd been up since just after midnight and worked nonstop through breakfast and lunch...and all of this on his birthday. Jake couldn't believe he'd had such a run of bad luck. He closed his eyes and tried to sleep. The bunk was never comfortable but damn it felt good as his mind relaxed, the empty barracks giving way to his thoughts. He couldn't believe it, but for the first time in a long time it was just him and Mira. He could smell her scent, and the beauty of her eyes caused him to lose his breath. More than anything he wanted to reach out and touch her.

The sound of heavy boots scattered across the room, forcing Jake to leave Mira for the time being. Men stormed into the barracks, cursing and bitching about the day's events. It seemed an extended march had been in order and no one was happy, least of all the head ass. "What's this," Donnie said with a snarl and as he stopped alongside Jake's bunk. He pushed upwards on the edge of Jake's mattress, causing Jake to roll sideways. "He's sleeping while we march our asses off." Not everyone understood what he said, but they got the point and some of them joined in, bitching about and deriding the nap they had disturbed. Donnie slammed his pack onto the floor, his anger emerging like a wave that neared shore. "The son of a bitch won't even get out of bed," he snapped.

Jake took a second to scan the room, starting with Donnie. It seemed quite a few men backed him as many pushed in close. Jake slid off the bunk and stood nose to nose with ole Donnie boy. "Son of a bitch," he questioned.

Donnie reddened just a bit. He knew you never called anyone a "son of a bitch," well not to their face. So he deflected the retort by adding, "So in two months that's the first words you've understood?"

The men supporting Donnie laughed, but Jake wasn't amused. Jake stepped back, taking in the crowd that railed against him. Jimmy and Luther pushed through the men and stood with Jake. It was now three against sixteen or so with a handful abstaining and diving into their bunks. "All right," Jake said, bobbing his head as he spoke. "If that's the way it's gotta...." But before Jake could finish, another man crossed over followed by four more. It seemed the Mississippi Five didn't like being on Donnie's side either. "Pig's Eye," Jake said appreciatively. Pig's Eye was Clayton Walker, and his family owned a pig farm near Meridian Mississippi. As for the other four, well, they also hailed from Mississippi. Ever since the five first arrived they had stuck together like glue, and Pig's Eye was their unofficial leader.

"Don't worry," Pig's Eye said. "I ain't understood a word he's said either."

Jake's shoulders broadened just as a smile did the same.

With a name like Pig's Eye you'd think a fellow could fight, but what happened next surprised even Jake. Pig's Eye let out a yell...... and it sounded a lot like a pig. He began jumping up and down and pushing into people.

"Thank God he's on our side," Jimmy thought. And if you could have read Donnie's mind, you'd know he wished the same.

Pig's eye was relentless, growing louder and more agitated by the second. He threw a punch, just a random blow that grazed JC's shoulder. You would have thought JC had been hit by Joe Louis as he fell into the crowd behind him. He rubbed his shoulder as he regained his feet and disappeared behind the row of men. But Pig's Eye wasn't finished, egging the other Mississippi boys on. Soon they all began to hoot and yell, and it sounded like the Rebel Army making a charge at Bull Run.

Jake had never seen anything like it, but figured it to be a form of psychological warfare. And there's no doubt it was working. Donnie said something to Jake, but the Mississippi Five drowned the words. Truthfully, unless it was "I surrender", Jake didn't want to hear it because he wanted to bust Donnie's chops more than he wanted his next breath. The Mississippi Five continued and within minutes they had worked everyone into a frenzy.

Pig's Eye bounded backwards a few steps then charged forward, and it was as if he were trying to take flight. He spread his arms and sailed head first into the crowd, taking six men to the floor with him. Jake glanced over just as Pig's Eye took his maiden flight and it proved to be a mistake. Donnie saw an opportunity and slugged him in the jaw, a solid blow that caused Jake's arms and legs to go rigid as he fell backwards. No one from behind caught him and he slid into a footlocker. His eyes crossed, and then went dark.

Jake must have been out for more than a few seconds, because when he awoke the room was chaotic. Jimmy had two men on him, both wailing away. He covered his head with his hands and Jake knew without question that he couldn't fight. Luther had a man on his back and one on each leg, but wasn't fighting back. And as for the Mississippi Five, well, they were beast though way outnumbered. Jake had to get back in there and turn the tide. He stood on wobbly legs and rubbed his jaw with a hand that came back with blood. "That son of a bitch," he thought. Jake ran towards Jimmy, thinking if he could get those two off of him then they both could fight. He grabbed one of the men by the shirt, spun him around and cocked his fist. And boy-oh-boy did it ever hurt when Donnie punched Jake in the left ear. Jake didn't see him coming and the blow landed flush. Jake stumbled sideways and collapsed onto the floor. Perhaps a few seconds longer than the first time, but when Jake awoke things had deteriorated even more. The Mississippi Five were all losing, Jimmy was all but done, and another man had jumped on Luther. Jake would later lament that if he hadn't seen it with his own eye, just one eye because blood trickled down and pooled in his other eye-socket, he wouldn't have believed it. But big Luther had had enough.

Like a vicious storm Luther let loose. He began throwing men across the room like bales of hay. He stormed from one end to the other, men jumping on him only to be slammed to the floor, others throwing punches into his stomach and back and head to no avail. Luther crushed each assault, repelled every contender, and smashed every face he swung at. The Mississippi Five now had better odds and another pig's yell brought them to life. Pig's Eye got both hands around JC, dragged him from beneath a bunk, and did his best to kill the little bastard. As for Donnie, well Jake was going take care of that one.

The struggle proved enormous, more exhaustive than Jake thought it would be, but he finally managed to stand on his own two feet. And Donnie was straight ahead. Jake walked sideways, kind of like John Wayne walks, but still ended up in the same place as Donnie. Jake shook his head, trying to clear the cobwebs. Donnie had no cobwebs and like an experienced boxer he threw jab after jab at Jake's wobbly head. Jake's nose now bled, joining his jaw and eye. Then his lip flowed, followed by the other eye. There was nothing left to bleed from but Donnie kept hammering away. Well, he kept hammering away until Chief Petty Herschel Caster walked into the room. Caster began yelling and pushing people apart. A tough man, hardened by years of service and who really knew how to fight... well he thought he knew how to fight until he met with the wrong force. Luther continued to be that raging bull, and when Chief Petty pushed him from behind Luther spun and leveled an uppercut to his chin. The punch lifted Caster off the floor and everyone watched as he bounced twice on the concrete, slid ten feet, and ended up beneath a splintered bunk. No one uttered a word, but everyone stopped throwing punches.

Chapter 28

Sweat soaked, Chief Petty Caster awoke... and moaned. In his boxers and in his bed, he moaned again as he touched his jaw. "What hit me," he mumbled. He rolled to his side and then back flat, on his back... his entire body ached.

Chief Petty screamed obscenities the entire way to the recruits' barrack. The words flowed naturally and hit a feverish pitch by the time he slammed the barrack's door open. "You bunch of low life pieces of shit!" he yelled as he stormed into the room.

The men had cleaned the room, doing their best to right broken bunks and busted footlockers. But the ten broken beds, two broken hands, four busted footlockers, and countless dislocated fingers and bloodied noses suggested that not everything was in order. Lounging around as if nothing had ever happened, Donnie and Jake sat on the same bunk, playing cards and reminiscing. Caster yelled and sailors jumped to attention and scrambled to the front of their respective beds.

Caster walked a tight line, rubbing at his jaw every few seconds. He stopped in front of Luther and stared upwards. "I ought to have you court-martialed," he spewed.

Luther stared straight ahead, his eyes wide and his mouth shut.

"Canfield, you're a low life maggot. The scum of the earth! There's nothing about you that makes the Navy proud." Caster poked a finger in Luther's face as he continued. "I'll have you…"

"Chief Petty," Jimmy yelled, breaking Caster's stranglehold on Luther. What Chief Petty was doing wasn't right, and hell or high-water Jimmy couldn't let it go on. "I started the fight. It's me you need to yell at."

Caster quieted and rubbed at his jaw again. His eyes remained fixed on Luther before he shuffled away and headed for Jimmy. A slow walk, deliberate in nature, Caster made his way to Jimmy and nosed up to the sailor. Jimmy didn't flinch or cower, realizing that Caster couldn't dole out any punishment that would keep him from protecting his friend. "So Clark wants to be the hero," Caster said. Caster shook his head. "No," he said, "it wasn't you. You don't have it in you! So which one of you pieces of shit started this fight?"

Jake picked up the mantra. "It was me, Chief Petty."

Now that was something Caster could believe. Cullen had been nothing but trouble since day-one and he closed in for the kill.

"No Sir," Pig's Eye said from the other side of the room. "I'm the one. That's what we do in Mississippi. We bust people up!"

Jake smiled ever so faintly as Caster halted his approach.

"It wasn't either of them," another Mississippi boy said. "I did this. I started the fight."

Caster stepped back. "Anyone else want to volunteer?"

Men began to raise their hands, and even Donnie shared in the blame.

Chapter 29

Chief Petty Caster eventually reached his goal for punishment and relented, granting a twenty-four-hour pass to the men. Perhaps he had no choice, after all the men only had three days before shipping out. But whatever the case, the break came at a crucial time as the fleeting moments of freedom would be their only salvation. After all, the Pacific lay ahead.

"Where you headed," Pig's Eye asked Jake and Jimmy and Luther. Men had washed and primped and splashed on gallons of aftershave for this moment.

Jake shrugged.

"Well, watch out for JC," Pig's Eye added. "I hear he's gunning for you!"

"Yea, that'll be a heck of a cat fight," someone else added, "with plenty of scratching and hissing."

Like the entire squad, JC was also in the room, and the little weasel added to the assault. "If I'd known Cullen couldn't fight, I'd have crawled out from beneath that bunk and took him."

Everyone laughed, except Jake. Jake had endured the wrath of the entire squad since the fight. Even Donnie played along and Jake could hardly stand it. He needed a beer and time for his ego to heal. "Just a few beers, no drama and no trouble," Jake said to Pig's Eye. Jimmy was good with that and Luther agreed to go along, but nothing more. Luther lived in a dry county and grew up in the shadows of Rock Creek Baptist Church, and alcohol was as foreign to him as China. But as for Jake and Jimmy, being the devout Catholics they were, they assured Luther that a few drinks were okay. They even agreed to say ten extra Hail Mary's for their friend the next time they repented. The Hail Mary's did little to sway Luther's stance but he trusted Jimmy and smiled and agreeable smile.

For the most part the men on leave hooted and hollered and acted like idiots while in the bars and on the streets of Corpus Christi. As for Jake and Jimmy and Luther, however, they were the exception and headed in a different direction. As they walked along, a breeze stoked the midafternoon heat and the streets of Corpus Christi became even hotter. It always seemed to blow out of the west here in Texas, like an oven door that had been left open in an already warm kitchen. "I say we find a quiet place," Jimmy said.

Jake nodded. "A few beers and no trouble," he reiterated.

Strip joints, pool halls, dance clubs with loud music blaring from open doorways, and a host of pitchmen and scantily clad women doing their best to entice young men to enter and spend their money, lined both sides of Ocean View. Jake and Jimmy would occasionally poke their heads in a doorway, look at each other, then move on. It took a while, a walk down the entire length of the strip before they found the right place. Jake looked at the hanging shutter and tattered roof. He studied the building as if he'd just returned home, and smiled. Jimmy liked it as well and walked to the door and opened it. He could see the bar and the row of empty stools positioned across its front. And just beyond that was the perfect backdrop, open windows with a view of the gulf. He turned to Jake and raised his brows in an approving manner.

Jake studied Luther, watching the man who grappled with such decisions. He took Luther by the arm, realizing he needed help taking that first step, and guided him forward.

"Hey Jake'ee boy!" someone shouted.

"Crominy sakes," Jake thought as he turned to see Donnie and a host of his friends hurrying towards them.

"Jake'ee," Donnie yelled again.

Where the hell Donnie got Jake'ee from no one knows, but the man somehow believed that he and Jake were now best friends and could take such liberties.

"You don't want to go in there. It's a dump," Donnie said with machinegun rhythm.

"Yea, we kind of do," Jimmy added.

Donnie and his gang closed the last few feet that

separated them and Donnie stood next to Jake. He swung an arm over Jake's shoulder and squeezed. He spoke into Jake's ear. "That Jimmy fellow is bad news." Donnie either had a head start on drinking or couldn't handle his liquor, because he slobbered on Jake's shoulder.

Jake pushed back but Donnie only squeezed harder. "Let go of my neck," Jake said. Donnie was playing ruff and Jake quickly had enough.

Donnie let go and stepped back. "Come on buddy, let's go have some fun," he said. "I know this special place." He put a finger to his mouth. "Really special," he added.

"We're just gonna have a beer and call it a night," Jake said in response. Jake stepped toward Jimmy who still had a hand on the door.

"Cullen!" Donnie yelled.

Jake stopped, took a deep breath, and turned to face Donnie. Jake stared at Donnie, waiting for a reply.

Donnie softened, and then giggled. "You have to see what this stripper can do. It's amazing," he said. "Besides, I owe you a beer."

Jake pointed to the rundown bar in front of them. "Come on in and I'll let you buy me one," he said.

Donnie swayed, grabbing the man next to him by the elbow in order to steady himself. "I'll buy you one but you got to see this girl. She can pick up dollars without using her hands!" Donnie smiled while looking for approval in Jake's face. But the smile disappeared as his brows inched inward. "You telling me you don't like girls?" Donnie turned to his gang. "Hey, Cullen don't like girls." All of them laughed.

Luther said a few kind yet forceful words to Donnie, and his tone left little room for misunderstanding. Donnie's gang crowded in close.

Jake studied the men at Donnie's back. The Mississippi Five weren't around and he and Jimmy and Luther were heavily outnumbered. On top of that, Chief Petty had promised to throw them in the brig if anyone stepped out of line. Jake turned to Luther. "It's ok Luther," he said in a soft voice. He turned back to Donnie. "Tell you what. We'll go to the club and if the stripper can't pick up the dollar, were leaving, no questions. If she can, then we'll stay and drink."

An exuberant Donnie extended a hand to make it bonding. "Deal," he said.

As if drinking weren't enough to send him to Hell, Luther now worried about having to go to a strip club. His face showed the strain of such decisions and Jake couldn't help but feel sorry for him.

"Don't worry," Jake said to Luther, "you stay outside. I got this!"

The club proved to be the underbelly of all strip clubs. A dirty, poorly lit, watered-down-whiskey, smoke-filled hole in the wall about the size of a railway car, sitting on a plot of dirt not much bigger. A neon sign above the front door read "Lola's".

Once inside, a tiny stage wrestled everyone's attention to a single pole with an overaged stripper clinging to it.

"That's the girl," Donnie said with excitement. "That's Lola!" There were two other sailors in the room but when Donnie and Jake and everyone except Luther walked in and packed the joint, both men left.

Donnie raced to the stage before anyone else. "Baby, you remember me?" Donnie gushed. The group crowded the stage and catcalls and whistles begin to echo off the walls. A box-top turntable rested on the end of the bar and Lola swayed to the pace of the music it played.

"I sure do," Lola said as she knelt down and kissed the top of Donnie's head.

"I told the guys about you. And my friend Jake here, he couldn't wait to see what you can do."

Lola turned her attention to Jake. "Why hello sugar," she said. Fog from cigarette smoke clouded the room and Jake rubbed his eyes. Lola mistook this for admiration. "So you like what you see?" she asked.

Jake didn't want to say yea and he didn't want to say no, so he answered as if he didn't understand the question. "Ma'am," he asked.

"Ma'am?" Lola said, her voice changing from sultry to angry. Undoubtedly it had been a long day at the office. "Look," she added. "I ain't your momma and my time is money. So if you want to see what I can do, I suggest you put a dollar down."

The guys crowded even closer, even Jimmy who figured what the hell. Lola moved to the edge of the platform as Jake reached into his pocket. Lola continued to sway with the music, her body an exotic instrument, her facial expression no different than a perturbed school-teacher. The sexy voice returned. "Well Baby...."

Jake smiled before tossing four quarters onto the stage.

Everyone, including Lola, stared as the coins rolled in circles before dying on the wooden planks.

"What the hell is that," Lola muttered. She stopped swaying and lashed out with her foot, trying to kick Jake in the face, the toe of her shoe narrowly missing.

Jake dodged the attempt and stepped back, not wanting to give her another shot. "That's a dollar," he said.

"You little bastards," Lola yelled. "Hey Ronnie!" she hollered in the direction of the bar. "Get these bums out of here!"

A baseball bat and two minutes later, they were all on the street.

"Just had to be a smart ass, didn't you Cullen," Donnie said.

Jake shrugged his shoulders. "You agreed to the rules," he said. "I put the dollar down and now we're going to a quiet bar." Jake and Jimmy and Luther turned to walk away.

Donnie grabbed Jake's arm and was about to bust him up when a vise, a mammoth clamp encircled his arm. Luther's hand found its way to Donnie's forearm. "Stay out of it chief," Donnie stammered. He should have said something different, perhaps more gentile, as Luther applied vast amounts of pressure, damming the flow of blood to Donnie's hand. Donnie's body bent and contorted in an effort to ease the pain. And in a matter of seconds Donnie had seen the errors of his evil ways.

All and all it ended up being a nice evening as Jimmy and Luther and Jake looked out and across the gulf. "Looks a bit like home," Jimmy said.

Jake agreed but didn't agree, and tilted his head from side to side as he pondered Jimmy's statement. "It's almost perfect," he said with a smile. He held his empty beer in the air. "Got any hot ones?"

The bartender responded with an odd look before shuffling to the back room. Moments later Jake and Jimmy popped the tops on warm beers and took long swigs. For the rest of the evening the three sat quietly and stared out the windows, their thoughts taking each of them home.

Chapter 30

Ralph could hardly contain himself. He just completed his fifth game as starting pitcher for the Camp Parker Falcons and smiled as he headed to the dugout. Colonel Webster stood just beyond third base and said, "Good game son," as Ralph drew within earshot.

"Thanks," came from Ralph. The two men had become close friends over the past months, allowing the rigidity of Army etiquette to allay in times such as this. They spoke daily and Ralph even had dinner with the Colonel and his wife on a regular basis. Webster became a mentor and Ralph found a friend.

Webster wasn't alone on this afternoon and quickly introduced Stan Weise. Both men smiled as Ralph shook their hands.

"Great game," Weise said.

Ralph smiled, always appreciative of a pat on the back.

"You know who this is?" Webster asked Ralph.

Ralph had no idea, never seen or heard of the man. "No Sir," he responded.

Both Weise and Webster's smiles broadened. "I'm a scout with the Phillies and I came to see you play. Old Web has told me a lot of good things about you but I didn't believe it until today. Truth is you may be better than advertised."

You could have knocked Ralph over with a feather. He paled, looking to Webster for assurance and Webster gave an acknowledging nod.

"Your good kid, really good," Weise added. "You may have the liveliest arm I've seen in years and who ever helped you with your control, I may want to talk to them about being on our staff."

Ralph couldn't believe this was happening. "My brother taught me," he blurted. "And I'm sure Toke will be happy to help."

Weise grinned, his statement about adding staff members purely rhetorical. "Well, let's get you in camp and see what you can do first, then we'll talk about your brother. We're in last place right now, but with an arm like yours we may have the pieces to make a run at the pennant next year."

"We'll have to see about that," Webster said to Weise. "You know there's a war going on and Ralph's on my payroll."

Weise knew he couldn't buck the Colonel because he too had served under the man. And just like Ralph, he'd also been an outstanding baseball prospect. "Right,

175

Colonel," Weise said. "But as good as he is... I'll wait."

The men spoke for nearly an hour, the same amount of time it took to drink a bottle of rye whiskey. Ralph could have spent the night talking about his future in the Majors, but the Colonel called an early end to the backroom negotiations. Ralph had become somewhat of a son to the Colonel but that didn't mean a soldier's duties would be neglected. Ralph was in charge of a chain of radio towers along the northwest ridge of camp, and he and his crew serviced the towers on a daily basis. A Signal Corp couldn't function if it couldn't communicate, and both Ralph and the Colonel understood the importance of such operations. Besides, Ralph wanted to write a letter home... he had a lot to tell them.

***

Chief Petty Caster gave his men the last order they'd ever receive from him. He instructed each sailor to write a letter to their family, just one, and to keep it simple. There would be no talk of how they trained, who they trained with, destinations, dates, or the Navy as a whole. The sailors listened and Jake thought this to be an easy task since he knew very little, although he could give some pointers on peeling potatoes. Besides, he'd already written one letter home a few weeks earlier and there wasn't a whole lot more he could say.

Jake said 'I love you' six times and 'I miss you' another seven or eight, but that was pretty much it. And truth was it sounded an awful lot like his last letter. After all this time apart, he found it hard to believe that he didn't have much to say. He glanced over to Jimmy, and Jimmy had written less than him. So he turned his attention to Luther who worked on his second page. Jake leaned over, hoping to find a few nuggets he could use as his own. But Luther was writing to his Dad and that didn't help. So Jake told Mira not to worry and that things were going great. He even said that the men in his outfit had a big turnout for his birthday and had given him several gifts. He just didn't tell her that it was two black eyes and a loose tooth.

Chapter 31

The night roused with little purpose, moonless and black. Toke eased the skiff along, the breeze stirring with a softness that gave birth to delicate ripples across the water's surface. The skiff continued forward, the fat-lighter wood burning brightly in the steel cage that extended more than two feet in front of the bow. Toke stood on a platform, just behind the burning wood, a ten-foot wooden pole in his hands. He eased up on the poling motion as the skiff slowed even further. He twirled the pole in his hands, like a majorette spinning her baton, and the opposite end now jutted towards the water, the steel tines of the gig pointing at its target. "Swoop," was all the sound the gig made as it penetrated the water and into its prey. Toke lifted the gig, the eighth flounder of the night thrashing about, and shook it free in the boat's bottom. He smiled as he turned the skiff to the south and headed for home.

The boat nosed onto the beach and Toke jumped off the bow before pulling it further ashore. The fat-lighter had burned hot and bright but neared its end, the smoke trails disappearing into the black. As the last glow faded, he used the dying moments to string the flounders onto a line. "Pop, pop, pop," sounded just a short distance away. Hairs stood on Toke's neck as panic pulsated through every vein. No doubt it was gunfire. "Dear God," he thought, realizing the shots came from near his house. He dropped the stringer before racing up the slope of the beach. He stumbled in the sand but soon gained his feet and onto a path that led home. Toke breathed hard, his arms pumping, his feet carrying him as fast as they could.

More gunfire echoed in the night. Toke was close and the bullets sounded like they were right on top of him. But he didn't care and he didn't let up, as Laura was his only concern. Toke careened around a pine tree, his shoulder scraping the bark. He moved as fast as a twenty-year old, even though his lungs burned like a man in his late forties. He could hardly breathe, but straight ahead was the opening that surrounded his house and he pressed even harder. More gunfire and he could now see the flashes from the barrels igniting the night. As Toke reached the end of the path he could see the outline of his house. "Just a few more feet," he thought.

Toke tripped, his foot slamming into the side of something that lay in the middle of the path, but not a root or plank or metal. Whatever caught his foot was soft and large and rounded. He stumbled, his momentum carrying him forward and face-first into the dirt. Toke rolled twice and ended up on his back. His remaining breath had been knocked from him and he sat up, gasping for air.

A flood lamp, the kind he'd seen the airmen toting, flicked on, the light illuminating the yard as if it were morning. Toke turned his eyes from the glaring light and gasped at what he saw. There were two bodies lying motionless to his right and another to the left of those. He twisted and looked over his shoulder, from where he had come, and stared at yet another body that straddled the path.

Horror brought tears, but Toke would never have time to lament as his attention would be wrestled away when someone from behind the lamp yelled, "He's still moving!" Toke spun back to face the lamp as gunfire erupted yet again.

Chapter 32

The screen door to Willy's bar sprang open and in walked Peter. Peter hesitated as he scanned the room, his eyes eventually coming to rest on Saul. "Where's Willy," Peter asked.

Saul had ventured in just ahead of Peter and replied, "Willy stepped out back just a second ago." Last night the entire village had been brought to its knees by the merciless killings. It was now a given, misery plagued the once tranquil Island and people were giving serious thought to moving away.

"What happened last night is a hell of a note," Peter said.

"If things don't get better soon, this place ain't gonna be fit to live in," Saul added.

Peter mumbled an agreement before joining Saul at a table. "Should we start anyway?" Peter asked. Saul nodded in agreement before standing and heading behind the bar. He returned with a bottle of whisky and two glasses. Deciding that wasn't enough, he went back to the bar and retrieved another glass. "Just in case Willy comes in, wouldn't want him to think we started without him."

Peter smiled in agreement. "First one's on me," he added. Both men laughed as Saul poured them a large one.

The screen door opened a second time on this afternoon and neither Peter nor Saul would have believed it if they hadn't seen it with their own eyes. Standing in the light of the open door was Lieutenant Brantley, disheveled and downright pitiful. I mean pitiful! The man all but staggered in, his gape no more than a dragging of his feet. His eyes were bloodshot with bags beneath so large that a man could fit a nice size lemon in them. And his hair... well his hair looked like a mockingbird had made her nest in the middle. Brantley willed himself to a chair next to Peter and fell into it. He struggled to keep his head from sagging as he said, "Rotgut."

Peter looked at Saul, but neither spoke.

"Rotgut!" It seemed to take every ounce of Brantley's energy to get the word out.

With great hesitation, Peter slid his glass of whiskey toward Brantley. Brantley snatched the glass from the table and drank the entire contents in one fell-swoop. The jolt seemed to revive the Lieutenant. "Another," he said with increased vigor and as he slid the glass back. "I haven't slept in forty-hours," he added. "And... and... and I've seen things that can't be unseen." As soon as the glass returned to his side of the table he took a swig. "And where the hell is Toke Cullen?"

Saul frowned. He knew Toke spent last night floundering and that Brantley would lock him up for the rest of the war. "Toke ain't here," Saul said. "Somebody said he moved to Coden and he ain't never coming back!"

Brantley finished off the second drink before speaking. "Well someone needs to tell his wife because I just left there and she said he'd be here!"

Both Saul and Peter grimaced before Peter jumped into the fray. "Wait a minute," Peter said. He was loud and forceful and appeared to be angry. "What about last night? Who's gonna answer for that?"

For the first time since straggling in Brantley demonstrated some real energy and righted himself in his chair. "What are you getting at?"

"Ya'll killed five more goats last night and that makes......" Peter paused as he counted on his fingers. "And that makes nine. And three of those were mine! Now, don't get me wrong, had those been hogs or cows I might be onboard, but goats are tough to eat." Peter wrinkled his nose. "They're all gristly."

"Gristly," Saul said in agreement.

Peter continued and even shook a finger in Brantley's direction. "So, when I go to Brookely and complain, there's gonna be a lot of explaining to do. You mind me, a lot of explaining!"

Brantley leaned back in his chair. He gave a sideways

stare at Peter, doing his best to size the man up. "What are you trying to say?" he asked.

Peter didn't let the Officer see how nervous he truly was when he said, "You leave Toke and everyone else alone, and maybe all this goes away. Maybe!"

Brantley nodded, understanding the score. "You know that's blackmail and I could have you locked up for that."

"Yea, well he don't care," Saul blurted. "Go ahead and lock him up, see if we care!"

Peter shook his head in disbelief. "Not the time for that," he said to Saul.

"Oh," Saul replied.

Peter turned back to Brantley. "If we got a deal then we can drink on it. If not, then let's just see who gets in the most trouble."

Brantley couldn't believe he was being shaken-down by an uneducated local, but the man had big ones. Brantley stared at the glass before raising his eyes to meet those of Peter's. "Pour me a double," he said.

***

The room overflowed with sunlight but Toke lit a candle anyway, figuring he needed all the help he could get. Laura was the one who'd always taken care of the praying and going to church and stuff, but last night had rattled him. He could no longer hide behind laughter and jokes, and genuinely feared for his family's future. Jake had been gone for months now and the dread of each passing day grew. And with the gunfire from last night, Laura could have been injured as well. He needed to help. So here he was, next to the church altar and lighting a candle that stood more than four-feet tall. He whispered something as his eyes studied the emblems on the candle, before heading to the front row of pews and kneeling.

Toke had always attended church, believed in God as much as everyone else, but never kidded himself or pretended to be as devout as most. But now, well now he truly needed God and his first prayer would be for God to not hold that against him.

"Well...." a voice from behind said just as Toke closed his eyes.

"God," Toke openly replied.

"Don't be foolish," Father P. K. Malone added.

Toke knew it was Malone as there was no way of mistaking that Irish lilt. When the priest spoke, it sounded like a lullaby, a beautiful and calming voice that lifted and fell with each syllable. As for Toke, he didn't know whether to keep praying or take a nap. "Um," Toke acknowledged. It was never any secret that the two didn't get along, even people from communities as far away as Heron Bay and Mon Louis Island knew this, so the two never pretended or bothered with niceties.

Malone continued to stand next to Toke, studying the top of his head and envying the thick black hair. Malone ran a hand through his own hair, a thin and silvering testament to his age. "Might you move over," he finally said.

Toke took in a deep breath and slid sideways. Malone settled in next to him, made a sign of the cross, then closed his eyes and took a moment of silence. Toke kept his hands clasped together and in front of his chin, a reverent position if nothing else. He stopped praying once Malone interrupted, though looking back he may have never really started, and now wandered if it'd be best to leave before an argument ensued. He realized that God may never answer his prayers if he argued with a priest, in a church, while praying!

"Now," Malone said as he finished his prayer. "It must be something mighty powerful to bring Toke Cullen to church on a Monday."

Toke couldn't argue that point. Laura had been coming to church every day since Jake shipped off, and he expected her to walk through the door at any moment. He hoped she would, to save him from such a predicament. "Hold it," Toke said to Malone. Toke clasped his hands tightly and muttered a prayer for Laura to walk through the door. As he finished, he looked over his shoulder and stared at the door. "About right," he muttered.

"What's that," Malone asked.

Toke continued to study the door. "Hang on," he said with aggravation. The door never opened and he relented.

Malone smiled, his eyes softening to the moment, his

heart and kindness rising up inside, his compassion becoming much more than his intolerance of Toke. "I pray many times a day," he said. "And I always pray for those boys."

Toke righted his gaze and now stared at the candle that flickered in the drafty church. He nodded as Malone continued.

"I have faith in the Lord and faith that he'll bring them home safely."

Toke couldn't believe he was about to have this conversation, but he did. "I wish I had your faith," Toke conceded.

"It's there for you," Malone added. "In your heart you know what God wants from us."

Toke turned sideways and inspected the priest. "I don't get it," he said.

"Well let's look at that boy of yours," Malone began. "I heard a story of when the two of you crossed the channel on a foggy morning and Jake fell overboard. He would have drowned if not for your actions and God's will. God gave you the strength to save him, because God is not through with him. I truly believe that he has plans for the boy, even if he is just like his father."

Toke smiled at the barb, admired it in fact, and it made him feel better. "Being like Toke Cullen ain't all bad you know."

"Well that's something that even God may have trouble deciding."

Toke chuckled and decided he was losing this battle of wits because the priest had home-field advantage.

"Shall we pray?" Malone asked.

The priest had lifted Toke's spirits and given him hope, and Toke wanted nothing more than to pray. For an hour the two prayed, only pausing for discussions about God and his will. Neither man was kneeling by the time they ended their prayers, and had long since moved to a sitting position because of their aching knees. "Tell me Father. What does P. K. stand for?" Toke asked.

"Ahh," Malone said. "Now it becomes personal."

Toke shrugged, and waited.

Malone told Toke his name and Toke laughed. "Now don't be funning me," Malone added, "it was me father's name and his father before him." There was a pause, the men adjusting their thoughts now that the discussion drifted from spiritual. "Now what about you, surely Toke isn't your given name?"

Toke was actually upbeat when he said, "No, it's Charles Ruben."

"And you go making fun of me?" The two began to laugh, and if Laura had actually walked through the door she'd have believed a miracle occurred... or she'd faint. "We're a fine lot," Malone added. "Two Irishmen and not a respectable Irish name between us." They both laughed again.

"I'm only half Irish," Toke added with a chuckle.

"None of us are perfect," the Priest said wryly.

Toke nodded, having been bested yet again. "Well Father...I'm not sure which half, but one-half of me says it's gettin late and that it needs a beer, and the other half ain't putting up much of a fight. Whatcha say?"

"Nooo..., never touch the stuff," Malone stated matter-of-factly. Toke flinched at the comment and Malone sensed it. "Beer that is," the Priest added.

Toke smiled while arching a prospective brow.

"But a touch of scotch may be in order."

Toke's smile grew as did the arch. After another series of prayers and one more sign of the cross, they exited the church and headed in the direction of the rectory.

Laura heard the voices, the melody of two wailing baritones long before anyone walked in the side door. One voice belonged to Toke, no mistaking that, but the other confused her. The two men were singing some sort of Irish melody and it sounded like some weird version of 'row, row, row your boat'. They had the same rhythm and tune but seemed to be singing at different interludes. And Toke's words neither matched nor rhymed. One moment he was singing about fishing on the reef, the next about playing baseball and slapping her brother Nolan in the face. Laura shook her head as the side door flew open and Toke sauntered in.

"Oh, me baby mullet, me eyes are softly," Toke belted before raising his voice to a crescendo, "upon thee......" He extended an open hand in Laura's direction and she rolled her eyes at the effort.

He was drunk, nothing unusual, but Laura's jaw dropped as Father Malone stumbled in behind him...... also drunk and also singing. "And your beauty will haunt me wherever I go...." Malone sang as he finished the real version of Bridget O'Malley.

The two men quieted, both staring at Laura, awaiting her praise...... But Laura just stood there, apron around her waist, her arms crossed and her brows scrunched together.

"Ahh... me lovely wife," Toke said in his best faux Irish accent, "as pretty as a filly in me Irish meadow."

"Ohh......," Malone added, "a fine sentiment for a fine woman indeed."

Laura took in a deep breath before releasing it through her nose. Toke had corrupted yet another and this time it was her priest. On top of that, she could now die because she'd seen everything. "Well," Laura began in her best fake Irish accent, "me husband and me priest, a fine pair the two of you are." She smiled... she smiled and it was breathtaking and heart-pounding and charming. "We'll be having dinner in a moment," she added. "So sit down and I'll fetch ye a drink," she added as a chorus to the song. Malone moved past Toke and headed for the table, and Toke, well Toke just stood there in unworldly admiration.

Dinner proved to be a blessing in such unsure times. They spoke and laughed and even cried together. Malone shared his wisdom and strength and compassion as he comforted the parents of a young soldier. He measured his responses and exposed his own fears for those serving oversees and for the world in general. He captured the room on this night, and the hearts that beat within.

Chapter 33

"It looks......" Sherry circled Mira, the keen eye of a fashion-queen scrutinizing every nip and tuck, tugging at every hem and seam. "Tight," Sherry finally concluded.

"Tight?" Mira replied.

"I think your Momma's hips are definitely in your future," Sherry added.

Mira stared at herself in the mirror. She didn't want to say it out loud, but the damn dress Sherry had given her was tight. "Must be the dress," Mira said. "It's new, right?"

Sherry rolled her eyes skyward. "Don't worry, once this party thing is over we'll get you some exercise and have some real fun." Sherry's tone was upbeat as she turned away and headed toward the window. Sherry's belongings lay next to the window sill and she retrieved two items from her overnight bag. Within seconds she spun to face Mira and held them up for approval.

The girls stood in Mira's room, at her parent's house, on the Island, and Mira frowned. Mira stared at the clothes in Sherry's hands. "You want to go swimming?"

Sherry shook her head. "Well... maybe. I don't know about swimming but after the party we're taking a blanket to the beach and spending the rest of the day."

"Why do we need to go to the beach?" Mira whined. "I haven't spent a lick of time with my family in months. Can't we just stay here?"

Sherry tilted her head back, lifting her nose in the air. "No, we can't," she said defiantly. "I have one last day with you and they have the rest. I want it to be just me and you. Besides, I'm more fun than any of them."

Mira scoffed at the notion of Sherry being more fun, but decided not to make a big deal. Mira had finished her schooling and Sherry, well let's just say Sherry hadn't taken her studies quite as seriously and would be headed to school in the morning. "Okay," Mira relented, realizing that after tomorrow she didn't know when they'd see each other again.

Sherry skipped the few feet to her friend and flung her arms around Mira's neck. "We are gonna have so much fun," she whispered in Mira's ear.

Peter tapped at the bedroom door. "Got a minute," he asked his daughter.

Having been given her cue, Sherry squeezed Mira's neck once more. "I'll see you in a bit," she said, before exiting the room.

Peter smiled, and as always it put Mira at ease. "You

193

look lovely," he said. "And I'm so very proud of you."

Mira returned the smile.

Peter walked to Mira's bed and sat on the corner. He patted the spot next to him and Mira took her place. "You've worked awful hard," Peter said. "And I wish I could give you something worthy of your effort."

Mira shook her head, tears instantly forming. She'd been more emotional lately with Jake and the war and school coming to an end, and it didn't take much for her to cry these days. "Don't Daddy," she whispered. "I have everything I need."

Peter tried to smile but the attempt failed. "Well," he added... his voice cracking and a lump forming in his throat. "As a Dad, we always want more for our children." Peter nervously rubbed his hands together while searching for words. "I want you to be happy but I don't know if what I have will do that."

Mira put an arm around her Dad's waist. "You don't have to give me anything," she said. Mira shrugged... a hopeful gesture. "But whatever it is, it'll be perfect."

Peter's face had weathered over the years, a life on the water having carved chasms down both cheeks and along his chin. But his eyes remained his truest feature, soft and gentle and fatherly. He took in a heavy breath as he reached into his back pocket and produced a small jewelry box and a letter.

Mira stared past the box and at the letter, knowing who had written it.

"Toke gave it to me a few days ago," Peter said.

194

Mira never reached for either item. Instead, she laid her head against her Dad's shoulder and cried.

Chapter 34

Mira's eyes widened. Piles of food and presents, her parents and Toke and Laura, Sherry and Ted, her Aunt Rebecca, everyone from the Island and dozens more from the Bayou and Heron Bay, had come together for this touching gesture. She looked at the sea of smiling faces and wanted to cry. But she braved the moment, looked to her Mom and Dad for strength, and waded into the center of the room.

It probably set a record of some kind, the amount of fawning that Mira endured. She must have hugged a hundred necks and opened nearly as many presents. She received thousands of kind words, smiled and laughed and gushed over every moment. She was charming and warm and lovely in every sense. But she was also alone, even in a room of a hundred. As Mira opened the final gift, her thoughts returned to Jake and the letter she laid on her pillow. She promised herself she'd wait until she had some privacy before reading it, and now prayed she could hold out. "What," Mira said.

"I said," Sherry said, "don't you think that's a beautiful scarf?"

Mira stared at the scarf. "Yes," she said with a smile. "It's absolutely gorgeous."

Sherry took the scarf from her hands and placed it with the other gifts. "If you'll excuse us," Sherry said to everyone. "I think Mira needs a break." Everyone understood and Sherry took Mira by the hand and led her to the door. "You okay?" she asked, once outside.

Mira nodded. "Just a little much."

Sherry turned around and looked through the open church door. "I'll be right back," she said. Within minutes Sherry returned and prodded Mira towards her house.

"But what about everyone," Mira protested.

"I took care of it. Now let's have some fun," Sherry responded.

"How?" Mira questioned.

"Don't worry, it's done."

Sherry dropped the blanket and flung her arms skyward. She let out a high pitched shrill punctuated by "God I love this place!" She closed her eyes, her face aglow with the sun's warmth, and smiled broadly. "Don't you just love this?" she murmured. Mira never replied. Sherry turned to face her friend. Mira was chewing on something while digging through a bag, shuffling through the snacks and left overs they'd brought along. "Don't you just love this?" Sherry asked with more authority.

Mira never looked up as she continued her plundering of goods. "Yea," she said in a soft response.

Sherry raised a brow. "You remember how tight that dress was, right?"

Mira lay on the blanket, propped up by her elbows, and watched as Sherry walked along the shore. She breathed slowly as her body gave in to the tranquility of the deserted beach. The sun gave a warm smile as waves, small repetitive rollers capped on the beach, surrounding Sherry's ankles before retreating to the gulf. An occasional seagull called from overhead and the water blinked with a million sparkles. Yep, Sherry had been right about coming here as Mira sank into the afternoon and allowed her troubles and worries to vanish.

"That water is freezing," Sherry said. She walked from the water's edge and now stood over Mira.

Mira looked up, shielding her eyes with a hand while studying her friend. "I can tell," she said.

Sherry brought her eyes to her own body, looking down and studying the pointed-tips of her breast.

"No," Mira said snidely, "not that. I'm talking about the goosebumps on your legs."

Sherry looked further south before smiling. A moment later she stepped toward the blanket, anxious to stretch-out next to her friend.

"Hold on," Mira said. She pointed to Sherry's feet.

Sand caked an inch thick on top of her toes and around her ankles. "Wipe 'em off," Mira added, sounding like her Mom.

The day continued to warm, just as the afternoon paced slowly by. Mira rolled over, onto her stomach, while Sherry sat Indian style, next to her. Sherry must have picked up a hundred handfuls of sand before letting the grains slide through like an hour glass. "I'm bored," she whined.

Mira rolled onto her side, facing her friend. "This was your idea," she said.

Sherry arched a brow, followed by a thin, snake-like smile. "I know," she said.

Mira watched, dumbfounded, as Sherry pulled one of the straps of her bathing suit over the tip of her shoulder and down her arm. She then then did the same with the other side. The girl was topless, on a beach, in public.... well it was kind of public in that perhaps someone may walk up. "What are you doing?" Mira bellowed. Mira leapt to a standing position and began scanning the horizon, looking for onlookers.

Sherry was also quick to her feet, her dazzling smile no longer her most prominent feature. "Now it's your turn," she said with a mischievous grin.

***

Ted eased himself into a chair and pointed across the room. "Who's that," he asked.

Saul looked over his shoulder. "That's Lieutenant Rot Gut," he said of the man sitting at a table by himself. "It seems he spends more time in here than he does with his squad."

"That's just pathetic," Ted said.

"Yea, it's pretty pitiful," Peter interjected. "I just don't know about this younger generation. But that's what Toke can do to a fella."

Lieutenant Brantley may have been across the room but it was only eight-feet and he could hear every word. So he mustard some pride and stood from his chair. He tugged on his uniform, straightened his tie, and gathered his belongings, which consisted of a bottle and a glass, and headed out the back door. He'd be doing the rest of his drinking in private.

Ted had never been a drinker, didn't like the taste, but he could see how a young man could fall into such a trap. When it came to the Island, to being with Peter and Toke and everyone else, it seemed natural. Over the past year he too had spent a lot of time here, but he was a grown man who made sound judgements, and he realized what was most important. He had no better friends in the world and perhaps this was his family now and that this would be the best place for both him and his daughter. Lord knows he loved everything about the place, especially the people. He laughed, as Toke started with a story that only he could tell.

"Just me and Willy," Toke said. "It's always just me and Willy except on the evening Ole Saul straggled in and decided to stay. I knew something was up, because Saul never stays."

"Well I can't never stay," Saul chimed in. Saul tilted his head downward while rolling his eyes upwards, as if he were a child seeking forgiveness. He looked to Ted. "I always got things to do. Ted, aren't there times when you have things to do?"

Ted chuckled before leaning back in his chair and taking another drink.

Toke continued. "In any case and as it so happened, we were drinking and the next thing ya know Willy was drunk and doused the lamps and headed out back. He didn't say a word! And there me and Ole Saul stood, in the pitch black. It took a while, but we figured out that Willy was trying to tell us something. So as we stood in the dark it set me to thinking that going home had to be better than standing in the dark. So I said, 'Come on Saul, going home has to be better than standing in the dark'. Ole Saul agreed, so we headed out the door and damn if it wasn't blacker out there than in here. And with Saul being scared of the dark and all..."

"I ain't scared of the dark," Saul emphasized. "I just couldn't see an inch in front of me... that's all. Besides, I couldn't tell what way was up let alone see a trail or know which way to head." He looked over at Ted. "Wouldn't you be hesitant if you couldn't see?"

Ted laughed a little hardier as Toke nodded agreement and smiled. "Yep, he panicked," Toke said.

"I didn't panic," Saul added. "I just couldn't see and I didn't know what we were going to do... that's all. And when you don't know what your gonna do it kinda gets to ya. You understand, don't you Ted?"

201

Ted's laughter increased as Toke continued with the story.

"Well, no one knew these paths better than me," Toke said, "especially the ones leading to and from Willy's bar. So I said to Saul, 'Saul, I know these paths better than anyone, especially the ones leading to and from Willy's bar, and I got an idea'." Toke raised a finger in the air, but Saul couldn't see it. "Give me a cigarette."

"What?" Saul asked, his words disappearing into the night.

"A cigarette," Toke confirmed.

Saul fumbled in his shirt pocket and produced a pack. He slid a cigarette out and extended it the direction of Toke's voice. "Here," he said.

Toke couldn't see either, but reached out until he found Saul's arm then traced it to his hand. He took the cigarette.

"Now what?" Saul asked.

"Well damn Saul, a fella needs a light."

Saul fumbled in his pocket once more before producing a box of matches. He struck a match, the glow illuminating their faces and the cigarette that dangled from Toke's lips.

Toke didn't smoke very often, as we already know, but as Saul placed the flame beneath the cigarette Toke inhaled, long and deep. He held the smoke for a while before releasing it. "I don't smoke very often," Toke said, "but when I do I really enjoy it."

"Now what?" Saul asked. "Want a drink to go with that?"

Toke gave that some serious thought, but finally said, "Just follow the light and it shall lead you home."

The cigarette burned bright, the overcast sky providing no other option, and Saul followed its glow. Toke took another puff and let it go. They were approaching a curve in the path and Toke said, "Just ahead, crooked knee."

"Yea, I know about 'crooked knee'," Saul replied. "For gosh sakes, you act like I never seen Dauphin Island!" Saul looked to Ted. "Even you know where 'crooked knee' is, don't you Ted?"

Ted's face reddened as his laughter increased.

Having navigated 'crooked knee', Toke said. "Just ahead, Mainer's Oak, be careful with the roots."

"Yea, yea, I know about the oak and the roots. What is this, some kind of guided tour?"

Within moments they survived Mainer's Oak and moved steadily towards home. Toke breathed in yet again, the cigarette glowing at peak performance. "Got the bayou straight ahead," Toke added. There were plenty of bayous that cut into the Island, forming inlets for mooring and hosting a myriad of animals and aquatic life. But the one ahead dug deep into the north side and a man had to walk quite some ways to the south to steer clear.

"Yea, yea, yea, I know about the bayou," Saul said with aggravation. "Enough with the tour, let's just get

home...... I don't like it out here, it feels like rain."
Again, Saul looked to Ted. "You don't like to get caught
in the rain either, do ya Ted?"

Ted could barely contain himself.

"Well the bayou was coming up," Toke continued with
his story, "and I took another drag on that cigarette."
Toke looked skyward, contemplating the moment. "That
sure was a good cigarette," he reflected. As Toke
inhaled, Saul could see the side of Toke's face, the
cigarette glowing brighter than ever, and it gave him
comfort. The men picked up speed and within seconds
they were at the bayou. At the last moment Toke veered
right while flicking the cigarette to his left.

"Dang it," Saul cursed, as he stumbled head first into
the bayou.

"Dang it," Saul cursed while sitting at the table. "I
ruined my best pair of britches when I stumbled into
that mud."

Toke and Peter laughed, and Saul was happy he could
play along.

Ted laughed as well, but the real joy was from the
smiling faces and the warmth of such unique
individuals. "Why not move here," he thought. "They are
my family." Ted laughed yet again as he picked up the
bottle and filled his glass. He then held the bottle in the
air as a gesture. "Toke?" he asked.

"Maybe in a little while," Toke answered. "If I start now
I'll never see dinner."

Ted doubted that, knowing how much Toke could

drink. But he let it go because he liked Toke the most. He had never met such an easy-going person, someone who liked you for no other reason than to be nice.

***

"I love you," kept repeating in Mira's head. Jake's lips were soft against hers, his face as wonderful as she remembered. The fact he was home, safe, the two of them in bed and alone, his kisses, his touch, their breathless bodies intertwined, it was too good to be true. Mira stared deep into Jake's eyes as he ran a hand through her hair before bringing it to her cheek and then her body. She moaned... a delight she hadn't felt in months. "I love you," she whispered. Jake whispered the same words, and Mira could only believe that this was a dream. Jake showed no restraint, his hand finding the perfect spot. Mira arched her back and moaned even louder as deep breaths began to surface.

The shadow... Mira believed it was a shadow, like a heavy cloud crossing the sun on a bright day. She struggled to understand how, or what, as Jake and her were less than an inch apart. Mira jerked, her body gasping, her eyes opening... and she screamed! "It's okay," Sherry whispered before allowing her lips to meet Mira's once again.

Mira pushed back, flipping Sherry from on top of her and off to the side.

"What," Sherry exclaimed. "You said you love me!"

Mira shook her head while scrambling to her feet. Instinctively, she tugged at the side of her bathing suit that had been pulled down, exposing one of her breast. "What the hell are you doing?" Mira cried.

Sherry shook her head while extending a hand. "I love you," she said with a tearful plea. "I am so in love with you."

Mira stepped back, her hands animated. "No, no" she said, "I don't love you, not like that! And I can't believe you brought me out here thinking you could..." Mira's face took on a look of disgust, "...that you could touch me like that. What's wrong with you?"

***

The front door to the bar rocketed open and the long thin shadows of late-afternoon raced inside. Ted leapt from his chair, knocking it over as he rushed towards the door. Ted reached his daughter just as she swooned... plucking her up before she could fall. "What's wrong?" Ted asked in a panic. A sobbing Sherry said nothing.

Peter and Saul were quickly at Ted's back. "Where's Mira," Peter asked, fearing the worst.

Sherry muttered, an inaudible phrase, and began weeping.

"What's wrong? Where's Mira?" Ted kept repeating.

Peter wasn't about to wait around and disappeared through the door, followed by Saul.

"Tell me what's wrong," Ted begged.

"I want to go," Sherry whispered.

Ted looked over his shoulder and to Toke before

refocusing on his daughter. "Go?"

Sherry pushed both hands into her Dad's chest and squirmed in an attempt to be put down. Ted obliged. "I want to leave! We're leaving," Sherry yelled.

**

Mira sat in her bed, a kerosene lamp nearby. The flickering light distorted the writing on the envelope, but it didn't matter because she'd read the words a hundred times. It had been such a horrible day and now staring down at the letter she wasn't sure it was over. She breathed deeply, doing her best to dispel her fears. Earlier, her Dad found her dragging everything she and Sherry had toted to the beach, back towards their house. His panic had been real and his pestering of what went wrong, bothersome. But Mira never told her Dad what happened, and never would. It wasn't something a parent should know. All of it, the entire afternoon turned into the second worst day of her life. Jake remained but a dream, she'd lost her best friend, and every day she felt sicker and more tired than the one before. The world was no longer a beguiling wonderment, and she no longer felt welcomed in it. Another heavy breath just so she could steady her hands. She opened the letter and began to read. Three and four times she poured over the letter, trying her best to make sure Jake was okay and not just putting on airs. Having decided everything was fine, she began writing a letter of her own.

May 10, 1942

Dear Jake,

Remember that no matter what happens in this world I'll always love you. It breaks my heart just thinking about it, so let's move on to everything else.

Life's changing and I've changed as well. Mom and Dad threw a graduation party for me today and there must have been a hundred people stop by. Even some of the airmen stopped in and it was a real surprise! We had a lot of food and fun.

I guess I'm a Nurse though I don't feel much like one. For the first time in my life I don't know what's going to happen tomorrow. I've planned 'til this day and now I don't know. I wish you were here so we could talk.

Everyone is doing fine and gives their love. Your Mom and Dad are doing well also and want you to come home soon. I see them a lot more since I've moved back to the Island. I plan on getting a job as soon as possible but haven't started looking just yet, maybe next week. I need a break, some time to sort things out.

Thank you for the letter. I loved every word and I'm glad to hear you're so well liked by the men in your unit. They must be a swell group. Since coming home I've been thinking about Will a lot, and not a day goes by that I don't miss him. But I don't have to tell you that.

I didn't forget your birthday and I even have you a present. I wish you were here, it would be so much easier in person. I don't know how else to give you your present, so I'll just say it. I love you, I always have, you know that, and I'm pregnant. I haven't told anyone yet, not even my parents, I'm afraid to. But if I wait much longer they'll figure it out. I think they'll understand, at least I hope they do. Anyway, I wanted you to be the first to know and to tell you that we miss you.

Be careful. We love you and we need you to come home so we can be a family.

With all my love,

Mira

Chapter 35

Like autumn leaves in a brisk afternoon breeze, the graduating sailors of Naval Base Corpus Christi scattered in every direction. As for Jake, Jimmy, and Luther their luck held as they stepped off a train in San Diego, California. The three had survived training as a group and for now they remained together. Their fortune had been both good and bad as they no longer had to deal with Donnie or his cousin or their henchmen, but they also lost sight of the Mississippi Five. Pig's Eye and the others had proven to be good friends and wherever the Navy sent them Jake hoped they survived the war.

The port in San Diego was alive. Thousands of men poured in and collectively funneled in one direction. The destination of sailors, soldiers, airmen, and marines were the large hulking ships that stood as granite in the calm waters of the port. Men offloaded from railcars, buses, and trucks and gawked at the inevitable. Jake gulped as he looked upwards, the ship he was ordered to board more than five stories tall. Dwarfed by the ship's enormity, three doors just above the dock lay open and awaiting its cargo. Gangplanks bridged the distance between dock and doors, and men were divided accordingly and marched on board. Jake and Jimmy and Luther settled in, and hours later the ship began to move.

It was no pleasure cruise, just seven days of heat, sweat, and body odor. The rooms resembled large stalls with a hundred or more men packed inside and amidst bunks and makeshift hammocks stacked three and four high. Men dined where they slept and on cold meals, mostly bread and cold-cuts and fruit. Bathrooms were limited and the lines that formed never diminished. Perhaps this was the military's big plan, making it so miserable that by the time soldiers saw action it was a relief.

***

"I look quite the professional," Mira thought as she stared at herself in the mirror. With a baby-blue skirt, neatly pressed white blouse, and high heels which made her look taller and by some miracle, leaner, her spirits lifted higher than they'd been in weeks. She had an interview this morning and she aimed to impress. Peter and Bess and Mira ventured to the Bayou the day before and the three stayed the night at Rebecca's. It was just past seven in the morning when everyone wished Mira good luck and she drove away. Shell Belt Road took her to the main road before heading out of the Bayou and towards Mobile and Southern Hospital. A Catholic founded institution, Southern did a wonderful job of healing all who needed assistance, and she couldn't think of a better place to work. It had been a dream and early goal of hers, and she wouldn't let it slip away.

Mira sat in a hall and chatted with other ladies who were there for the same reason. She didn't worry though as she knew what she could do. Her confidence soared. She held a folder containing her school records and letters of recommendations from the Dean of Medicine at Mobile College and Doctor Meyer, and one more from the Arch Bishop of Mobile. Father Malone had helped with the letter of commendation from the Bishop when he introduced the two at an Easter service last year. Mira impressed on that Easter Sunday, just as she would today.

Doctor Madison sat behind a large desk, the sun shining brightly through a large window that overlooked a crowded and bustling street below. The head of medicine at the hospital made introductions, including Mother Tamera, a Nun who held a lofty position within the hierarchy of the hospital, and the three settled in their respective places. The interview would be administered by both, and nursing would be but a portion of the criteria for employment. This suited Mira perfectly as she'd always been a devout Catholic and believed herself to be an expert in the field. Either way, she had a decided advantage over many of the other applicants.

The two reviewed Mira's files at length and voiced satisfaction with her credentials. The Doctor put her through the paces and posed medical questions as well as observations that required thought to solve. Mira aced the inquiry and grew more positive with each passing moment. The Doctor finished and gave an approving nod to Sister Tamera. The Nun blinked her eyes as she conceded the doctor's observations, before scanning Mira's files once more. She flipped the pages, looking for any weaknesses. The papers before her laid out Mira's entire life, from baptism, to schooling, to confirmation, and to now. "You seem well suited, both spiritually and medically," Sister Tamera said with a warm smile. "Do you feel there is anything else you have to offer?"

Mira's head spun in dizzying circles, the room tilting from side to side. Nausea flooded her stomach. She closed her eyes, focusing on keeping her breakfast down.

"Young Lady," the Nun said.

Mira stood on wobbly legs.

"Are you ok?" Doctor Madison asked.

Mira shook her head. "I'm going to be sick," she said as she found a waste-basket at the edge of the desk and vomited. There was nothing else she could do. The Doctor stood from his chair before reseating himself as Mira left to find a bathroom. With a wet cloth in hand she stared at herself in the bathroom mirror. "What have you done?" It took longer than she hoped, but she finally returned to the room and her seat.

Sister Tamera left in the meantime but returned with a damp cloth and handed it to Mira. "Just in case," Sister Tamera said.

Mira thanked the lady and awaited the inevitable.

She knew it was over.

"Have you been ill?" The Doctor asked.

Mira shook her head as she sat bent over. "I'm sorry," was all she could say.

"Is it nerves?" the Nun inquired.

Mira never looked up but shook her head yet again.

"Are you pregnant?" the Doctor asked pointedly.

For the first time in her life, Mira felt ashamed. She wasn't sure of why, she just was. She never said a word as the Nun repeated the question.

Mira held the damp cloth to her lips and nodded slowly. The Nun and Doctor studied each other as Mira's face, and future, rested in her hands.

"Are you married?" The Nun asked.

Mira raised her head and looked at them both. "No I'm not," she said without wavering.

"A soldier," The Doctor said with assurance.

"Yes, he's a soldier as well as a lifelong love. We've loved each other since we were kids and are engaged."

The Nun closed her eyes for a brief second before giving the bad news. "I don't think we'll be hiring you," she said. "It wouldn't be in the best interest of the Church or the hospital to have an unwed pregnant nurse taking care of the needy. I trust with your Catholic upbringing that you understand."

Mira stood, nodded to the Doctor and Nun for their time and walked to the door. She started to open the door, it would have been easy to just walk away, but she turned and addressed the Nun. "Yes, I understand. I understand that the father of my baby and I love each other very much. We're engaged and when he gets home we'll be married. As for my Catholic upbringing, I always thought God loved everyone and forgave those that needed it. I'm not asking for my own forgiveness, but yours. I'm ok with what I've done."

***

Bess and Rebecca dug in the soil alongside the house, a potted hibiscus next to them. As Mira pulled in the drive Bess dropped the trowel and shed her gloves. Rebecca did the same and the two met Mira at the car as she rolled to a stop. Bess knew immediately though Rebecca missed all the signs. "Well," Rebecca asked. Rebecca had taken a lot of pride in her niece, the way she sculpted and cultivated her into a presentable young lady. And nothing would make her happier than Mira's success.

Mira stepped from the car and shut the door. Bess wrapped her arms around her daughter and held tight. "It's okay," she said. "There'll be plenty of other opportunities.

"How... what happened?" Rebecca demanded.

Mira shook her head as tears formed in the corners of her eyes, and it made her eyes look larger than they really were. "I'm sorry."

Bess smiled. "Oh child, there's no need to be sorry. It's just one job."

Again, Mira shook her head. "No, not that......."

Bess studied the one person she knew best but couldn't see past the veil.

"I'm pregnant," Mira whispered.

Rebecca fainted, stumbling sideways and falling to the ground.

"Good Lord," Bess said.

Perhaps it would have been better had Rebecca remained in her catatonic state, because when she awoke you'd have believed the devil himself appeared. "How could you?" She yelled. Then the horror struck in earnest. "When did you? And in my house?"

Bess gave her sister a sideways glance which Rebecca didn't appreciate because she had nearly has much invested in Mira as Bess did. She helped raise this young woman and this kind of conduct shouldn't be condoned. Rebecca glared at Bess before storming off and disappearing into her home

"Don't worry," Bess said, "your Aunt will be fine. She'll be over it in no time." Bess brushed her daughter's hair away from her eyes and gave a warm and seemingly complicated smile. "Does Jake know?"

Mira sniffled. "I don't know. I told him in a letter but I don't know."

Bess again put her arms around her daughter, but this time she hugged her like she did when she was a child. Rebecca had no children of her own and couldn't understand that this was still Bess' little girl. "You're gonna make a wonderful mom," she whispered. "And Jake, well, he's a Cullen and he'll keep things lively."

Mira let out a laugh that broke the stream of tears.

For hours Bess and Mira sat on a bench in the yard, an honest conversation about life and what's expected of a Mom. For the most part Peter watched from the kitchen window until he could no longer tolerate Rebecca's incestuous high morals. When he left the house he said nothing, heading to the bayou to check on his skiff. He hoped his wife and daughter would soon join him because he would never step in that woman's house again.

Peter poled the skiff as a soft breeze stroked his back. The day warmed to the point of being hot but he didn't care. He was headed home and would pole his skiff across a sea of lava to get there. I don't think two words were said the entire way and Mira was thankful for the reprieve.

"Mira," Peter said as he tapped at her bedroom door.

"Yea Daddy," Mira replied. She sat down her pen and paper, another letter for Jake.

Normally, when Peter and his daughter had these kinds of talks he would sit on the edge of the bed, but not tonight as he remained at the door.

Mira smiled... the light from the lamp making her Dad's eyes sparkle. She'd never been scared of her Dad and by the expression on his face, tonight would be no different.

"I hear we have a baby on the way," Peter said.

Mira nodded.

"When do you think it's due?"

Mira had given that some serious thought since realizing she was pregnant, and said, "Late September."

Peter walked to the edge of the bed but retreated to his original spot. He rubbed the stubble on his chin, the coarse hairs scrapping against his palm. "A child for the holidays," he said. "I like that."

Mira shook her head. "No Daddy, a grandbaby for the holidays."

Peter liked that even more, and it showed with the broadest smile his daughter had ever seen.

Chapter 36

Mira, Bess and Toke and Laura...the table was set. Cups of coffee rested in front of each and the conversation ventured far from smooth and easy. There had been urgency in Bess and Mira when the two stopped by the Cullen house, and that urgency hadn't yet been explained. Laura fidgeted, Bess fidgeted, Mira smiled and uncomfortable smile, and Toke drank his coffee.

From Mira's side, ripples of panic flowed beneath the surface and washed across the table's wooden veneer. She needed to get the words out before she hyperventilated. So she closed her eyes for a second, concentrating on slowing her breaths, and began. "Mr. Toke, Ms. Laura, I have something to tell you."

"Is Jake ok? Did he say something in his letters?" Laura had been looking for a reason to panic, and the secrecy of this meeting lit the powder-keg.

"No Ma'am, nothing like that." Mira quickly stated. She didn't want this session to start with even more anxiety and added, "He's quite fine. He really is."

Laura nodded with thankfulness. "As long as Jake's ok, we can get through anything."

Seeing an opening, Mira said, "I'm glad, because...... well, because Jake and I are going to have a baby."

Laura's face flushed and her breath escaped her, so Toke took up the cause. "Of course you're gonna have a baby. Hopefully you'll have several. We want plenty of grandbabies." A huge smile crossed his face.

Bess shook her head in disbelief just as Laura grabbed Toke by the sleeve. "No Toke, I think she's saying she's pregnant... now!"

Toke shook his head. "No, no. She said she's going to have a baby." He half snickered as he raised the coffee cup to his mouth and drank.

"Ms. Laura's right, I am pregnant," Mira clarified.

Maybe he had a stroke, who knows, but both of Toke's eyes begin to twitch. He blinked repeatedly with the left and then the right as if sending Morse code. "Well then," he said.

Mira didn't know what to think of the episode, she only hoped Jake didn't inherit whatever that was.

A quiet and subdued Toke slid his chair back, stood and walked next to Mira. He knelt beside her so they'd be face to face. "You," he whispered, "and our boy are going to have a baby?"

Mira nodded and Toke smiled a toothy grin. "We're gonna have a grandbaby," Toke said with excitement.

"Ah, a little bambino," he added. "Mia Momma, she gonna be so proud."

"Not now Toke!" Laura stated.

Mira and Laura's eyes locked. Mira and everyone else knew who ran the Cullen household and she awaited the verdict. "Surely her faith is the only thing that could be in the way," Mira thought.

"Does Jake know?" Laura asked.

Mira nodded. "I sent him a letter a while back. "I'm sure he does by now."

Laura sighed.

For over a year there hadn't been any good news for the Islanders. First there had been Will's death, then the void of those serving so far away. Pain stabbed at the community and something good needed to come from all that has happened. Laura broke the trance with Mira and looked to her good friend Bess. She smiled. "I can't believe we're going to have a baby running around our houses," she said, her voice rising with excitement.

Toke joined in, now speaking as an Irishman, "Ah, me little babby." He was so confused.

Chapter 37

Father Malone made himself as comfortable as he could in his rocking chair. He crossed his legs and it somehow diminished his presence, as if he'd shrunk. He tilted his head and looked at the lady closest to him. Bess sat in a chair a few feet away, a drab expression upon her face. Next to her was her daughter, Mira, and flanking Mira sat Laura. Malone, never a man to be nervous, rubbed at the crucifix that hung from his neck. "So ladies, what do I owe this pleasure?" He smiled as genuinely as possible.

Bess looked to Mira and then to Laura before turning to the priest. "Let's not pretend you don't know," Bess began. "The good Lord knows how small this Island is and how quickly gossip travels."

"Gossip?" the Priest question.

Bess feigned a smile. "Not all of its gossip," she added. "So let's get to it."

The skin on Malone's forehead formed wrinkles as he

listened.

Bess studied the intense gesture coming from the Priest. "You can cut it out, it'll make all this a lot easier." Bess looked to Laura, her aggravation mounting. "Fine, then I'll spell it out," she said to Malone. "What we want is for you to marry Jake and Mira as soon as Jake gets home."

The wrinkles vanished. "Well now," Malone said with a bit of cheer. "I think that's a fine idea, just fine."

Bess cut her eyes to Laura then back to the priest, but neither lady spoke.

Malone made a point to look each of them in the eyes. "Is there something else," he asked.

Again, the three women passed glances as Malone waited. "You do know I'm pregnant," Mira interjected.

Apparently Malone hadn't heard the gossip, or truth, or whatever, and he nearly fell from his chair. With his composure lost, it appeared as if Malone would rub clean through his crucifix. After a moment his hand relaxed and he stood. He stepped away from the women and studied a picture of Christ that adorned the wall. "God called me into service more than thirty years ago," Malone said, his eyes focused on the golden aura that highlighted the depiction of Jesus. He turned back to the women. "And I've done a fair job of what he's asked. I've obeyed his laws and the Church's doctrines... they are one in the same." Malone waited, hoping the ladies would get the point.

The ladies understood the point but none of them

agreed with the point, so they said nothing.

"Very well," Malone continued. "As I'm sure you are aware, I'm bound to uphold the rules of the Church..." still no reply. "...that is the oath I took when I joined the priesthood." Malone held out his hands as if to beg for understanding, and still no takers. "You realize I can't do this," he added.

"I've always wanted to be married in the church," Mira said with excitement. "And on a Saturday!"

"And once the baby's born we want a baptism as well," Laura said.

"Wait, wait," Malone stammered.

"Yes," Bess said, "we can't have a child not being baptized. And of course first communion," she added.

"No, no," Malone said. "I can't do any of those things. Surely you understand that?"

"Well I think this went well," Bess said as she rose from her chair and stepped toward the door. The others followed suit.

Malone raised his voice. "Stop," he yelled. "I will not be a part of this! I will not break my oath!"

Laura walked near the Priest and Malone noticed the pattern of wrinkles that now streaked across her forehead. "I do hope you change your mind," she said.

Chapter 38

Sweat ran down both cheeks and onto his collar, his green shirt darkening a shade. The stress of the past few weeks culminated with this one day, and he wanted nothing more than to go home. He stopped in the trail and looked over his shoulder for movement, for anything out of the ordinary. The trail wound and bended like a snake, the line of sight limited to about twenty feet in each direction. He needed to see more, for his own safety. "Just a few more feet," he thought as he picked up his pace. The trail from Toke's house to the church was less than fifty yards, but it had been an intense walk as he stopped in front of the church and glared at the door. Toke played it cool, humming a soft melody. "Mighty fine church," he said. As soon as the words left his mouth he spun a full ninety-degree, expecting to catch someone watching him. But he saw nothing, no movement and no sounds. Scared to death, Toke knew it was now or never. So he turned and headed for the church door. After a few feet and glances in every direction, he changed course and broke into a full sprint. He headed toward the rectory next door. Within a few feet of the house the front door swung open and Toke leapt, clearing the single step and sliding through the opening. As Toke screeched to a halt, Father Malone slammed the door behind him.

Malone was immediately on top of Toke. "What do you have?" he thundered.

Toke held up a finger, a request for a moment to catch his breath.

Malone would have none of that and grabbed Toke by his shoulders and shook. "What do you have for me?" The lullaby-lilt had vanished. Toke didn't think a man should ever be afraid of a priest, but this one scared him. Toke reached into his pocket and produced two biscuits, wrapped in wax paper. The biscuits were smashed, but the Priest didn't care. He snatched them from Toke's hand and devoured the bread. "Is that all, is that all you could get?"

"Yea, that's all," Toke said. Nervous, Toke used the fingernail on his right thumb to clear away the dirt beneath his left-hand nails. "I need to go," he begged. "I'm afraid to be caught here."

"Afraid? Afraid?" Malone stammered. "They're starving me out and you're the one who's afraid?"

Toke cocked an eye. "Well, yea. If they find out I'm helping you, I'll end up like Saul." It seems that ever since a priest had been living on the Island that the women had taken care of his cooking and laundry needs. So when Malone refused Bess and Laura's demands, the help ceased and the ladies decreed that anyone who helped the Priest would pay. And poor Ole Saul made the first mistake by attending Mass, and he didn't eat for a week. "Just let me go," Toke whined. "I'm not like you, I'm fond of eating."

"I need more," Malone insisted. "Look, I have nothing." The Priest turned and scanned the room. "No stove, no food, me clothes are in shambles....and, and,"

Toke truly believed a tear came to the Priest's eye as he continued.

"And no scotch!"

"Oh," Toke said as he put his hand to his mouth and staggered backwards. The thought of not having any liquor hit him right in the gut.

"And not a soul will take me to the mainland!"

A rustling-sound outside the door caused alarm and Toke threw himself against the wall, his back hugging the planks. Both men hushed and listened. "Oh, Lord," Toke whispered. "I knew this was gonna happen."

"Hush," Malone insisted. Malone eased to the window next to the door and slid the curtain a fraction of an inch to the left. With one eye peeking through, he watched. "There, right there" he whispered with enthusiasm. "That's what I want!"

Toke scrunched his face, like he'd eaten a sourball. He then moved to the window so he could see. "That cow?"

"Yes," Malone replied. "I want that wonderful, beautiful cow."

"You can't have that cow," Toke said. "That's Julius' milking cow."

"I don't care," Malone railed. "That cow, any cow. Just get me a cow!" Father Malone hooked a thumb in the waistband of his pants and tugged. "Two inches," he said to Toke. "I'm nothing but skin and bones and you're the only one who can save me."

"Well," Toke said. "You could save yourself. You could marry those kids and baptize the baby."

The lilt returned, and a high and mighty lilt at that. "Oh," Malone began. "So you've become one of them. They sent you here didn't they?"

"What," Toke replied. "No, they didn't send me here and I've always been one of them."

Malone ran a hand through his hair, the fight inside of him fading. His strength vanished and he trudged to his rocking chair and plopped down. "I'm sorry," he whispered. "I'm terribly sorry. It's the hunger in me belly."

"It's okay," Toke said.

Malone fumbled through some papers on the table next to his chair. He wasn't sure what he was looking for but found one-quarter of a piece of peppermint candy. He cradled it in his hands as if it were pure gold. "Me last one," he said just before tossing it into his mouth. The old man sighed as he rolled the hard-candy from side to side with his tongue. "Remember when we drank those two bottles of scotch and ended up at your house for dinner? That was a fine meal!"

Toke didn't reply.

"And remember all the things we talked about that afternoon? The first time you and I ever came to terms." Malone stared at Toke's pensive expression. "About how we'd be best of friends from now on and look after one another......" Malone's words faded.

"Well, it does sound like me but I don't remember," Toke said. "It's not a secret that I tend to make promises when I drink." Toke rubbed the back of his neck. "But truthfully, I had too much that day. I don't even remember going home for dinner."

"Oh," the Priest added, his mind and body and spirit defeated. "Ooohhh," the Priest said, his mind and body and spirit suddenly lifted. "So you don't remember, do you?" Malone eased further into his chair and breathed with the resolve of a man who truly knew Christ. "Well then, I think we have our answer. You bring the ladies by tomorrow, say noon, and we'll put this business to rest."

Toke smiled, thankful this was over and that he could leave. A quick survey of the yard from the window and he ducked out and disappeared down a trail.

Chapter 39

Malone felt more in charge on this day. It was a sunny Sunday morning and he'd just finished Mass, just him and God and Grandma Nelly. He smiled because he'd had more people at Mass today than any Sunday since his involuntary hunger strike began. And now, well now he awaited Toke and Bess and Mira and Laura. He eased into his rocker, picked up the Bible, and waited.

Toke led the way, a bottle of scotch in his hand, followed by Bess with a bowl of shrimp stew, Mira with cornbread, and Laura with an apple pie. "Oh dear Lord," Malone said as he spied the liquor. Then the smells came, the food so close he could taste it. "Oh Lord...please give me the strength," he whispered. The Priest struggled to remain calm, squirming like a little boy who needed to pee. His mouth went dry and he couldn't even summon enough spit to swallow. Malone breathed as deep as he could before he continued, focusing on the task at hand. "Well." His voice was high, very high. He cleared his throat and began again. "Well, it seems you've come fully armed?"

"You look a bit thin." Bess' said, her barb hitting the mark.

Malone bit his tongue and instead of lashing out he said, "Nothing to worry with, I've been meaning to lose a few pounds." Malone glanced over to Toke, the linchpin to his entire plan.

Toke didn't like that. He didn't like any of this. "Father, I think I'll let you and the ladies handle this one," he said. He set the bottle of scotch down and stepped in the direction of the door.

"Hold it mister," Laura stated. "You were asked to be here for a reason and you'll be here."

Toke grunted before returning to his post.

"I'm glad you decided to stay," Malone said to Toke. "Besides, you'll be happy to know that I have good news."

"Good news?" Mira asked.

The Priest again struggled to contain his emotions, the smell of food wafting through his mind, the taste of scotch stirring in his kidneys. "Yes," he said to Mira. "You and Jake are going to be married in the church and your baby welcomed into God's arms."

The women looked at each and burst into laughter, dancing around the room and congratulating themselves along the way. "Thank you Father, thank you," Bess repeated.

"You've done a wonderful thing," Laura added.

Toke said nothing, knowing it couldn't be that easy.

Malone waited for the elation to subside while accepting the gratitude. "A piece of cornbread, if you don't mind, and maybe a touch of scotch to wash it down," he said. He ate the cornbread and downed the scotch before continuing. "Now then, I think everyone owes Toke a great deal of thanks."

Confusion swamped Laura's face, her bottom lip curling on the corners. "Toke," she questioned.

Confusion swamped Toke's face. "Toke?" he questioned.

Father Malone raised his brows, "Yes, Toke."

"Whatever you did, thank you," Bess said to Toke.

Mira was about to thank him as well when Laura interrupted. "What'd you do," she asked her husband, crossing her arms in the process. "This ain't some game you can pull!"

Toke shrugged.

"Oh, don't be modest," Malone said to Toke. The Priest held up a hand before Toke could reply. "Just let me handle this," he said. Father Malone looked at Mira and the smile on her face let him know that he'd made the right decision, that when it came to the human spirit it wasn't always black and white. "I've never doubted the love you and Jake share. It's a wonderful comfort having two young people care for each other so deeply. And it's an equal blessing to have someone like Toke looking over you. The humility of this loving father and soon to be grandparent has inspired me."

232

Laura wanted to believe the Priest, wanting it more than anything, but skepticism had yet vacated her brain. "Did he really inspire you," she asked Malone.

Malone smiled warmly, his jawline more angular than three weeks ago. "Yes. Toke saved a soul by giving his own." Malone gave a thoughtful pause, a nice addition to the forthcoming climax, before announcing with great pride, "And you'll be happy to know that he agreed to become a faithful sheep in our flock."

"I did what?" Toke stammered.

Father Malone nodded. "Yes, he agreed to be a pillar of the Church, to attend Mass twice a week and to do so soberly. And of all the selflessness a man can offer, none could offer more than Toke has. He's agreed to give himself to God so that his grandchild can be blessed with the same virtue."

Laura looked at Toke, tears forming in the corners of her eyes before releasing and sliding down her cheeks. Toke staggered sideways and then backwards a few steps. He raised his arm to his forehead and erased a line of sweat that formed above his brows. Laura continued the admiration, her tears sincere and honest. And Toke, well, one look at Laura and he knew it was over. Laura walked to her husband. "Did you really do that," she whispered.

"I guess I did," Toke replied. Laura began to sob, and Mira and Bess did the same. Toke kissed one of the tears on his wife's cheek. "I'd do anything for you."

The ladies plated the food, poured another glass of

scotch and left the men alone. As soon as the women stepped out, Toke turned to Malone. He scratched a spot behind his left ear and squinted with his right eye. "Did I really agree to all that?"

Malone gave a huge grin. "You just did!"

Chapter 40

They survived eight-weeks of basic training, were eventually herded out west on a three-day train ride, held prisoner for a week at sea, and once the ship ported they remained crammed aboard for another four days. And now that they've disembarked and taken up quarters at Naval Station Pearl, Jake finally had a reason to smile. He held up a letter, flaunting it in front of Jimmy and Luther. Jake could hardly contain himself, his hands fidgety as he read the return address over and over.

"Read it aloud," Jimmy said. "I wanna hear!"

Jake smiled, more than happy to do so. Jake ripped the end of the envelope off, being careful not to damage the contents. He squeezed the top and bottom of the letter and blew inside the opening. The envelope puffed open like a sail that had gotten its wind. Jake peeked in, a single sheet of paper neatly folded. Jake slid the letter out and began reading to Jimmy and Luther.

July 3, 1942

My Dearest Jake,

    We love you and we pray you're doing well. And we're so happy Jimmy is with you. Tell him his parents miss him and that we all love him.

    As you know, things have changed a lot lately, especially with Mira. Wait, your Dad keeps bugging me so let me get what he has to say out of the way first. He says those airmen are ruining this place and he wonders if we aren't the ones suffering under a dictator. And he's tired of eating goat, hah, hah. He also thinks they're too friendly with the girls around here, but you already knew that. Your Dad says they make eyes at everyone in a skirt and that one of them was caught winking at poor Aunt Bell the other day. And while we're on the subject, I think something must have happened between Sherry Larson and one of them. You know how much she likes the boys, and I think she may have went too far. She and Mira had gone to the beach a few weeks back and Sherry left the Island crying. Mira wouldn't say a word about what happened and no one has seen Sherry since. But back to Mira. Everyone is relieved to know that she told you everything instead of you having to hear it from someone else. And I guess it'll all be over by the time you get home. It took some doing, with all the shenanigans and backdoor business going on, but Father Malone agreed to perform the wedding. You can thank your Father for that! And Mira sure was happy when she found out she'd be married in the church, and on

Saturday. But the Father did say he ain't gonna wait forever. He wants all this nasty business behind him, sooner rather than later, and I think it's safe to say we all agree. If you're thinking it'd be better if you were here, I'd have to agree, but God has different plans and he'll bring you home when he's through with you. So hang in there. Finally, I want you to know that when Mira came clean, a huge burdened was lifted. It's important to understand that she did the right thing even though it doesn't always feel that way.

We love you! And tell Jimmy we love him too.

Love, Mom and Dad

Jake stared at the page. "What the hell," he said. He flipped the letter over, to see if he missed anything. "What the hell!" he added. Jake looked to Jimmy and Luther and neither man wanted to state the obvious. "I got to go," Jake said as he leapt to his feet and grabbed his duffle bag. "I got to git' home and fix this before it's too late."

"Grab him," Jimmy said to Luther. Luther did and Jake squirmed and fought to get loose. He even used some of the moves the military had taught him, but to no avail.

Jake gave up the fight but continued to stew. "Let me go," he said to Luther. Luther never budged. "I said let me go!"

"Jake," Jimmy said. Jimmy put a hand on each side of Jake's face and directed his eyes to him. "You have to let it go. If you try to leave they'll arrest you before you get off the base."

"I don't care," Jake said. "I have to see her."

"She's moved on," Jimmy added. "She's found someone else and she's happy. Just let her be happy."

Jake began to cry and Jimmy motioned for Luther to let him go. Jake fell into Jimmy's arms, his sobbing uncontrollable. "But I love her," he cried. "I've always loved her.

Chapter 41

Mira and Peter sat on the middle bench and Toke poled. Peter looked out across the bay as small clouds cast shadows on the surrounding water before moving on and dragging the shade with them. This was Toke's usual run for the mail though the three had bigger fish to fry. Having shoved off from the Shell Banks just after daylight they fully expected it to be dark by the time they returned home, even with the use of Julius' car.

Toke gave one final push and the bow of the skiff grounded to a halt on Cedar Point. The three jumped off and within minutes Toke and Peter found a shade. This wasn't their first trip over and the two napped while Mira walked along the shore, her thoughts her only company. For the first time in months she felt good, even great. Her strength had returned, along with her mental endurance, and optimism prodded her spirit. With school over and everyone now knowing about the baby, she slept better and ate better and laughed and sounded like her old self. And if today worked out like she hoped, it would leave Jake as the one missing piece.

The mail arrived as scheduled and Toke threw the bag in Julius' car. Mira climbed in behind the wheel, and both men realized this was a good thing. The three made their way into west Mobile and Mira pulled to the curb. Peter and Toke stepped out. Mira leaned over and spoke through the open passenger-side window. "Two hours," she said. She held up two fingers so there'd be no misunderstanding.

Peter and Toke nodded.

She was about to drive off when she gave a second thought as to who she was actually talking to, and added, "If I come back and I have to look for ya'll in a bar somewhere, I'm gonna tell Momma and Ms. Laura!"

Toke laughed at the threat but soon shut up when Peter said, "She's not kidding, she'll do it."

Mira drove east and soon pulled into the parking lot for the County Health Department. Mira wanted a job, she needed to help, but didn't know if anyone was willing to take a chance on an inexperienced and awfully pregnant nurse. But she gave it her all and when the interview concluded, was happy with her efforts. It turned out the Health Department had one opening and they extended it to Mira. They needed a nurse who could call on those who had no means of making it to the actual Health Department building. It would require traveling the county and assisting and serving as midwife and such when needed. Mira couldn't think of a more perfect job until they told her she needed her own transportation. Mira spoke up, about to ask the

Administrator for more time to consider the offer, but declined the job instead. Her only hope would be Rebecca and she wouldn't crawl, or have her mother crawl, and beg for help. Mira thanked the man and drove back to the other side of town.

Mira laughed as she rounded the corner. Toke and Peter had been shopping and both toted colorful bags from some of the finest stores in Mobile. She slowed and watched as Peter opened one of his bags and Toke peeked inside. Toke placed a hand over his heart, like he'd just seen the most precious gift in the world, and smiled. Peter smiled just as brightly, pleased with the results. And as the men jumped in the car, they never stopped yapping. Mira interrupted. "You ladies have fun?" Neither man minded the quip and continued their conversation as they headed south, back to Cedar Point. As soon as the ladies ended their tongue-wagging, Mira told them that she'd been offered a job. She then told them that she declined it. When asked why, she lied. She realized that telling the truth would hurt them more than any lie she could think of. It was her father, and her baby's grandfather, and though they had little they had a wealth of pride. They were cut from the same cloth, believed in family and taking care of one's own, and the fact they weren't financially able to help with buying a car would be a slap in the face. So she said the work load would be too much with her pregnancy so far along. Both men agreed and soon the car ride south became terribly quiet.

"Slow down," Toke said from the back seat. They were in Alabama Port and almost to Cedar Point, when Toke

241

added, "Turn right."

Mira frowned.

"You thinking what I'm thinking," Toke said to Peter.

Peter thought for a second. "Yea," he said, "the Bayou."

***

Mira sat on the center bench and stomped her feet so hard that Toke thought his skiff would come apart. She screamed as loud as she could before standing and screaming some more. Toke feared she'd taken the fever, but Peter knew his daughter and smiled. Dauphin Island rested straight ahead and Mira stepped up and onto the bench, the boat rocking beneath her feet. She spread her arms skyward and yelled as loud as she could, "God I love this place!"

Toke and Peter had been right and following a brief meeting at Doc Meyer's office, Mira was employed as of July 28, 1942.

Mira pulsated with joy and as soon as she eased off the boat she raced home. She wanted nothing more than to tell her Mom the good news. From there, she had other plans. As for Peter and Toke, they pulled the boat ashore, unloaded the bags and walked to the crossroads. Peter asked Toke, "You heading to the bar later?"

Toke shook his head. "Nope, gonna be with the misses tonight."

Peter held his bags in the air. "Think I'll do the same,"

he said.

Toke took the path to his house while Peter headed down his.

The next morning everyone gathered at the church, as Mira had requested. Last night Mira told her Mom the news before rushing out of the house in secrecy. She didn't return for more than two hours but by the time she walked in she sported the broadest smile her mother had ever seen. She kept tight lipped about where she'd been or what she was up to, and Mom and Dad let it go. And today, well her excitement spilled over, stirring the room with anticipation.

Father Malone quieted the group, said a prayer, and turned it over to Mira. "I want to thank everyone for coming," Mira began. "These past months have been hard and I wanted to talk to everyone about doing something for our boys overseas." The room was silent as the glow from the morning sun warmed the sanctuary. "I think there are things we can do to help. If it's okay, I'd like to suggest we gather in groups, of five or six, and write letters to each boy. That would make about ten letters to each." Mira waited for a response. "I can't imagine a better gift than each of them hearing from someone other than their mom and dad. If nothing else, so they know we love each of them." The silence continued and Mira wondered if she had overstepped her boundaries.

"I think it's a lovely idea," a lady in the audience said. "Two of my nephews are over there and if I can do anything to help then I'm in."

"Me too," someone else said. "And I think we should include some small reminders of home as well." Soon, the entire group was on their feet and eager to dive into the project.

Malone stepped next to Mira as the crowd broke into groups. "You're doing a wonderful thing," he said.

Chapter 42

Pate Carter stood shoulder to shoulder with twenty-seven Marines as the landing-craft headed toward the small island. It was early morning on August 7, 1942 and the island of Tulagi, in the Solomon Island chain, was officially under siege. Dozens of landing craft moved steadily across choppy waters, the waves thrusting men from side to side, the sandy beachhead drawing ever closer. "Five-hundred yards," an officer yelled. Pate gripped his rifle, his eyes fixed on the grey wall of the vessel. For some reason, men didn't look at each other in moments like this, each mustering the strength to rush into an enemy stronghold. But never-the-less the boat plowed on, a relentless pace. Sweat ran down Pate's cheek, his mind grappling with nerves and everything he'd been taught, everything needed to be a good Marine. Three short bursts from a whistle, a hundred yards left. Men readied themselves, all of them now facing forward, awaiting the moment when the door would flop open. Pate stared at the back of the man in front of him, the silence of twenty-eight lives causing his head to ache.

A flash of light, or perhaps it was that moment when you snap out of a dream. Whatever happened Pate was unable to comprehend as he fell forward, like all the men in the landing craft, each one slamming into the person in front of him. Men began scrambling, trying to right themselves. A strip of shallow coral reefs grounded the vessel, as well as dozens of other landing craft. The reef hadn't been plotted on maps, a result of poor reconnaissance. The landing craft reversed its direction and turned to the north before swinging around and making another attempt at the beach. Men fell forward again, the front of the ship grounded once more, this time unable to move. Someone in the rear made a decision and the door swung open, exposing the beach some fifty yards away. Whistles blew and men jumped out of the vessel, some landing on the reefs, twisting ankles and cutting themselves on the sharp coral, while others missed them all together and landing on sanding bottom. Pate ran forward, becoming one of the thousands of Marines that exited their craft and charged toward shore. After clearing the reef, the water deepened before turning shallow again. Men struggled with backpacks and heavy ammo and rifles, and by the time Pate reached the beach deep breaths swamped his lungs. His legs burned from racing through water and salt from the ocean stung his eyes. And there was still an enemy to contend with.

The Marines quickly took up positions, assessed their strengths and casualties, and wasted little time before moving inland. The beach landing had been easier than anticipated, though things quickly changed. Pockets of Japanese soldiers plagued the approaching Americans who skirmished regularly and at close distances. Small battles raged as the outnumbered Japanese retreated further into the jungle. The Marines pushed hard and the Japanese would eventually make their final stand on a hill on the southern end of the island. As daylight and the hues of a setting sun shortened the advance, the Marine Corp decided to halt until morning. So, like everyone else, Pate dug in, burrowing a pit in the middle of a sandy island in the middle of the Pacific Ocean. The Marines eventually formed a line with squads spaced fifty-feet apart and posted sentries. They knew it would be a long night.

Chapter 43

A sliver of moon and billions of stars sparked the sky, their glistening lights shimmering off palm fronds and the waxy leaves of exotic plants. Deep within the jungle the heart of the night began to beat, insects and creatures uniting into an orchestrated crescendo. Pate lay against the embankment of the foxhole, the moon and stars peering through the jungle canopy, spying as he nested in the sand. Pate ran a hand along the embankment. The sand was thicker and coarser than back home, yet familiar and comforting. He leaned back, and the cool-damp-sand soothed his aching body but did nothing for his rumbling stomach. He hadn't eaten much throughout the day, nerves had seen to that, and it was finally catching up with him. His stomach railed. "Johnson," Pate whispered.

Private Johnson lay against the opposite bank, and the mention of his name caused his right eyelid to flip open. "What," Johnson whined as the eyelid closed.

Stevenson stood guard and gave a harsh whisper,

telling the men to pipe down. Pate crawled to Johnson and lay next to him. "Got any rations left," Pate whispered.

"Hush," Stevenson said. There had been urgency in his voice and the others took notice. Pate and Johnson and the fourth man, Private Marelli sprang to the embankment and peered over. The jungle, thick and sprawling, its waxy leaves twisting and turning in the breeze, the faint light from the moon and stars, culminated into a world of deception. Stevenson pointed and the four glared, their eyes straining to make out what they could not see. Two minutes passed and not a word. Twice that amount of time came and went then doubled again, and yet no one moved. Finally, Johnson shook his head. Stevenson silently agreed and his body eased.

"Go home Joe!" The voice, high pitched and nasally, echoed through the jungle.

Hairs stood on the back of Pate's neck, his eyes flicking back and forth examining every twisting leaf and shadow. "Dear God," he muttered, struggling to swallow. Pate had never heard a Japanese speak and never imagined they would sound like that.

"Go home to your girl and we let you live."

Pate's hands strangled his rifle, his knuckles turning white. Sweat streaked down the side of his face as patches of his light-green uniform turned dark. Sand caked to the damp spots of his uniform and along his arms. He clinched his teeth so tight that they may actually crack and break. The barrel of his rifle rotated across the landscape, braving the night, daring it to blink. He had fired his rifle dozens of times throughout the day and seen dead bodies on both sides, but he didn't know if he had actually killed anyone. He didn't want to know.

Voices continued to rise and fall in the distance, resonating through the valley, unnerving a remarkably beautiful night. Pate's entire body jerked, thinking he saw movement, and he nearly pulled the trigger on his rifle. Sweat stung his reddening eyes as he tried to focus. He fixated on a spot before tapping Johnson on the arm. The two glared, unblinking, as the voices faded to silence. Pate aimed his rifle at the spot and waited.

He was silent, so silent! A Japanese soldier raced toward the hastily built bunkers, the bayonet at the end of the man's rifle glistening in the faintest of light. Fast and soundless, the soldier closed the seventy-five feet between jungle and bunker in a matter of seconds. Pate fired a shot and was soon joined by the others in the hole. The approaching soldier fell forward onto his right shoulder, almost like a deer that had been taken down by a hunter, as gunfire erupted from all the bunkers, bullets ripping though and disappearing into the entanglement that was the jungle.

"One soldier, just one?" Pate questioned. The gunfire died and officers assessed the situation. It proved to be a one-man diversion, as a small group of Japanese soldiers flanked the Marines. Bayonets at the ready, the handful of Japanese charged. From the right a Marine cried out. Pate turned, looking for the enemy, eager to fire a shot, but couldn't. The enemy had made it into their hole. The barrel of Pate's rifle, still in motion and swinging to his right, deflected a blade meant for him. The Japanese soldier's momentum knocked Pate backwards and his rifle from his hands. The enemy soldier stumbled past Pate and landed on his stomach. Pate flipped over, on top of the man's back. Brutal and violent... and oddly silent, the two men waged war. The enemy soldier was much smaller than Pate, almost frail. Pate could feel every bone in his back and shoulders, but the man had strength and a determination to live. Pate thrust a forearm in the back of the man's neck while his free hand fumbled with the sheathed knife on his side. And even death proved silent.

Breathless, Pate rolled sideways before falling backwards and into the embankment. He stared at the motionless soldier, hating what had been forced upon him. It took a minute or so, perhaps a bit of shock to wear off, but Pate finally noticed Johnson's crumpled body at the bottom of the hole... blood gushing from his side. Stevenson acted quickly, applying pressure to the wound as Marelli pulled Johnson slightly upright. Marelli yelled for a medic. Within seconds a medic and aide appeared, the two crawling over the edge and into the hole. The medic looked at Stevenson and hitched his eyes in an upward motion. Stevenson understood and retreated to his lookout position. Quietly, the medic and aide tended to the bleeding soldier as they awaited a stretcher from the rear.

There had been two Japanese soldiers in the hole and both were killed. When the fight began Pate never saw the one that got Johnson, but he saw him now as he and Marelli rolled the two bodies up and out of the hole.

Pate forever changed on that night, just like every other man who'd fight in this war. He had killed and nearly been killed, and with all that had happened he could only think of his Dad. Julius never talked about the war around his son, but the Island was small and Pate had heard plenty of stories. The stories always glorified the battles, given reasons to be proud of a man's actions. But his Dad's eyes told a different story, a story of grief, stricken by heartache. Pate had spent his life looking into those eyes and only now did he understand. This would be the longest night of Pate's young life as he sunk deep into his hole.

By morning Pate rallied his spirit, and it was good that he did. What lay ahead for young Pate was more enemy entrenchments and fanatics, those who chose to die when faced with surrender, and countless acts of cruelty. From here on out he had no choice but to fight tooth-and-nail for every inch of land, to do so for his country and the man who stood next to him, and of most importance...... because he was a Marine.

***

Julius put on his best face as he handed Alice the letter. Alice smiled, broad and happy as she sat at the kitchen table, studying the exterior of the letter. Julius took a chair across from her and leaned back. Alice brought her eyes to meet those of her husband's and he forged a smile. Julius knew what the letter would say, just as he knew all the things it wouldn't. But Alice never needed to know. With trembling hands, Alice opened the letter and began to read aloud. Alice cried a lot, even though care had been taken to ensure a bright and cheery letter. Perhaps it was her son's voice she could hear, his words closing the distance that separated them. As Alice finished, she wiped at her tears and sighed. Julius stood from his chair, walked next to her and put his arms around her shoulders as she began to cry once more.

Chapter 44

Jake received two things on September 24, 1942, his orders assigning him to a ship for training and a letter from Mira. Jimmy and Luther received their orders as well and were thankful for the change in venue. The two had been listening to Jake cry for the past few weeks, foiled three escape attempts, and eventually had to get tough and slap him around a bit. They'd had enough, and no matter where the Navy sent them it had to be an improvement. Packed and ready, the next morning would bring more than just another day.

Jake sat on the edge of his cot and stared at the envelope. The damn thing looked like it'd been run over by a tank. Ripples and ridges creased the exterior of the letter, and apparently it had been misdirected many times. Jake rolled his eyes upwards, to meet those of his friends. "Well here it is," he said with disgust. "What a lifetime of love going down the drain, looks like." Jake traced a finger across the envelope's bumpy surface. "May 10, 1942," he said. He stabbed a finger into the paper. "And right there is her name! Like it ain't nothing to it!" He twisted at the waist and tossed the letter on the bunk. A second later he picked it up. "You read it," he said to Jimmy while extending it with his hand.

Jimmy shook his head.

"Then you read it," he said to Luther.

Luther didn't need to shake his head because he had no intentions of reading it and Jake knew it.

"Fine," Jake stated. "I'll read it!" Jake tore open the envelope but didn't have the strength to remove the letter. He began to cry.

"Give me the damn thing," Jimmy said, "anything to get this over with!" He snatched the envelope from Jake, removed the letter and unfolded it. He began to read aloud.

"Dear Jake," Jimmy began.

"I can't stand it," Jake yelled. "I just can't stand that she has the nerve to say 'Dear Jake'. It ain't right I tell you."

Jimmy turned his head sideways so he could see Luther. He gave a disapproving glare. "Anyway," Jimmy said, returning to the letter. "Remember that no matter what happens in this world I'll always love you."

"Yea right!" Jake exclaimed. "Just a big fat lie! They're all lies! Who the hell does she think she's fooling?"

"Jake, do you want me to read this or not?" Jimmy asked. "Because I'd just as soon throw it in the trash."

Jake quieted. "Yea, though I don't know why."

Jimmy reset himself and continued. "It breaks my heart just thinking about it."

"Oh, I bet it does," Jake said under his breath.

"So let's move on to everything else," Jimmy continued. "Life's changing and I've changed as well. Mom and Dad threw a graduation party for me today and there must have been a hundred people stop by. Even the airmen stopped in and it was a real surprise."

"God damn it!" Jake yelled has he jumped to his feet. "I knew those dirty bastards were up to something. When I get home I'm gonna butcher every last one of them...."

"Sit down and shut up," Jimmy said with aggravation. Jake never moved so Jimmy motioned for Luther to handle it. Jake soon obliged and plopped back down. "I ain't telling you again. Stay seated or me and Luther's gonna give you a beating." Jimmy was adamant and Jake nodded in understanding. "Now then," Jimmy said, searching for his spot. "We had a lot of food and fun. I guess I'm a registered nurse now though I don't feel much like one. For the first time in my life I don't know what's going to happen tomorrow. I've planned 'til this day and now I don't know. I wish you were here so we could talk."

"Talk or stab me in the back," Jake questioned.

"Damn it Jake!" Jimmy said.

Jake looked up to Jimmy. "Is that in the letter or is that your words?"

"Me, I said it. So just shut up and let me get through

this!" Jimmy shook his head in irritation before continuing. "Everyone is doing fine and gives their love......" Jimmy read on, each word grinding into Jake's brain, "...... God I wish you were here, it would be so much easier in person."

"For God's sake, just say it woman!" Jake yelled.

Jimmy pressed on. "I don't know how else to give you your present, so I'll just say it. I love you, I always have, you know that, and ..."

"Please Lord," Jake begged. "Just let this be over!"

"And I'm pregnant." Jimmy looked at the words again, reading them to himself.

"Oh dear God, I just knew it!" Jake wailed. "What? Wait a minute," Jake continued. "What did you say?"

"She says she's pregnant," Jimmy stated.

Jake snatched the letter from Jimmy's hand, his eyes racing to find the spot where she said she was pregnant. Jake read it over and over. "She's not seeing someone else. The news Mom talked about was this. She's pregnant and she loves me! She's pregnant and she loves me...... oh God, she's pregnant."

Chapter 45

Smoke from the fire circled like vultures before ascending into the deep-blue sky. A coffee pot rested on a makeshift grill, the water inside shy of boiling. Pate picked up the pot and poured a cup. He sipped his coffee. Pate stared across the rocky terrain, his eyes venturing across the Pacific Ocean and past the dozens of warships that sat motionless on the horizon. Another sip of coffee, bitterly strong but welcomed. Pate had always been able to look past the warships, beyond the vast ocean that separated him and home, but today, well today he struggled. Dauphin Island remained in his thoughts but he could no longer see the tall pines that scraped against the clouds or the surf that roared onto shore. He shook his head, trying to oust the battles and bombs and deaths that suffocated his memory. Pate finished his coffee, some of the grounds catching in his teeth, but Dauphin Island never appeared. He thought of pouring another cup but decided against it. It seemed the Marine Corp had an abundance of coffee and bullets, and little else. Like every other Marine, Pate had been on half-rations from the first day he landed on a beachhead, and the shadow from his stark frame stretched out like a fence post on the mountainous landscape. Pate's eyes sank deep into his features and his jaw was razor sharp. His platoon had been instrumental in the taking of another island, a name he didn't care to remember. The fighting was heavier than before with more hatred and more deaths. And for Pate, well he knew this wasn't the end.

***

Doc Meyer walked out of the room, taking care to close the door as quietly as possible. It was October 4, 1942, and he hadn't smiled so broadly in months. The Lea's and Cullen's were anxious, and the smile allowed the four to let out a collective sigh. "Both are fine," the Doctor said. "The baby's as healthy as a horse and Mira just needs some rest. Let them sleep for a while and everything will be just fine." The Doc cocked an eyebrow. "I'm going home, but if you need something then come fetch me." Everyone thanked the Doc as he left the house and headed to the beach. Julius would see that he made it to the Bayou safely.

Toke hugged Laura and Bess and Peter did the same. "Let's fix some dinner," Bess said to Laura. "I think we could all use some food." Laura agreed and the ladies disappeared.

With the ladies gone, Peter shrugged his shoulders as if to ask Toke 'what they should do'. Toke smiled and Peter understood. The two of them headed out to spread the word. They were now the proud grandparents of a healthy baby boy.

Mira sat up in bed, the baby breastfeeding while Laura and Bess sat in nearby rocking chairs. The cramped bedroom was hot and stuffy, but no one complained. Mira had slept most of the night, only waking when the baby needed feeding, and she felt better on her first full day as a mother. Laura took the baby as soon as it finished and patted its back. The baby gave a loud burp and everyone laughed. Laura couldn't take her eyes from the little thing, proud and happy and trying to decide if he looked more like Jake or Mira. She hoped to see a glimpse of her son in the baby's face. Deciding it may take more than one day for the baby's characteristics to develop, she said, "At least he burps like Jake." This brought another chorus of laughter.

Bess' chair sat next to the head of the bed and she extended a hand. Mira accepted it with hers. "I love you," Bess said to her daughter. Mira smiled. Mira had given a lot of thought to her life over the past months and the one thing that always held true was her family. She loved her Mom and Dad but it was more than that. People from all over the island had brought her diapers and a crib and everything else a person needed to raise a baby. She again smiled, thankful for so much love.

"So," Bess said.

"So what," Mira replied.

Laura stopped humming to the baby long enough to ask, "Have you decided on a name?"

Mira smiled once more. "I think so," she said. The two ladies waited. "Joseph William Cullen," she said.

A tear came to Bess and Laura's eyes. Joseph was Bess' father name and William needed no explanation. "I think it's a wonderful name," Bess said. "So what are we going to call him?"

There could be only one answer. "Will," Mira replied.

Laura stared at the baby she cradled, his tiny arms stretching out in front of him. "He looks like a Will," she said with a smile.

Chapter 46

The strain of war spread like an infectious disease, and Pate wasn't immune. Dysentery and half-rations cut into his features just as a mason cuts into stone. He once stood six-feet tall but his bent frame, wrecked from countless hours in bunkers, had bowed his back. His features were muted and his mind chaotic. He only wanted a moment's peace.

Like a hermit, Pate hunkered in yet another bunker on another island in the Solomon Island chain. He removed his helmet and placed it upside-down next to him. He ran a hand across his brow. Even in October it was as hot as Hades in the South Pacific. There was no changing of leaves, no brisk winds from the north, and no signs of fall. But even with the lack of seasonal respite, baseball and the game between the Island and the Bayou pricked at his mind. He wasn't even sure if October had yet rolled around on the calendar, but in his bones he knew the game neared. Pate stared at the pile of sand mounded in front of him. He shook his head, doing his best to remember last year's win. Yea, it was there, and he recalled that he'd been instrumental in the victory. He smiled as he hoped the Islanders were giving it to them yet again. "What a day," escaped his lips. He also remembered other things about that day, especially Sherry Larson. Easily the prettiest girl he'd ever seen, he'd shown her picture so many times that the guys no longer cared to see it. They had their own dream-girls back home and the sight of Sherry made them pale in comparison. Pate enjoyed the way the guys doted over her, because she was his girl. He had kissed her, on the lips, and he figured that had sealed the deal. And boy oh boy, what he wouldn't give for one more kiss?

"Mail," a soldier said just loud enough for the soldiers to hear. Heads popped up beyond the holes in the earth, like prairie dogs that had been put on alert. Men watched as a soldier dragged a mailbag in their direction. The man disappeared into foxhole after foxhole, asking the same question every time he slid down an embankment. "Who's the lucky son a bitch named Carter?" He didn't get his answer until he entered Pate's domain.

"Here," Pate answered with anticipation. The man held a bundle of letters, as if they were a football, before tossing them in Pate's direction.

"Christmas came early for somebody," the soldier said before slivering away. Pate smiled as the sight of home returned.

***

"Eleven," Jake shouted. He looked to Luther, who also held a letter, then back to Jimmy. "How the hell did you get eleven and I didn't get any. Has to be a mistake!"

Jimmy smiled, happy to be the center of attention. "I guess they like me more," he replied. Jake returned the smile, happy for his friend. The three men sat at a picnic table that overlooked Pearl Harbor, the afternoon breeze a constant friend. The tables rested in neat rows on neatly mowed grass and seemed to be at contrast with the war, an obvious hold-over from more peaceful times. Jake studied Jimmy and the bundle he clutched, but Jimmy didn't seem eager to unfurl the contents and read. He cut his eyes to Luther. Truth was, Jimmy and Luther had become best friends since day-one and Jake envied them. The two would talk at length, and if given the chance they vanished for hours at a time. They didn't need Jake and that must have been how Jimmy felt when Will was still alive. A quick observation of Jimmy and Jake understood. "Okay Luther, let's hear it," Jake said. Luther was happy to oblige though one wouldn't know by his expression. He did, however, open his letter and begin to read.

"Wow," Jake exclaimed once Luther concluded. Luther's father had written something beautiful and reflective and amazing. The letter mixed quotes from the Bible with country colloquialism, bridging life on a farm with love for a child. Luther's Dad had infused God's will with the path and lessons to becoming a man, and the words became a passage from father to son. "Wow," Jake repeated. The three men would eventually get to Jimmy's letters, but for now Jake wanted to hear more.

"Read it again and tell me about home," Jake pleaded. Jake got what he wanted and listened as a man moved from the shadows of life and into the bright autumn sun.

***

Pate counted thirteen letters and let everyone know.

"What are you, the governor of Alabama," Stevenson asked.

"Not yet," Pate replied, "but I'm still young." Pate untied the twine that held the bundle together and the letters spread out like a deck of cards. "That sure is something," Pate added.

Marelli and two other soldiers stood guard at the top of the bunker. Marelli glanced over to Pate. "Yea, it's something," he said. "Now start reading. I have to hear about these people you're always yapping about!"

Pate smiled at the comment. He'd gotten used to Marelli and his harsh view of anyone not from Brooklyn. But then again, when your life depends on someone, you can get used to anything. Pate used his knife to slit one of the letters open before stabbing the blade into the ground next to him. He read the opening line aloud, "To Pate, from Mira, Saul, Father Malone, Alice, and Toke." The smile on his face was shameless.

"So it takes five people from Alabama to write one letter," Marelli quipped.

"When I'm done with mine you can read yours," Pate retorted.

265

Marelli hadn't received any mail and answered, "Nice Carter, real nice."

"Well, because I have so many maybe I'll let you read one of mine," Pate snapped.

Marelli flinched before falling backward into the hole. He lay at Pate's feet, blood pouring from his chest. It was one gunshot... but there was never just one gunshot and within seconds a full-on firefight erupted. Pate dropped the letters into the sand, picked up his helmet and slammed it atop his head as he dove into the bank. He scrambled for his rifle, taking a moment to stare at his friend. Japanese soldiers slipped through openings in the thick underbrush and charged. Gushing from several fronts, the enemy took up positions and returned fire, providing cover as others stormed forward and into a hail of bullets. The four remaining men in Pate's bunker fired, reloaded and fired again.

Men rushed to die as the roar of gunfire drowned the last breath of humanity. The war had always been dire, but the battle for Guadalcanal would be the most dreadful of them all. Rifle barrels heated to the point of scorching, the determination to kill stronger than the will to live. Another salvo and another man in the bunker caught a bullet in the upper chest, the impact driving him backwards and into the opposite bank. He slumped against the embankment, the last of his blood pumping from his body within seconds. Pate yelled for the soldier, but the man never moved. Pate's focus returned to the battle as three enemy soldiers continued their rapid advance. He fired, emptying his rifle yet again, and an enemy soldier tumbled to the ground.

Pate's hand fumbled in his pocket for another clip of ammo as Stevenson and the others continued the attack. Within seconds another enemy had fallen. The lone Japanese soldier drew near and screamed the high-pitched word that all of them scream when charging. But the cry turned guttural as a bullet found his stomach. Air escaped the man's throat as he stumbled forward. With one final purpose in life, the soldier tossed something in the direction of the foxhole before crumpling to the earth. The grenade landed with an unmistakable thud, the ordinance burying an inch deep in the bunker's underbelly. Pate dove just as Stevenson did the same. Stevenson landed first, his torso straddling the grenade, as Pate slammed atop his back.

Chapter 47

The twine went in one opening, around the back and through another opening before crossing under and looping over the first. Toke then cinched the twine tight and began again. There were two large holes in his cast-net, thanks to something submerged behind Willy's bar. Just one throw off the back of Willy's deck and an afternoon of work lay ahead. Toke tossed the hand-line over a tree limb and hoisted the net. He pulled the bottom of the net open and hooked it on a nail in a tree, a few feet away. The cast-net resembled a hula skirt, flared open at the bottom before tapering upward to a thin waist.

Toke finished the patchwork of the hole and stepped back to admire his work. The plastic needle, three-inches long and a half-inch wide, remained in his right hand, the coil of #9 nylon-string nearly gone. Toke smiled and then frowned. The patch was good, but then again the net was nothing but patches. He'd have to sew a new net before long. Toke stepped forward and unhitched the net from the nail and hooked it in a new spot, exposing the second hole. As he opened his pocket knife and began to cut away the frayed and broken ends of webbing, he heard an outboard engine. He listened for a moment before closing the knife and placing it back in his pocket. He headed for the Shell Banks.

The walk to the Shell Banks was only a couple of hundred-yards and Toke made it in time to see a skiff round the point. And no one could mistake the skiff that raced into view or the man steering it. The bright-yellow skiff looked like an enormous banana skimming across the water. Henry Thomas sat on the rear bench... his eyes focused forward, his hand clutching the throttle of the powerful sixteen-horsepower air-cooled engine that roared at top speed. All people from the Bayou liked to show off, this was just a fact, but Henry took it to a whole new level. Toke knew the dumbass and knew his decisions were created by two things. One, he was a dumbass, no way around it. And two, he had left his wife for a younger woman and the middle-aged crisis had affected his dumbass brain. "Dumbass," Toke thought as he studied the boat and its three occupants. He recognized Jim Cowl right off, but didn't know the other. As the skiff turned toward shore, Toke took notice that the man sitting next to Jim was an officer, Army or Navy or something, and his pulse quickened as the tips of his ears began to burn.

Henry slowed the motor and a wave, caused by the boat's wake, raced to catch up with the skiff. The wave lifted the boat on its shoulders and carried it safely to shore. Toke squinted, trying to figure out what was different about Henry. He chuckled, noticing that the sixty-four-year-old man had cut his hair into a crewcut-army-style that all the boys were wearing. "Dumbass," Toke whispered.

As the boat nosed onto shore Jim jumped off, followed by the soldier. Henry killed the engine but never moved. Henry had never lost anything on the Island or had any kin living here, and he'd just as soon see it sink into the Gulf and take everyone with it.

Toke walked to the beach and studied the men, the sincerity upon their faces and the seriousness of their silence. Toke's heart pounded with thundering explosions as they shook hands. The soldier was a captain or colonel or something, Toke didn't know what the insignias on his lapel actually meant, but he understood the cross that covered his pocket.

"Toke," Jim said, "this is Barry Goldman......Army Chaplain."

Toke labored to breathe. He couldn't nod or speak or move...... and he couldn't hold back the tears that were mounting. The only thing he could do was wait on the next words to be spoken, which he knew would be devastating.

***

Although an island, Hawaii looked nothing like Dauphin Island, and although an island the locals were nothing like those back-home. But Jake brushed the differences aside because a new home awaited, the USS Porter (DD-356). The 381' Destroyer rested peacefully along Battleship Row, the American flag at her stern rippling in the wind, her grey bow stamped in yellow with the numbers 356. The lead ship of her class she carried a crew of 194 men and could run at an impressive 35 knots. She was sleek and beautiful and deadly.

The Porter set to sea on October 16, 1942 and Jake never imagined a world so large. Back at school on the Island they had a globe that showed the Pacific Ocean, and though impressive it had its boundaries. But now he understood just how large it truly was, seeing how a ship could run as fast as the Porter for days on end and not see land. "Surely," he thought, "this world is big enough that we don't have to fight over it". But we were fighting over it and by the fifth day the Porter waited just off the coast of the Marshall Islands. She'd soon join Task Force 16, and from there...... the war and the Solomon Islands.

Both Jake and Jimmy had seen plenty of ships back home but could not have imagined the sheer size of an aircraft carrier. The two stood at the stern of the Porter as she merged with Task Force 16. The experience made the hairs on their necks stand as they gazed at the enormity and strength of the USS Hornet and USS Enterprise. The Hornet plowed effortlessly through five-foot seas less than a thousand yards away while the Enterprise could be seen miles off the port. "How does something like that not sink," Jake asked.

Jimmy shook his head. "No idea, but if it floats I'm sure your Dad could pole it across the bay."

Jake responded, "I'm not too sure, but he'd tell you he could." Both men laughed.

***

Palm fronds and cedar limbs brushed against the men as they walked away from the Shell Banks and into the village. They turned right at the crossroads, the walk as somber as pallbearers. Toke shed tears as he and Jim and the Chaplain made their way along the dirt paths of the Island. The day, warm and pleasant and something God certainly planned, never offered any help, never allowing the pain to escape with the breeze.

Toke led the men past his house, the closest one to the Shell Banks, then past the church and to a yard cluttered with engine parts and broken lumber. He pointed to the front door and the men nodded graciously before walking up and knocking. Alice Carter appeared, a screen door separating her and the men. Toke wished he'd never seen the expression upon her face because it would haunt him for the rest of his life. Alice, an ever-timid woman, collapsed before either man could speak. Jim pulled on the screen door and knelt down. He lifted Alice's head. Alice wasn't physically hurt, and Jim nodded to the Chaplain that she had only fainted. But she was hurt, and when Alice awoke her wails ripped at the world.

Julius drove a nail, reattaching a plank along the back of his shed. He spent a lot of time behind the house these days, after all he and his son built a lot of memories there. Julius started another nail, holding it between his fingers while tapping the head with his hammer. He paused, listening, thinking he heard something. Julius dropped the hammer and raced down the side of the house. "Alice," he yelled as he neared the front. Julius slowed, noticing Toke in the yard and then the two men at the door.

Jim Cowl held tight to Alice, her body twitching and fighting to get away. Julius came to a full stop, his expression a painful account of war. He didn't know if he could help his wife... his thoughts reliving the day when he and his son delivered Christmas gifts to the Gorman's. He remembered the smiles on that day and the trip home when his son said, "I love you Dad". He'd give anything to hear it once more.

Toke stepped in Alice's direction and Alice glared at him. Her arms flailed and her feet kicked outward, as if she were trying to kick Toke in the face from fifteen-feet away. Over and over she screamed, now pointing a finger at Toke and wagging it in the air. "He brought them here. He killed my boy! He killed my boy!"

"No," Toke whispered. "No."

Alice continued the mantra that bellowed loud and frantic, "He brought them here! My boy, you killed my little boy!"

As Jim and the Chaplain dragged Alice inside the house, Toke leaned over, placing his hands on his legs just above his knees. "Dear God," he muttered, "why would you allow this." Toke never understood why there had to be so much pain in the world or losses so great, but what he now saw changed him forever. When this war broke out Willy said that he wouldn't let them take his boys. He said he'd seen enough war to realize what it can do to men and families. And only now did Toke understand what it was all about.

Private Daniel Pate Carter died of wounds sustained during the battle of Guadalcanal, on Saturday, October 3, 1942...... the first Saturday of the World Series.

Chapter 48

"Julius," Willy said. Julius sat on a bench in the shed where he and his son had cut thousands of boards over the years. The saw, a few feet from him, sat as silent as Julius, as did the generator just outside the double wooden doors. Sunlight streaked into the room, finding its way between cracks in the planked siding. Darkness mostly covered Julius' face, not unlike his mind and soul. "How you doing? How's Alice?" Willy continued. This visit, just coming here, took a monumental effort on Willy's part. His own desperation had been slowly strangling him over the past months, stealing his existence.

Julius stirred, moving his hands from his lap to his hairline and combing it back. But he said nothing.

Willy understood the silence, he had lived it. Willy's head drooped as he thought of Will and the day he lost him. "It don't get any easier," he said. "I wish I could say it does, but it don't."

"Then why you here," Julius asked.

Willy wiped away a tear as he lifted his head and shrugged his shoulders. "Because it's you."

Julius looked at him expectantly, his eyes sagging at the corners.

"Because we fought our war and we understand these things happen." Willy began to cry, the tears streaking down his cheeks. "Because I lost my son as well." The words were barely audible but he had said them, something he thought he'd never be able to do. "I want you to know that I understand. That I've walked in your shoes and I've seen how hateful the world can be. And that I live with that same hate...... I live with it every God damned day."

Julius held up a hand while shaking his head. "There's nothing anyone can say that's gonna bring my boy back. And there's nothing you can say to ease.... there's just nothing you can say!" Julius looked at the giant saw blade that protruded upwards and between two large planks that skirted each side of the blade. He stared at the blade, reliving all the times he and his son had sawed planks together and the countless hours they'd spent working in silence because of the noise. He wished he could have those times back. "He's my only child and they didn't have the decency to send him home! They buried him on some God-forsaken island!"

Julius' body began to shake, his tears uncontrollable. Willy sat down across from Julius, a dusty spot along the stacks of wooden planks, and quietly cried with his friend.

Chapter 49

No sir, Jake no longer had KP duty...... he was now doing laundry and cleaning heads. Jake folded a towel and placed it on top of the stack. He couldn't believe his luck and figured that if he stayed in the Navy much longer that they'd have him wiping the Admiral's ass. He thought about that and shivered. He folded another towel, the last one, and transferred the pile to a tote. Someone else would take it from there. Jake grunted as he stepped through a bulkhead and into another compartment. The room that held mops and disinfectants was straight ahead, and from there, well...from there the head awaited. He reckoned if every man on this ship had to clean toilets for just one day that their aim would improve. As he reached the storage room, he twisted the handle and swung the door open. He stared at his weapons, trying to decide if he should go with the big guns or just a peashooter. He decided on the peashooters and grabbed toilet brushes and disinfectant. The big gun, the mop, would have to wait until the skirmish with the toilets was over.

The Porter turned hard to port and Jake stumbled sideways. He could hear the engines as they ramped up and the ship pitch forward. Simultaneously, the off-white lights dimmed and a red warning-light began to glow. The intercom came to life with five bursts from a horn. "What the hell," Jake thought. He knew Jimmy was only two compartments away and he wanted nothing more than to get there. Jake paused, realizing that he couldn't leave the compartment. Everyone had a spot and he and his mops were at theirs.

Like the drums of a tribe on the warpath, deep thumps could be heard from the upper deck. The antiaircraft guns ratcheted up, the shells poking holes in the sky. Jimmy was an auxiliary firefighter and rushed towards his designated spot. As for Luther, well he was topside, a gunner's mate, and Jimmy worried. Luther would be in the middle of it all, working as a loader for one of the guns. "Keep your head down," Jimmy said to himself. "And don't be a hero."

It was the morning of October 26, 1942 and the battle for the Santa Cruz Islands had begun.

Sweat ran down and dripped from the tip of Jake's nose, his body anxious and taut. He reflected on the many times he'd been to the beach and the sound of being beneath the water as a large wave rolled you towards shore before breaking onto the sandy beach. The roar of the gulf and the force and energy of a wave was like nothing he had ever known... until now. He heard a "thud," and within seconds the bulkhead of the ship came to life with feverish tremors. As the tremor faded there was another explosion, this one bigger, closer, drowning the sound of the anti-aircraft cannons and forcing the ship to list and mercifully bow down. Jake stumbled and fell into the hull, his shoulder meeting steel. He pushed himself upright, unsure of his next move. The lights, already dim, blinked as if they were giving some kind of signal, telling him to run somewhere, anywhere. A five-hundred-pound bomb penetrated three decks of the carrier Hornet and exploded, and moments later a second bomb exploded on the top deck. Fires raged aboard the carrier, the large hulking ship slowing to a halt as its engines fell silent. The Hornet lay motionless and smoldering and vulnerable.

As rapidly as the percussions traveled the ocean's depths, they ceased. The roar of antiaircraft guns fell silent and only the hum of diesel engines could be heard. The battle cruiser Porter turned sharply and Jake placed his hand to the wall for balance. Moments later the ship slowed to what Jake believed to be a complete stop. The vessel buoyed in the open Pacific, weathering the brilliant blue water that swelled and then rolled beneath its dull grey exterior. Jake relaxed, rubbed at his shoulder and thought about his friends. The hatch door to the next compartment had slammed shut and he swung it open. He ducked his head while stepping over the bulkhead and moved into the next room. He could see the steps that led to the upper deck and Jimmy standing next to them. "Thank God," he said as he ran to his friend.

"I don't like this," Jimmy said. Jimmy tossed Jake a life-vest and Jake slipped it on.

Prior to the attack, aircraft had surged from the deck of the Hornet and headed for the Japanese fleet and the Japanese had done the same, almost simultaneously and in two waves. And as for Jimmy and Jake, they were below deck, blind as bats and biding time in a metal tomb. They had no idea that a second wave was about to strike.

Chapter 50

Jake glared up the stairwell that led outside before turning to Jimmy. "I'd rather be out there," he said.

Jimmy nodded in agreement as antiaircraft guns began to beat once more. But Jimmy knew what to do and replied, "No, we gotta stay put." Jake acknowledged the statement and hunkered down as Jimmy retreated to a nearby firehose-reel.

The Hornet's engines restarted and the ship was under partial power when the second wave of enemy planes hit. The remaining battle-cruisers circled the Hornet, providing cover for the wounded behemoth. Bullets and shells stormed into the face of enemy aircraft as losses mounted on both sides. The onslaught proved enormous and the defense massive. As the battle raged and Japanese bombers were knocked from the sky, an enemy pilot made a desperate attempt. With his plane fully armed, the Japanese pilot aimed for the nearly motionless carrier, ramming headlong into her side. The Hornet, already ablaze, became mortally wounded. The Japanese eventually broke off the attack and the guns fell silent once more.

A squadron of American TBF Avengers neared the Japanese fleet and a group of Zeros soon filled the sky around them. The American torpedo-bombers had little hope against the faster and more agile Japanese fighters and within seconds two bombers were lost and one heavily damaged. As bombers continued to their targets, the damaged plane turned and limped toward the Hornet.

The crippled Avenger was in route and it wouldn't be landing on the Hornet. The Carrier's landing deck was splintered and the ship listed as she took on water. The bomber would be instructed to ditch and the Porter ordered to rescue the airman.

The Avenger pilot decreased his forward speed as the plane glided a few feet above the water. The undercarriage of the plane cut into the top of a wave and the plane jerked forward, the propeller nosediving below the surface. The torpedo, still attached to the bottom of the plane, dislodged during the landing and the bomb did what it had been designed to do. The bomb's propeller engaged and the torpedo bounded forward, speeding toward the ship that had come to its rescue.

The explosion ripped through the hull of the Porter, storming through the ship like an army of angry giants. Jake could feel the instant and searing heat that flashed through the rooms just as he could feel his body being lifted and hurled headlong into a wall. As smoke billowed, thick, choking, and black, the hulking ship rolled to its side and water flooded into its hull. Bulkheads buckled as men raced from the decks below and towards the surface.

"Jake," Jimmy yelled. Jimmy's head pounded, his ears ringing so loudly that he couldn't hear his own words. But he kept yelling as the suffocating black-smoke increased with each passing second. Jimmy stumbled forward and collapsed only a few feet from the stairs that led to safety.

Luther stepped away from the gun and searched for his friends. Men swarmed from the inferno below, crowding the starboard side. They hung onto rails and each other as the ship slipped further into the sea. Luther spun in circles, searching. The battle had been intense and horrific, the sight of the Hornet and other vessels being torn to pieces, and now his friends were missing. Chaos spanned the deck and Luther focused.

The USS Shaw spearheaded towards the Porter and nosed alongside the battered vessel. Men began to leap from the injured ship, some falling into the water, others making it safely across. The Porter listed again and men crowded the rail, fighting for their lives and the man beside them.

Black smoke raced from the decks below, hostile and consuming. Luther turned from the chaos and headed down the stairs that led to the ship's bowels. Smoke strangled Luther's breaths and his eyes burned and watered. As he reached the bottom step he spotted Jimmy, lying in a few inches of water. He reached down and lifted the head of his friend. Jimmy mumbled something as Luther dragged him to the steps and propped him up against its rails. Jimmy's face was the target and Luther's hand caught it square. Jimmy roused. He couldn't believe he was looking into Luther's big brown eyes. He turned his head and pointed in the direction he'd last seen Jake. Luther acknowledged the motion and ran in that direction.

Luther found Jake lying in a small crevice where the steel had buckled and pinched inward. Jake's head gushed and blood streaked across his face. With a serene nature, Luther's body raged against the smoke that tried to claim his life. He lifted Jake's lifeless body and carried it to the stairwell. He lay Jake next to Jimmy, face down, before rolling Jimmy onto his stomach. Luther lay down next to his friends, his body starved of oxygen. Luther breathed, each breath stoking the fire that burned his throat and lungs. His vision waned and all he wanted was to sleep.

Just off starboard, the Shaw's deck lay cluttered with men. Everyone had been rescued from the Porter's deck and the Shaw backed a safe distance away. Smoke from the lower deck of the Porter circled and spiraled in its escape, forming a black obelisk that reached into the heavens. Sailors' sat quiet and motionless, mourning the loss of their ship and crew members. As the Porter inched ever closer to the water's surface, the sinking feeling in their stomachs became as deep as the ocean's depths. Their loss had been devastating, the eerie quiet of a sinking vessel merciless. Luther burst through the black veil, stumbling out from the blinding haze, a man clutched in each hand as if they were suitcases. The deck of the Shaw came to life, a huge roar escaping into the air, men leaping to their feet and each of them cheering and hooping and yelling.

The Porter listed and Luther fell to his knees. He took time to breathe in fresh, God given air before finding the strength to stand. He lifted his friends, their feet dragging the wooden planks of the deck as he carried them away from the smoke and toward the Shaw. The rescue ship reversed its engines and made another advance on the Porter. Men continued to shout and hoot, waving their arms and encouraging Luther in their direction. And they continued until the fireball that raced outward and skyward, blinded the sun. Below, the fire found the ship's magazine and the explosion ripped through the Porter's remains. Wood splintered and steel melted as the bright, instant flash rose like the morning sun.

Fifteen sailors lost their lives on the Porter that day, and 381 Americans in all. The Hornet would be scuttled, destroyed by her own fleet so the Japanese couldn't claim her, and the Porter lost to the sea. When this battle began, the United States had only two carriers in the entire Pacific theater, and the Enterprise, the lone remaining carrier, had suffered her own damages.

Chapter 51

It rained more than an inch the night before and Toke now sat on the center bench of a skiff, using a homemade bailer to swipe at the water that had collected in the bottom. Toke often tended to the boats that moored at the Shell Banks, and today was no different. He collected water again and again and moved from boat to boat. He'd be done shortly and would head home for a nap afterwards.

"Get out," a gruff voice said.

Toke looked up and stared at Julius Carter, his arms filled with a large canvas bag and quilts. "Just being neighborly," Toke replied.

Julius stared at Toke. "Don't matter, leave the water in her" he said. "I just need to get to the other side before she sinks."

Toke's brows closed inward as he sized up Julius' reply. "Is everything okay," he asked.

Julius' face contorted, his jaw clinching tight and his

mouth moving to one side. He looked as if he may cry, or scream, or climb aboard and kill Toke. Julius had been but an apparition since his son's death, he and Alice remaining in their house, doors locked and answering to no one. The Islanders did everything they could to help but nothing worked because nothing mattered. And now, well now Julius stood on the shore while Toke sat on the bench of his skiff wondering what to do. Finally, Toke stood and did as Julius wanted. Julius climbed aboard... stumbling as he did and losing the armful of quilts that fell to the wet bottom. "God damn it," he muttered.

Toke was about to help when Alice walked up from behind. She handed Julius the cloths she carried as well as some framed pictures. As she handed the pictures over, Toke noticed they were of their son including one with him in uniform. "Need any help," Toke asked.

Julius made busy with readying the boat and neither he nor his wife replied.

"Anything I can do."

"You can come along if you want," Julius said.

"What," Toke replied.

"We're not coming back, ever. Do you want to go or not?"

"I can't leave Laura and...." Toke almost said Jake and Mira and the grandbaby, but realized that everything the Carter's were doing surrounded the loss of their child.

287

"No," Julius said. "Just to Cedar Point! You can have the boat cause' I won't be needing it."

"I can't accept that," Toke replied. "I just couldn't."

"So be it," Julius said. "I'll set her adrift once we're across and let God be damned with it!"

Toke shook his head. This was insane. Julius had lived his entire life here and now he was leaving everything. It just couldn't be happening.

The engine to the boat started and Julius gave half a wave as he backed away from shore.

"Wait," Toke yelled. "I won't take the boat but I'll keep it up until you come back for it."

Julius shrugged his shoulders as if it made no difference. Toke waded into knee deep water before catching up to the skiff. He jumped onto the boat's side, his stomach straddling the wooden board that made up its edge. He then swung his feet around and into the boat.

The small boat sped away from Dauphin Island in a rush... a rebellion that Toke never knew existed. But then again he still had his only child.

Chapter 52

Toke looked heavenly, into the bluest sky he'd ever seen, and shuffled sideways along the skiff's narrow deck. He moved no more than six-inches before lowering the oyster rakes back into the water. He was tonging oysters in Dauphin Island Bay and the shallow water afforded use of his short rakes. The stales, handles, were no more than ten-feet long and the steel rake-heads were half the size of a standard set. And everyone referred to the scaled down version as nippers. The only oysterman on the water this time of day, being that oyster catching was a morning job and it now ventured past noon, Toke lowered the nippers to the muddy bottom. He repeated the action dozens of times, digging into the oyster-bed before raising the rakes and dumping shells and mud onto the deck. Toke slept in this morning because of last night when he and Willy stayed up most the night talking. They had dimmed a lantern to the point of snuffing it out, avoiding the blue helmet Gestapo who'd just as soon kick the door in and shoot the place up, and it was the fifth-night this week they'd done so. And truthfully, the world seemed just a little better. But that was last night... and now, well now his bloodshot eyes ached and his head throbbed in the blinding midday sun. Toke cut his eyes to the deck of the skiff, the wooden facade piled high with oysters and mud, the weight causing the bow to tip deep into the water. Soon he'd have to cull the dead shells away and place the live oysters in a sack.

As the sun drifted to late afternoon, Toke decided one more stab at the bottom was in order. Toke dropped the rake-head below the water's surface... he hesitated. A sound, an outboard motor drew his attention. Nearly half a mile from the Shell Banks he could still see Julius' boat, the only one with a motor, and his internal alarms sounded. He twisted to the north and watched as a skiff rounded the point of Little Dauphin Island. As fast as the boat sped, Toke's pulse was even faster.

Toke could see the same three men in the same yellow boat, and he panicked. He hoisted the rakes, water running down the handles and across his hands, and tossed the heavy end, the end with the metal teeth, into the bottom of the skiff. The jagged teeth from the rakes gnawed into wood as the handles flopped against the bench in the center of the skiff. Toke scrambled for his pole and drove it into the bay's muddy bottom. Over and over the pole dug into the bay, Toke doing his best to outrace the motor boat.

Laden with oysters, the bow of Toke's skiff grinded to a halt some ten-feet from shore and he jumped over the side. Jim and the chaplain had since disappeared down a trail by the time Toke sloshed his way onto the sandy beach. He ran. He ran and he hollered, and he prayed the men would hear him and wait. Toke had no choice but to catch the men because no one, especially Laura, should ever have to endure what Alice endured.

But Toke didn't catch the men, he was too late. His time having run short, he stopped along the path that led to his house. He breathed hard, the cool crisp air of mid-November driving his breaths deep into his chest. He bent forward, the palms of his hands resting on his knees, tears welling in his eyes. He lifted his head and watched as the Army Chaplain knocked at his front door before stepping backwards and down the three short steps that made up his front porch. He watched as the screen door opened halfway and Laura's face appeared. He watched as his wife's entire body came into view, the small holes of the screen unable to hide the lines on her face or the terror in her eyes. Toke fell to his knees as the Chaplain spoke, the movement of the man's mouth destroying lifetimes. Laura's right hand went to her mouth, her left trembling. Toke watched as his wife shook her head, seemingly unable to understand. He watched as tears flowed unabated. Laura raised her hand and Toke watched as she pointed down the path and her lips spoke a name. Toke pounded his fist into the sandy earth, his tears crashing to the soil with equal force. "Dear God," he cursed. Toke never heard any of the words, but he knew, and his heart ached because it also knew. The Chaplain thanked Laura with a gracious nod before walking away. Toke struggled to his feet and followed after the two men.

As Toke walked past Laura he only wanted to hold her, somehow believing it would make all this a little easier. But Laura would have to wait, because Mom and Dad needed him more. Ralph, the youngest of the Cullen kids, had died while on patrol in the Ozark Mountains of southwest Missouri.

Chapter 53

The best oysters around could be found in Heron Bay, and Toke needed to get some. "Come on Willy, just a quick trip over in Julius' boat and we'll be back with a barrel in no time," Toke said.

Willy shook his head. "No, I got too much to do and it's too cold out," he replied.

"What about me," Saul said from down the bar.

"Come on Willy, Momma's been in a terrible way since......" Toke hesitated, his own struggles surfacing. He couldn't say it and wouldn't say it, so he moved on. "It's the only thing she likes and I need to get her some good ones!"

Again Willy shook his head.

"I'll go," Saul said.

"Do it for me and Momma," Toke whined.

Again Willy declined.

"I'll help Momma," Saul added.

"Would you pipe down," Toke said to Saul. "I'm trying to get Willy to go to Heron Bay with me."

Saul shuffled down the bar and nosed in close to Toke. "Let's do this for Momma," he said.

"She ain't your Momma," Toke stammered.

"Well she ain't Willy's either," Saul quipped.

Toke and Saul ran at top speed, only slowing as they made their way into Heron Bay. The chill of late November caused Saul's eyes to water and by the time the boat slowed he'd wiped at them enough to soak his sleeve. As the engine died Toke grimaced. A yellow skiff buoyed in the clear water, a half-dozen other boats nearby. "Let's get what we came for and get out," Toke said to Saul. Saul agreed and plunged his rakes into the water.

Henry Thomas stood on the stern of the yellow banana and tonged. He studied Toke and didn't like the fact that he was here, stealing oysters that rightfully belonged to the Bayou. "Good job Toke," Henry shouted.

Toke never acknowledge the bastard and went about with his tonging.

"Takes a big man to swindle a boat from a fella who just lost his son," Henry barked. The men in the other boats laughed and Henry felt like the big shot that he knew he was.

The barb Henry delivered dug deep into Toke and Saul. Julius was a close and dear friend, and his loss no joking matter. "You can shut the hell up," Saul shouted back.

"Sooo... oh Saul wants to play too," Henry quipped. "Well you can kiss my fat ass you piece of Island shit!"

"Come over here and say that," Saul yelled, "and I'll scalp the rest of that goofy looking hair on your head!"

Henry threw his rakes into the bottom of the boat and wrapped the cord around his motor. Perhaps two hundred feet separated the skiffs, and once cranked he'd close the distance within seconds.

"Oh shit," Saul said to Toke, "I think he's coming over!" Not only was Henry coming, but so were the other boats from the Bayou. "Oh shit, oh shit," Saul added, "they're all coming."

Someone from the Bayou picked up an oyster shell and flung it at Toke and Saul, people from the Bayou always started the fights. The shell arced, gliding on the wind and turning into the boat. It slammed against the side, the sharp bill of the shell cutting into the wood.

"Hey you bastard, you could hurt someone," Saul yelled.

The men from the Bayou laughed and began in earnest. Oyster shells came from every direction, one catching Toke across the hand and slicing him open. Saul and Toke returned the salvo but it was useless, there were too many of them. "Let's get the Hell out of here," Saul stammered as he continued with his bombardment.

Toke looked at Henry, who continued the struggle with his motor. Toke prayed he'd have better success as he leaned over and wrapped the cord around the motor.

Blood streaked down his hand and onto the wooden handle at the end of the rope. Toke yanked and the motor revved. It started on the first pull and Toke quickly turned the boat towards home.

As the oyster shells faded in the distance and the boats from the Bayou became nothing more than a hazy silhouette, Toke slowed the boat. The shell had cut deep into his hand and he needed to do something. "Needs stitches," Saul confirmed. Toke winced and shook his head. Saul understood not going for stitches but they needed to stop the bleeding. So Saul tore the sleeve from his shirt and wrapped Toke's hand before cinching the cloth tight. "It'll do until Mira can have a look at it," Saul said.

Toke helped pull the skiff onto the beach with his good hand and he and Saul headed inward. "That motor really saved us," Saul said. "It was a miracle it started on the first pull!"

"You think that's a miracle," Toke exclaimed, "when I first got the boat all I had to do was shake the rope at it and she'd start."

Chapter 54

The wheels squeaked a high-alternating pitch and it annoyed Jimmy to no end. He rolled his wheelchair through the neat row of beds and stopped next to Luther. Luther lay face down on starched white sheets, the back of his legs, arms, and neck a jigsaw puzzle of gauze and blistered and bloody skin. Jimmy studied the bloody bandages and open wounds. Luther endured the daily process of peeling bandages and burned skin from his body, and he ached from the process of healing. This wasn't the first day Jimmy rolled next to his friend, every day had been the same with Luther lying there, never complaining and never crying out from the pain that gripped his body. Plenty of men in the ward agonized over a lot less than Luther, including Jimmy, but then again none of them were Luther.

Jimmy poked Luther in the middle of the back. "Do you feel that," he asked. It seemed to be little consolation that the middle of Luther's back hadn't been burned, his life vest becoming an armament of blessings. When the Porter exploded the fireball burned quick and hot, a searing white flame that engulfed their bodies. But luckily, a term used with deepest regards, they were facing the water when the explosion burst through the deck and they avoided breathing the flames into their lungs. Had they done so they'd have died almost instantly.

Luther mumbled a word that sounded like "no".

"It looks better," Jimmy lied. He'd been lying to Luther since they awoke in the hospital at Pearl. He knew Luther was in bad shape, had overheard the doctors saying that he may never walk again, and he did everything he could to ease Luther's mind. The fire damaged tendons in the back of his legs, and then there was the scarring that would surely come. He stared at the back of Luther's head, along the neck line where thick black hair once trailed downward. He knew Luther needed to know, but wasn't ready to tell him just yet. He just couldn't. The man had given too much when he came back for him and Jake, and for that he'd lost nearly everything. "You'll be up in no time," Jimmy added.

Luther didn't respond as there was nothing he could say.

Jimmy looked out one of the large windows. The panes were opened in an upward position, the rising sun instantly adding warmth to the room. Palms stood long and tall just outside, their morning shadows three-times longer than their height. Jimmy reflected on his fortune, or perhaps a measured sense of self-pity. In any case, he'd been lying close to the deck and on the wayward side of Luther and Jake when the blast occurred, and most of the flames either cleared his body or were blocked by the two men. He couldn't explain it, but he escaped the worst of the injuries... at least the physical ones. His left ear, ankles and calves would take time to heal, but unlike Luther and Jake, he'd heal with little long-term impairment.

The sun continued its morning ritual and the hospital in Pearl brightened with each passing moment. It had been five weeks since the Porter sank and the scars of war needed time to heal while the souls of men would take longer. Luther said something, his face pressed into the white sheet, his muffled voice escaping with his breaths.

"Where's Jake?" Jimmy confirmed.

Luther's head nodded ever so slightly.

"Outside," Jimmy added. "I think he needs more time to accept everything."

Jake sat on a bench and glared into the blue sky, a letter from home clutched in his right hand. The sun's warmth glistened across one side of his face, a callous reminder of who he'd become. The other side of his face couldn't feel the warm rays, the bandages saw to that. The explosion came from Jake's left and his entire left side, down to his ankle, had been severely burned. He looked down to the letter, something he'd read a hundred times in the last week, and grimaced. Jake had spent the first three weeks in a comma and on a morphine drip, and just within the last couple of days did his mind clear. The letter he held was from Mira and it confirmed that he was a father, though he felt nothing like a Dad. Jake touched the bandages on his face, the white gauze hiding his disfigurement.

"You okay," Jimmy said. Jimmy rolled his chair next to Jake and looked out across the landscape. Everything in Hawaii seemed manicured, like a golf course, and the place was beautiful. "Pretty, isn't it," Jimmy added.

Jake said nothing.

"I think Luther's getting better."

This sparked a response from Jake. Jake owed Luther more than he could ever repay, having saved his life and all. And truth be told, he owed Jimmy as well. "I hope he heals all the way," Jake said with little enthusiasm. "At the very least he deserves that."

Jimmy nodded in agreement while waiting for the silence to drift in the breeze. "So you're a Dad," Jimmy finally said.

Jake turned and stared at Jimmy, his one eye struggling with the distance between the two. Jake shook his head. "I don't think I'll ever be a Dad," he said. "I wouldn't want anyone to see me like this, especially my son."

Jimmy shook his head in disgust. "You know," Jimmy said. "I've had enough. Here you are, alive, because of Luther and me...yes, I said me. And poor Luther caught the worst of it and may never even walk again and he ain't complained one bit. And you, well you have a beautiful fiancé and I'm sure she gave birth to a beautiful baby and all you can think about is poor Jake. Well you need to shut the hell up and be a man for once. If Toke was here he'd be ashamed of you, and if Ms. Laura was here she'd put you over her knee... and I'd help! And oh, by the way, what do you think Will or Pate would say if they could see you like this? Now get your ass up and do something about the situation. And if you don't......so help me if you don't.... me and Luther are done with you. We won't be friends with a coward!"

Jake glared at Jimmy but said nothing. Within minutes Jimmy threw his hands in the air before rolling away.

As soon as Jimmy disappeared, Jake uttered what amounted to half a laugh. Yea, his Dad would be plum ashamed and his Mom would be livid. Jake also realized that it could be worse, that he could have lost limbs or his sight...... or even died. But Jimmy didn't understand. When a man changes the way Jake changed, a disfigurement that no one could ever look past, it haunts you. Jimmy was hurt, Jake knew that, but his scars lay hidden from the world and that made a huge difference. Jake continued to stare at the sky, the softness of the clouds causing his mind to drift to Mira and the baby, and Will and Pate. "Pate," he whispered, the breeze of the island carrying the name to some final resting place. Jimmy received a letter from home about the same time as Jake's letter arrived, and Jimmy's Mom had told him about Pate, about how he died fighting at Guadalcanal and how he'd been buried on the island. She said everyone was upset that the Government didn't have the decency to send the men home so their families could be at peace. "God," Jake whispered, "how could they not send Pate home?"

At first Jake didn't know what he needed to do. He stopped at a bed and said a few words to the man lying there. The soldier couldn't respond, his body in traction and his jaw wired shut, but that didn't matter. Jake held the man's hand as he spoke and the man squeezed before Jake moved on. Jake repeated this over and over until he covered the entire ward. He smiled and joked with some and prayed with others. He unburdened his soul and listen as men did in kind. He gave of everything he had but received so much more.

"Well look at this," Jimmy said to Luther.

Luther tried to turn his head but couldn't. Luther muttered something.

"I think we got Jake back," Jimmy said with elation.

Jake had been blessed with one gift in life, the ability to talk, and over the coming weeks he spoke daily with every man who passed through. He wrote letters for those that couldn't and his smile and stories became legendary. The story about Will and the Manger grew to epic proportions and everyone who came through the doors, including nurses and doctors, laughed heartily at Jake's version. Some didn't know whether to believe all the crazy stories he told but they enjoyed them just the same. Jake had found a calling and it meant more to him than his own life.

Jimmy was anxious, like a man on trial who awaited the verdict. He'd been by Luther's side for weeks and been an accomplice to Jake's stories countless times, but he was now being ordered out. He received his orders on November 27, 1942 and he'd be heading home. The war wasn't over for him, after a few months of healing and physical therapy he'd be shipped out once again. But still, he would soon see home.

Now on crutches, Jimmy walked down the aisle once more, stopping alongside Luther's bed for the last time. This time it was different though as Luther sat on his bunk and Jake lay in the bed across from him. The doctors had to remove Jake's left ear due to infection, and his recovery remained slow.

"Looking good," Jake said with a smile.

Jimmy returned the smile, as if it were a warm embrace. "Yea," he said. "I guess it's these dress whites?"

"No," Jake said, his voice softening. "It's the man inside them." Jake truly owed Jimmy, the man who saved his life for a second time. Jimmy had been tough on him, and Jake loved him for it. Jake's face remained disfigured, but when he now looked in the mirror he saw a man that he'd never known. Jake could never recall a time when he felt more alive or more needed, helping men who truly needed help. It was hard to explain, and even harder to imagine, but war terrorized men long after the fighting stopped and they all needed help. "When you get home, kiss Mira and the baby for me."

Jimmy's smile broadened as his eyes filled with tears. But he wasn't ashamed. "I'll kiss everyone for you," he

303

replied.

Luther's size and strength were but a splintered existence of who he used to be, but his recovery had been remarkable. He could even stand and walk with assistance and his prognosis improved with each passing day. Jimmy leaned over and gently hugged Luther's neck. He held to his friend, a man he loved like a brother, and whispered in his ear. Luther smiled and the room seemed a little brighter. And with that, Jimmy said his final goodbyes and left for home.

"What'd he tell you," Jake asked as soon as Jimmy disappeared.

Luther smiled. Luther wasn't one to curse and the words 'darn' or 'heck' defined his limits.

"So he wants you to go home and marry Ruth just to piss her Dad off," Jake reiterated. Both men laughed.

Chapter 55

Jimmy arrived and jubilation erupted, the sight of his parents filling his heart with relief. After hugging and kissing they drove from the train station to the Bayou. As they made their way into the Bayou, goosebumps rippled across Jimmy's arms and legs, and it was fantastic! "Welcome Home" signs and smiling faces dotted the landscape, occupying intersections and front yards. Jimmy stared out the window, waving to those standing along the roadway. "What's all this about," he asked his Dad, his arm tiring as he continued to wave.

Saul sat next to his son in the backseat of Rebecca's car and his Mom sat in the front with Rebecca. Rebecca had been good enough to give them a ride from the station, and from the smile on her face she'd been happy to do so. "You don't know," Saul replied.

Jimmy shook his head.

"You're a hero!" Saul exclaimed.

Jimmy blinked, not understanding.

305

"Jake," Saul continued. "Jake wrote us a letter and told us how you saved his life. How you fought through the smoke and fire to save him!"

Jimmy believed he may cry.

As the car made its way onto Main Street and neared St. Michael's Church, Rebecca sounded the horn. Jimmy couldn't believe so many people had turned out. "Family is family, even if they live in the Bayou," he said to his Dad.

The car pulled into the parking lot of the church and people came from everywhere to shake Jimmy's hand. There were people he didn't know intertwined with family, friends, and even the Mayor. Father Young greeted the youthful faced Jimmy and asked everyone to quiet as he said a prayer for allowing the man to come home safely. Following the prayer, the Mayor said a few words about dedication and sacrifice before they all headed into the building for punch.

As the sun began to set, Julius' motor boat puttered around the point and nosed onto the beach. Jimmy glared at the dozen men who lined the beach, their eager smiles awaiting their hero. Jimmy basked in the moment, the Island, the friends and family, and stood from his seat to take a hearty breath of home. As he struggled to his feet he lost his balance and fell sideways and into the bench. His Mom reached for him but he waived her away. Jimmy neglected to use his crutches, and when the boat buoyed in the tide it proved more than he could handle. "I'm okay," he said as he wriggled to a sitting position.

Half a dozen men carefully hauled Jimmy over the sides of the skiff and onto dry land as the others dragged the boat ashore. Jimmy wanted to walk the path, as he'd done a thousand times, but the tips of his crutches buried in the sand. Someone soon fetched a wagon and the men drove him into town. "Just like a taxi in a big city, ain't it," Peter said as they moved along at a brisk pace. Jimmy laughed and the wagon-train soon pulled into its depot.

The Islanders had cooked and decorated and waited, and now the church erupted into laughter and joy and love. Everyone took care around Jimmy and not everyone hugged him for fear of hurting him. As for Jimmy, well, he enjoyed nearly every second. He knew that not all of it would be pleasant, and the conversation with Toke and Laura proved as difficult as he believed. For the most part he stayed clear of Jake's exact injuries. He felt there was no need to break their hearts before their hearts would truly be broken. So he smiled and assured them that Jake would be fine.

"Will he be home soon," Laura eventually asked.

Jimmy nodded his head. "I think so," he said.

That satisfied Laura, and her and Toke moved along.

Mira waited until the Cullen's said their peace before taking her time with Jimmy. She tilted her head, her eyes fixed on the man of the hour.

Jimmy stared at Mira, and the baby in her arms. And all of it was yet another reminder of how much things had changed.

Mira took two steps and Jimmy stood to greet her. "I was told I have to kiss you," Jimmy said.

A lump formed in Mira's throat and she didn't know if she wanted to laugh or cry. "Okay," she said after a few seconds.

Jimmy admired young Will, rubbing the little hand that poked out from beneath the blanket. "I can't believe Jake is a Dad," he said. "What a mess that's gonna be."

Mira smiled, before passing the baby off to Laura. As soon as Laura strolled away, Mira turned her full attention to Jimmy. "Can we talk," she asked.

Jimmy nodded in understanding and grabbed his crutches as the two headed out the side door. A bench rested in the moonlight, the evening-chill of December a reminder of the gifts God has bestowed. "It's good to feel the cold again," Jimmy said. Jimmy eased onto the bench. With a heavy moan he removed the crutches from beneath his arms and set them aside. He knew this moment would come and hoped he was prepared. Having given lots of thought about what he could say and how he should answer the difficult questions, he waited.

"So," Mira asked.

Jimmy looked upwards, appraising the moon and the stars that rested just outside its aura. He was not prepared for that question. "A little vague," he replied.

Mira wasn't amused but soften to the moment. As much as she needed to know about Jake, Jimmy also suffered. "I'm sorry," she said.

Jimmy smiled warmly and Mira sat on the bench next to him. She held his hand. "I'm so glad you're home," she said. "Ever since Pate and Ralph......"

Jimmy stole a glance and slid sideways. "Ralph," he questioned.

"Oh God," Mira whispered. "You don't know?" Mira told Jimmy what little she knew about Ralph's death, and the moment seemed to steal the radiance of the full moon.

"It's just gonna kill Jake," Jimmy said. "I can't believe it. I just can't."

The night meandered as the faint light from the moon clung to the struggles of life. "So how bad is he," Mira finally asked. She didn't want to know but she had to. Jimmy shook his head, the moon's golden hues softening his thin and rigid features. If it weren't for Jake, Mira may have fallen for a person like Jimmy. He was kind and gentle and compassionate. She loved his compassion, believed in it more than anything, and laid her head on his shoulder.

"The truth?" he asked.

Mira nodded, awaiting the inevitable.

Jimmy hesitated, searching for the right words. "It's not good," he whispered.

Mira pressed her head further against Jimmy's shoulder, as if it were shelter from a ruthless storm.

"His burns have disfigured his left side, including his face." Jimmy took a breath as deep as a canyon. "They

had to remove his left ear just a few days before I left...
infection."

Mira struggled to hold back the tears, hating herself
for asking the question.

"But Jake......" A lump formed in Jimmy's throat as he
spoke. "Well I can't believe who he's become and how
much he's changed!"

Mira didn't want Jake to change. She loved him for
him.

"He understands things that I don't see," Jimmy
added, "and helps anyone who needs help. His days are
filled with laughter and tears and pain and anger, and
somehow he's happy. He's become a man unlike any
man I've ever known."

Mira sat up straight, trying to understand what
Jimmy was telling her.

"I'm telling you, he believes in the human strength
more than anyone, more than a priest. And you may not
believe this....... but he's the real hero because he's
healed more soldiers than any doctor! He's the reason
why wounded men, those who've lost limbs and
friends......." Jimmy shook his head, steering his mind
from all the suffering he'd seen. "Those men have lost
everything and because of Jake they want to wake up in
the morning and live!"

Chapter 56

He needed help stepping off the bus, and the bus driver obliged. As Luther stepped down the three steps, he brushed the metal along the door and grimaced. The ride from San Diego had been excruciating, and he was only in Texarkana Arkansas. Even if a black-indian could hitch a ride, two hours remained. Luther looked upwards, the cloudy sky adding to the cold of January 10, 1943. Luther lifted his bag, resigned to his fate, and hobbled towards the train station.

***

Jake read the letter... it concluded with, "Love, Mom and Dad." But most assuredly his Dad had no hand in it. Jake shook his head before crumpling it into a ball and throwing it to the floor. His thoughts drifted as the paper rolled across the hospital floor, his mind grappling with another loss. Jake had uncles, lots of them, but Ralph had been more like a brother.

***

Luther sat outside the station, awaiting a train that wouldn't come for another two days. He didn't know if he could rent a room and decided he wouldn't even try. So he stood his duffle bag on the bench he sat on and laid his head against the coarse canvas.

***

Jake sat on the edge of a cot and wrote. He listened as an injured man dictated a letter to his girl back in Nebraska. Jake said nothing, doing his best to make it word for word. The young sailor stopped midway through and looked at Jake. "Do you think it's too sappy?" he asked.

Jake thought about it for a moment. "I have a fiancée back home and I write letters like this all the time, and I'm pretty sure she loves 'em. So no, I don't think it's too sappy."

The young man smiled appreciatively and continued.

Doctor Westin entered the ward and made his rounds, nodding to Jake as he did so. As Jake finished writing, the Doctor disappeared down the hall. Jake smiled as he handed the letter to the man and followed after the Doctor.

Jake believed he was healed. The infections were gone and the burns mostly scarred over. Plenty of men had come and gone, including Luther two-weeks earlier, and Jake worried. He worried that he may never go home. So, Jake tapped at the door to Westin's office and the Doc called him in.

Jake sat across from Westin, staring out the window,

across the green grass and water beyond, as the Doctor finished his morning paperwork. "Morning, Jake," Westin said, never looking up. "I'm glad you came by. We have some important things to discuss."

Jake hoped it would be good news.

***

The kiss was sweet and innocent, and Luther blushed from the peck on the cheek. He also woke up. Luther's eyes were as big as silver dollars as he looked up and into the dear eyes of his mother. He shook his head as he noticed his brother and sister close at hand, and just a few feet further stood his Dad alongside the man who started his military service.

Luther sat in the front seat, so he'd have the most room, as the man drove along a winding highway. The drive was mostly quiet, just as Luther liked it, though one question remained. Luther couldn't understand how they knew he'd be in Texarkana so he asked his Dad. John sat directly behind his son and didn't fully hear the question. He asked Luther to repeat and Luther obliged, a bit louder. John removed a letter for his shirt-pocket and passed it over the seat. Luther began to read.

December 26, 1942

Dear Mr. Canfield,

I've only fought in one battle and that's more than any man should have to fight. This war has stolen my generation and many young men, and I don't know that we'll ever be the same. For those of us who've survived

313

our souls have been changed, and I believe mine has changed the most. I wanted to say that your son is a fine man and the most decent person I know. Also, he's the reason I'm still alive. Luther saved my life, along with Jimmy Clark's, and we are eternally grateful.

When our ship was hit, Luther was topside. He could have transferred to another ship and avoided injury, but not our Luther. He came for us, to the decks below and searched until he found us both. We were unconscious and he dragged us out and onto the ship's deck just as it exploded. We all have burns and scars, and I'm sorry to tell you that Luther got the worst of it. There are no words to describe Luther's injuries, so please be as understanding as Luther say's you are. The Lord knows he's suffered more than any of us.

I've spent a lot of time over the past months trying to figure all this out... I don't know that I've succeeded. I talk with the wounded that come through this hospital and what I find most common is that this war and how men fight is often driven by fear. But that's not the case for Luther. His heart is his strength, and it has no room for fear. He is a gentle soul and a man I look upon as a brother.

I've been told that Luther will be leaving Pearl on January 1, 1943 and that he should be in the city of Texarkana in ten to twelve days later. Luther hasn't been told as plans often change for those who are injured. But expect him home soon as Luther is no ordinary man.

A Dear Friend,

Jake Cullen

***

Westin set his pen down and removed his glasses. "How do you feel today," he asked Jake.

"Okay," Jake said hesitantly. "Am I okay?"

Westin smiled. "Yes, I believe you're quite okay. You've healed nicely, and the scars shouldn't limit you much longer."

Jake shifted in his seat and squinted with his right eye, as if his eye was asking the question. "What scars?"

Doctor Westin turned and looked out the window, reassessing his thoughts. "The reason I called you here was to offer you a job. You have an incredible gift that not all of us share."

Jake gave a sideways look but said nothing.

"Jake," Westin continued. "I can mend bodies and treat infections and diseases, but you...you can heal. I envy your ability to bring men back into the light so they can see that not all is lost. Your gift, and it is a wonderful gift, needs to be used so that men can return to their lives."

"What gift," Jake asked.

Westin chuckled even more this time. He knew Jake and his antics...and he knew he had selected the right man for the job. "I've been selfish," Westin said. "I've kept you here because I want you to continue healing others. I want you to look at this as your job. In fact, I've personally spoken with the Secretary of the Navy and requested a position be created just for you. I think it's important and I believe that you feel the same."

Jake took a deep breath, and Mira and Mom and Dad, and even the baby he'd never seen, filled his mind.

"Give it some thought, take a couple of days," Westin said.

"Would I have to work here," Jake asked.

"I'd prefer it," Westin said.

***

For Luther's first Sunday home, Rock Creek Baptist neared capacity. Following the sermon everyone headed upstairs, where a potluck-lunch waited. Luther stared up the narrow stairwell, his Dad alongside him. Within minutes everyone retrieved the meals they'd brought and pews became the food line. Luther enjoyed the home-cooked meal.

Following lunch most of the parishioner's congratulated Luther once more before departing. Luther looked to his father and John shook his head. "Not everyone comes to church these days," John said.

Chapter 57

Three hours. The bus pulled out of New Orleans and headed towards Biloxi and then Mobile. Jake sat against the window, studying the tall pines and magnolias that rushed by. He could see home in the landscape, and he feared what lay ahead. He had a child he'd never seen and the most beautiful fiancé in the world... and yet it was his face and neck and body that made him lose his breath. A spider web-like scar spread from his left eye, covering the side of his face and neck before disappearing beneath his collar. From there it reappeared from beneath his sleeve and down his arm. He understood the world, and far too many times over the past months he noticed the peculiar stares. He imagined that Mira would feel the same way. Jake breathed deep, trying to change his focus to something else. He thought about stepping off the bus and whether anyone would be there to greet him. If someone was there he didn't know if he should hug and kiss the baby first or Mira. And what if Mom and Dad came along, maybe they should be first, or possibly Jimmy for saving his life. "What a mess," he thought. Jake had no way of knowing, but Jimmy was already gone, shipping out two days before he would arrive. Jimmy would serve the remainder of his hitch stateside until his discharge on May 4, 1944.

As the bus pulled into Mobile, Jake peered out his window... not a person in sight. So he stretched his neck and looked out the windows on the opposite side as the brakes squealed and the bus came to a stop. Quite a crowd gathered but not a soul that he recognized.

Jake stepped off the bus, the bright sun abating the chill of early February. The bus had been mostly filled with servicemen, and people all around him were hugging and crying and hanging on for dear life. He worked his way through the crowd and smiled. Julius' car rested in a row with all the others, and standing in front of it was Mom and Dad, Mira and the baby... and Willy. The baby was covered in a blanket and Mira shifted the child in her arms before handing it to Laura. She cried the entire way as she ran to Jake and fell into his arms.

The boat moved at idle speed, a fitting approach. The waters of the bay were calm, only a light breeze nudging them along. Jake held the baby, though he wasn't comfortable with it, and Mira laid her head on his shoulder. The two stared at the baby and his perfect nose and mouth and eyes. He was awake and somehow understanding of the moment. Mira lifted her head and looked into Jake's eyes. Jake turned his head so the scars wouldn't be as noticeable. Mira placed a hand on his chin and guided his face back to hers. She kissed him on the lips.

Dauphin Island towered in the distance and Jake marveled at the beauty. "She hadn't changed," he said to his Dad. Toke said nothing as he steered the boat. Jake handed Mira the baby and stood. "Do you mind," he asked his Dad. Toke smiled brighter than the sun as he killed the engine. Jake lifted the pole from the bottom of the skiff as his Dad took a seat with his Mom. The pole felt good, like the world had returned to its normal self. Jake stabbed the pole into the sandy bottom and shoved.

Jake and Mira weren't yet married and some things on the Island would never change. Until they were wed, Mira would stay at her home and Jake at his. A respectable courtship would take place and nothing more. The Lea's and Cullen's gathered for a quiet dinner on Jake's first night home. Jake had asked for oysters and mullet, and it seemed everyone from the Island brought a plate of each. He couldn't remember the last time he'd eaten so much. "I bet your gonna sleep for a month," Peter said from the opposite side of the table.

"No Sir," Jake replied. "Tomorrow I'm going to work."

Mira twisted sideways in her chair. "You mean fishing," she questioned.

"No," Jake replied. "I have a job to do, so I'm going to work."

Mira wrinkled her nose. "So, what is this job?"

"I work for the VA," Jake said. "I have a job in

Pascagoula at the clinic, helping injured soldiers."

Awestruck, Mira smiled and Jake believed he would melt. "I am so proud of you," she said.

Chapter 58

Jake tapped at the door before pushing it open and poking his head inside. The Lea's sat at the table, dinner in front of them. "Got a sec," Jake asked. Mira smiled and stood from her chair. Jake waved a hand in a downward motion. "Not you," he insisted, "Ms. Bess." Mira frowned at the notion and plopped straight down.

Bess eventually returned to the table, fixed herself another bowl of cabbage and ate in silence, an etched grin on her face.

"Well," Mira questioned.

Bess shrugged and continued with her meal.

"You and Jake meet in secrecy and you're not gonna tell me anything?" Mira added. Bess never answered and Mira ended her pursuit. In truth, Mira was happy about the events because in the weeks since Jake's return this was the first time he'd done something that was Jake like.

Mira wrapped her shoulders with a blanket, the boat

racing across the bay, the morning chill fighting to keep the sun from rising. For weeks she and Jake made the daily pilgrimage and the strain showed. The two would cross over before daylight, Jake would catch a bus to Pascagoula, she would go about her nursing with Doc Meyer's, and they'd return home about dark. And she wasn't through because of the baby.

Mira tied the bow to a pole and stepped off the skiff. Jake kissed her on the cheek and the two went their separate ways. Mira trudged towards the doctor's office and the day that lay ahead. By mid-afternoon Mira finished everything on her docket and headed for the boat. Jake always rode the one o'clock bus and she knew he would be there. Perhaps they would be home early.

Clouds streaked the sky, as if they had decided not to touch each other, and the sun made each one burst with different colors. Jake pulled his coat in tight, took a seat, and waited. Mira showed up early and Jake slid off the tailgate of the truck. "I've had a good month," he said as soon as Mira drew close. "Got any questions?"

Mira listened to the words but could only think it odd that a truck rested along the bank of the bayou.

Mira shrugged her shoulders. "About your month?"

"No," Jake replied. He slapped a hand on the fender of the truck. "About our truck?"

"Our truck?" Mira smiled as she ran a hand down the side of the truck. "Oh, I love it," she squealed before kissing Jake on the lips. "Where... how...."

"One of the doctors sold it to me.... he had no choice," Jake said.

The truck was old and worn and half the things on it didn't work. "It's so pretty," Mira said as she looked through the window and at the interior. She turned to Jake. "No choice?"

Jake smiled, the scar along his lip dragging the smile crooked. "He said I couldn't keep leaving early to catch a bus. Said he wanted me to work the afternoon as well!" Jake's chest swelled with pride.

Mira shook her head and walked away from the vehicle.

As soon as Jake caught up he wrapped an arm around Mira's waist. "It's okay," he said. "I got a good deal."

Mira continued shaking her head. She stopped walking and turned to face Jake. "I can't keep doing this."

Jake stepped back, giving Mira room and time to collect her thoughts.

"I'm dead tired," Mira began. "I don't see the baby as much as I want and I never spend time with you without an outboard-motor drowning the conversation. I just can't do this anymore!"

Jake smiled and Mira thought of walking away. "Well it's a good thing you got me," he said, "because I've taken care of everything."

Mira didn't have the energy for games or riddles,

something every Cullen took pride in. "What is it," she questioned.

"I've rented a house in Alabama Port," Jake said.

"No, we can't, the baby needs..." Mira uttered.

Jake held up a hand. "Please," he said softly. Mira quieted and Jake continued. "We have a house on the mainland to live in, to raise our baby, and we have a truck to take us to Pascagoula, and we have babysitters. And the last loose-end is taken care of." Jake paused, wanting his words to sink in. "Now you can ask all the questions you want."

Mira didn't know what to do, or what question to ask first, so she said, "Let's go home, and you pole so we can talk."

Jake did in fact have everything worked out. The house he rented had an extra bedroom and he'd already spoken to his Mom and Bess and both agreed to babysit, alternating their weeks. The truck was there to take both of them to work, and to Mira's surprise Jake had secured her a job at the VA in Pascagoula. And as for the final detail, Jake took time to speak with Father Malone and the two would be wed this coming Saturday, and following the wedding their child would be christened.

Chapter 59

Clean white linens stretched across each of the sixty-two beds. The first round of soldiers entered at eight in the morning, their wounds dressed, injuries treated, and medications prescribed, and now the next wave made their way to the beds. This process occurred seven days a week at the military ward in Pascagoula Mississippi. Two doctors, nine nurses, twelve orderlies, and Jake Cullen treated those that came here, their post surgeries and post war traumas a stark reminder of the scars that war imposed on its survivors. It was April 5, 1943 and the soldiers that entered the hospital needed these helping hands just to survive.

Jake spoke to a soldier whose leg had been amputated. The man lay on a cot, the sunlight streaming through an open window and lighting the side of his face. The man laughed at something Jake said before casting his eyes downward. Healing the minds of men was never easy, but Jake never gave up. "Got a picture of your girl," he asked the soldier.

The soldier rolled to one side and removed his wallet. He removed a picture and gave it to Jake.

"Quite a looker," Jake said.

The soldier gave half a nod, as if it never really mattered, his eyes fixed on the ceiling.

"It matters," Jake said instinctively. "Look at me," he added. The man continued to gaze at the white ceiling, as if it were some faraway place he longed to visit. "Look at me!" Jake demanded. The man turned his head and looked at Jake. "Do you see me? Do you see the scars?" The man glared at Jake's injuries. "Someone loves me in spite of this! It's a curse that I look at every damn say, but my wife and my Mom and Dad and friends and family don't care about any of it. They see me and the things I've accomplished and believe me... that's plenty good enough. I know you fought your battle and I'm proud that you had the courage to do so, and I ain't gonna lie to you, there are plenty more battles ahead. But the question remains, do you have any courage left?"

Jake and the soldier stared at each other for more than a minute before Jake turned away and looked across the crowded room. Jake held up a hand and whistled. Everyone, including doctors and nurses, paused from what they were doing and turned to look at him. Jake stood as tall as he could, so everyone could see him. He held the picture of the soldier's girl in his hand, the scars on his face and neck no different than many others in the room. "First, don't be too friendly with the nurses," he began, "cause one of them's my wife and they're all so pretty I been thinking about swapping her out."

The group of soldiers laughed.

"But I'll tell you what, as pretty as these nurses are I got a picture of a girl that's even prettier!" The men in the ward looked around the room, assessing the nurses. Jake had been tough on the soldier with the amputated leg, but he now looked down at the man and extended a hand. Jake's voice softened as he directed it at the soldier. "You can help me by helping them," he said. The man nodded in understanding and reached out and took Jake's hand. He stood on his one leg, wobbling as if he were a buoy in a rising tide. "Hang in there," Jake whispered, "I've got you." Jake addressed the crowd yet again. "Now I'm gonna pass this picture around, which belongs to this soldier." Jake held onto the man's belt, steadying him. "Just make sure he gets it back because everyone should have reminders of such a beautiful face." Jake handed the picture to a nearby soldier. The soldier stared at it for a long while before passing it to another soldier. The picture was a hit as men began to jostle for a look, whistling and hooting as the picture made it to them.

The crowd of catcalls grew. "Hey, that's my girl," the soldier with the amputated leg said in defense of his girl. He did however, expose a broad smile.

"Okay," Jake said to the crowd, attempting to quiet them. "I also got a picture of my girl and she ain't too hard on the eyes either. Now I want to see your girl, so get your wallets out because here I come!"

Jake always made a point to speak with every soldier who came through the hospital, but days like this were special. Men liked talking about their girls, and for the ones who didn't have a girl, well... the nurses had become quite proficient at soothing egos.

"Very pretty," Jake said to a soldier, the man lying on his back. The man's leg had also been amputated, just above the knee.

"She's my wife," the man said.

It was the bright smile on the man's face and the pride in his voice that made Jake smile. "You're a lucky man," Jake added before patting the man on the shoulder and moving to the next soldier.

A thin man, no more than twenty years old, sat on one of the cots, his smile telling his story long before Jake ever spoke to him. "I see you got something for me," Jake said as he drew near.

An even bigger smile broke out, red faced and near blushing. The soldier handed Jake his own special picture. It was a poor-quality picture, taken by a home camera, but Jake knew in an instant. Nearly a minute passed, no words, no sounds. Nearly another minute ground-by before the soldier spoke. "Is everything okay?"

Jake couldn't take his eyes from the picture.

"I said, is everything okay?"

Always keen to Jake's needs, Mira watched carefully from the other side of the room as Jake stood motionless and in silence, like a slate of granite.

The soldier reached for his picture, his once smiling face now a barren expanse, when Jake whispered, "Mary."

"Yea," the man replied. "How do you know my Mary?"

Mira walked across the room and now stood next to Jake. She too stared at the picture.

"What," Jake asked the soldier.

"How do you know my Mary?" the soldier repeated.

Mira uttered a word but Jake cut her off. "I don't think I do," he said. "She just looks like someone I use to know. An awful lot like her."

The soldier nodded as Jake returned the picture. "Well... she's really something," the soldier said with pride. "And I'll tell you, if you knew her then you'd never forget her. She's the prettiest thing you ever seen."

"How'd you meet," Mira asked, her voice a kind reminder of the work these nurses did.

The man's smile grew. "When I was overseas Momma took her in. She needed boarders and Mary showed up one day and never left." The man couldn't take his eyes from the picture as he spoke. "Before long Mary was helping with the other boarders, cooking and cleaning." The man looked up, "She's a good cook and hard worker and before you knew it she and Momma were best friends." The man nodded a distant and lonely nod. "I think both of them were lonely. I know Momma was."

"Well she's lovely," Mira said. "Where's she from?"

"Lafourche Parrish," the soldier replied.

"Are you married," Jake asked.

"Not yet, but we're engaged. Soon as I heal up we're gonna tie the knot. Momma already said she'd be proud to have Mary in the family." The man could no longer contain his smile as it seemed to stretch across the room.

"What's her last name," Jake asked.

It seemed like a lot of questions and an awful lot of attention to one girl, but the man never recognized all the probing. "Deneau," he replied.

The ride home always seemed to take longer than it should. The distance from Pascagoula to Alabama Port was only twenty-five miles but the old road and even older truck turned the daily trip into a journey. The sun had set by the time Jake and Mira headed for home and the lights on the front of the Ford struggled to clear a path on this moonless night. Mira drove, as Jake rarely did, and it only added to their relationship. Mira didn't mind driving and liked the control it gave her, and Jake was okay with that.

The two crossed into Alabama, passed through Bayou La Batre, and neared the small house they rented. Neither had spoken since they left the hospital, but both knew the question that lingered between them. "Do you think that was our Mary," Mira finally asked. She downshifted as they approached a small wooden bridge.

"Yea," Jake muttered.

"It wasn't a very good picture. It could have been someone else."

"It was her. I gave her that scar on the chin when.... you know when." Jake was referring to the schoolyard brawl when Mary nearly killed him. "And she had the scars that you and Doc Meyer closed up on her brow and jaw." Jake let that be... not wanting to relive that night. "Well, we both know it was our Mary."

"Maybe it would have been best to tell him the truth," Mira added.

"Mary died," Jake replied. "When she left the Island, she wanted to be dead so she could start over. We need to let her remain at peace. She deserves to be happy."

Mira couldn't see Jake sitting in the seat next to her, the dash light had never worked and blackness stifled the cab, but she could feel his presence and his compassion....and that was all she'd ever need.

Chapter 60

Willy cut his eyes before moving to the table and asking the men what they wanted to drink. "Whiskey," the two replied.

Willy shuffled back to the bar and poured two drinks. He was about to head back over when Toke asked, "What'd they say?" The men were strangers and the Island didn't get many strangers.

Willy twisted his head and Toke did the same, both men scanning the room in silence. Willy cocked a brow and leaned in. "Whiskey," he said with a laugh.

Willy returned to the table and sat the glasses down. He lingered at the table, the men doing most of the talking. After a few minutes Willy returned.

"What'd they say this time," Toke asked with anticipation.

Willy didn't scan the room this time but arched a brow yet again. "The black-haired fella asked about the whiskey, and......"

"And what? Was it about the box," Toke asked. Toke spun on his stool to make sure the box the men brought in with them was still there.

"They didn't say nothing about the box, just what kind of whiskey I gave them and where they could find the Carter's."

"Gracious," Toke added. "Well what'd you tell 'em?"

Willy took in a breath as Toke took in the remainder of his beer. "I told 'em the Carter's left more than a year ago and hadn't been back."

"Hmmm," Toke replied, a thoughtful expression upon his face. "Well what'd you tell them about the whiskey?"

Willy frowned. "What the hell does that matter?"

Toke gave him a peculiar look, as if Willy should have recognized the importance of this question. "Was it the good stuff or the cheap stuff?"

Willy shook his head in disgust before turning to face the back wall of the bar. He stared at the liquors that lined the shelf before turning back to Toke. "I ain't got no good stuff," he said.

"Right," Toke said, "just as I thought."

Willy wanted to laugh but suppressed it. Encouraging Toke was never a good idea.

Toke lifted his beer and brought it to his mouth, his eyes half closed as if he were in deep thought. As soon as he finished the remaining beer, Toke said to Willy, "I need some help."

Willy waited, knowing exactly what the word "help"

meant.

"Set me up with some drinks on the house," Toke said.

Willy rolled his eyes.

"Let's start with two whiskies and two beers."

Willy didn't understand the beers or whiskeys. "Why two beers and two whiskies," he asked.

Toke stood from his stool, shifted the waist of his pants, and righted his cap. "Well," Toke began, "the whiskies are for those two fellas and the first beer is so I'll go over and find out why they're here. As for the second beer, I got a feeling you're gonna want to know what they said."

Willy smiled as he obeyed Toke's request.

Chapter 61

"We don't get many strangers around here," Toke said.

The black-haired man looked at Toke. "Are you Mr. Carter," he asked.

The hairs on the back of Toke's neck stood. He glanced back at Willy and Willy raised a brow while sweeping his hands in a forward motion, prodding Toke on. Toke sat the two whiskies on the table, along with his beer, and pulled up a chair.

Eight whiskies and ten beers later, as well as the usual afternoon crowd that had filed in, Toke had his answer...and Willy was thankful as it was costing him a fortune. The men crowded around the bar as Toke ended the conversation and walked over. "Tough negotiating," he said. No one interrupted, waiting for the next words. "Another round," Toke added, "and I think we'll have our answer."

"Ohhhh," Saul said in disgust. "You ain't doing nothing but drinking all of Willy's liquor!"

"That ain't true... tell 'em Willy," Toke said in his defense.

Willy tilted his head.

"Well you can't get something for nothing," Toke added. Willy gave Toke another round and Toke went back in.

As the sun waned in the late afternoon, so did the conversation. Everyone standing at the bar watched as the man with the black-hair slid the box across the table, the box coming to rest in front of Toke. Toke pulled his hands back and leaned away from the table, as if the box contained the plague. He shook his head as the black-haired man continued to speak. Toke finally relented. The men stood, shook hands, and the strangers left without saying another word.

Toke found his way back to his stool, a defeated expression on his face, and set the box on the bar. He sighed as he took his seat, his head slumping forward, but found enough strength to lift a finger. Willy grimaced as he again placed a beer in front of Toke.

"Well," Peter asked.

"Yea," someone else said.

Toke took a long drink, an exclamation-point to a long conversation. "You may want to sit down," he said to everyone.

Everyone, including Toke, knew that Toke had the only seat at the bar. "Come on," Peter urged. "Tell us what's going on." Everyone in the bar grumbled the same response.

The two men had been in the fox hole the day Pate died. They told Toke the entire story, of how Pate and another man saved their lives, and of how Pate died a hero. Toke told them everything, including what was in the box.

Ever since Will's death, Willy had spent many restless nights... but tonight was different, a different worry filling his mind. He lay awake, thinking about Pate and Julius and Alice. He tossed and turned until about two in the morning when he decided he couldn't just lie there anymore. He had to do something.

Armed with a kerosene lamp, Willy walked to the kitchen table and set the lamp down. After finding the things he needed, he sat at the table and began to write. Willy addressed the letter to the Secretary of the Navy and went on to tell Pate's story and how he died. He concluded with "....and it's important to realize that a man from these parts ain't got nothing but his family and that the same is true for the boy's family because they ain't got nothing but him. A boy grows up here, and on his way to becoming a man he fills his lungs with the warm salt air of the gulf and feels the sand between his toes. It's not something a young man forgets, nor does his yearnings to return home ever stop, no matter where his travels take him. This young man needs to come home, and his family needs him more than you could ever know."

Willy read the letter and then made ten more copies. He'd eventually mail the letters, one at a time over the coming weeks, and he'd continue to make more copies and mail them until someone heard his plea.

Chapter 62

If anyone could help it'd be Doc Meyer, and Toke headed straight for his office. Meyer's nurse greeted Toke and after a polite exchange she disappeared into another room. Within minutes Meyer appeared, donning a smile and a doctor's smock that was just a shade whiter than his thinning hair. "Toke," Doc Meyer said as the two shook hands. "Who's sick?"

"No one," Toke said. "But thanks for seeing me," he added.

Doc Meyer appraised Toke, studying his apprehension and the box he clutched in his hands. "Then what can I do for you?"

Toke smiled, relaxing a bit. "I need to find Julius Carter. Have you heard from him?"

The Doctor nodded, weighing his thoughts. "Yea, I paid a house call on Alice a while back. But I don't think they want to see anyone from the Island. You may want to leave them be."

Toke extended the box, as if he no longer wanted the burden. Doc Meyer stepped back, both men now suddenly apprehensive.

"What is it," Doc Meyer asked.

Toke began poking the box at the Doctor, urging him to take it.

"Okay," the Doctor said.

"Just open it," Toke said.

Doc Meyer moved to the nurse's desk and set it down. He lifted the lid and set it aside, a sadness quieting the room. "They're in Grand Bay," he said without looking up from the box's contents. He replaced the lid.

Grand Bay might as well have been New York City for Toke. He had no car and Grand Bay was the better part of six miles away. "Okay," Toke said appreciatively. "Tell me how to get to his house."

"Hang on," the Doctor said before disappearing into the room from which he entered. He soon reappeared, his smock replaced by an aged green jacket. As they exited the office he grabbed his brown fedora from the hat rack and placed it atop his head.

Julius and Alice had taken up residence on two acres of land that Alice's brother owned. They had a small home, entirely circled by barbed wire. The property looked like it might have been a corral at one time and the nearby barn now serving as a house. Doc Meyer and Toke pulled up to the property's gate and stared at the house. There were no cows and the building stood in disrepair. Broken shingles hung by a thread along the eaves while a hole in the wall, where boards had rotted, gave the appearance of a child who had just lost their first tooth.

"Want me to go with you," Doc Meyer asked.

"No," Toke whispered. Toke sat in the car for a long time before getting out and heading for the house.

After knocking several times, Toke was about to leave when the door creaked open. Julius Carter stood in the open doorway, thin and unshaven. Julius had once been a powerful man, someone to be reckoned with, but not anymore. He looked eighty years old and frail. Julius stared at Toke, as if he'd never seen him before.

"It's me," Toke said. "It's Toke."

"I know who you are," Julius replied. "What do you want?"

Toke took a deep breath, hesitation a rare trait. "I've got something for you," he said. He extended the box.

Julius stepped back, out of the afternoon light and into the shadows of his prison. "I don't want it," he said. "Go away!" Julius slammed the door in Toke's face.

Toke's head drooped and his shoulders slumped. As he stepped off the porch the front door opened yet again. He turned to see Alice standing there. "Toke," Alice said.

The last time Alice had spoken to Toke she became hysterical, screaming over and over that he killed their son. Toke would never forget that awful day.

"Toke," Alice said again, her voice soft and warming.

"How are you Alice," Toke replied.

Alice nodded ever so faintly. "Got some coffee if you want," she said.

Toke smiled and headed into the home.

By the time Toke returned to Doc Meyer's car, the sun had cast its last shadow. "Everything okay," Doc Meyer asked.

"As well as can be expected," Toke said. "But I think it helped."

Toke told the Carter's about the men who brought the box to the Island and how Pate was a hero, a man who saved their lives, and about how they'd never seen such bravery or will ever forget what he did. The soldiers went on to say that as the fighting died that day, they returned to the foxhole and collected Pate's letters and shaving kit and decided that someday they would see that the item got home. It was the least they could do.

As far as anyone knows, neither Julius nor his wife ever returned to the Island. And only on occasion would someone run into them at a market or funeral. I guess this war was like most wars, stealing more than just another young man. It had silenced the Carter's dreams and their memories of a little boy playing in the sand or catching his first fish. For Pate's Mom and Dad, the waves that had majestically rolled onto the beaches of Dauphin Island quieted in the evening sun just as the breezes that once ruffled the branches of the Island's oaks... died to a whisper.

Chapter 63

Laura was sick, sicker than Toke could ever remember, and he worried. If anything ever happened to Laura he just knew he'd never survive... because he wouldn't want to. Toke looked at the rough waters of the bay, the north winds of February 2, 1945 howling across the open expanse. The winds had been steady for three days now and he knew he needed to do something, and soon. He buttoned his coat, turned, and headed for the house. Hell or high-water he was going to get Laura to the other side and to Doc Meyer.

Laura leaned over the side, unable to keep anything down. The boat rocked and swayed as it fought the seas that tried to sink it to the bottom. The boat pitched and Laura slid forward and off her seat. Toke reached for his wife but she held up a hand and repositioned herself. Again she leaned over the side, waves twisting and turning the boat to the point that her face touched the water. If they sunk, the frigid water would see that they'd drown within minutes. Toke's worry grew, but it wasn't the sinking that he feared. Everything, his entire life, had been about Laura.

It was the first time in Toke's life that he was happy to have made it to the Bayou. He quickly secured the boat and helped Laura off. Within minutes they were at the Doctor's office and a nursed rushed Laura into the sole examination room. Toke waited.

By the time the Doctor walked out Toke was a wreck. Doc Meyer smiled and it put Toke somewhat at ease. "So everything's okay," Toke asked.

The Doctor bobbed his head from side to side as if to say yes and no. "Depends on how you look at life," Doc Meyer replied.

"Huh," Toke questioned.

"Sit down," Meyer told Toke. Toke did as requested. "It seems," Doc Meyer began, "that you are a father to be."

Toke fell to the floor... and didn't move.

***

On August 6th, 1945, Laura screamed just as Little Boy did the same.

Nearly everyone on the Island milled about in the Cullen yard as Laura gave birth, it also happened to be the same day that a nation, tired of war and death and of sacrificing, raged against its enemies. While one person entered the world, some seventy-thousand left.

Toke wrenched his hands together, glanced over to Bess and Willy and Peter, then wrenched his hands some more. "You got to quit that," Peter said. "Your gonna ware 'em out before they have a chance to hold the baby."

Toke tried to smile, but the comment only made him more nervous. He didn't like holding babies, afraid he'd somehow hurt them. So he did the only thing he could and tucked his hands beneath his armpits.

Doc Meyer smiled as he and Mira walked out of Toke and Laura's bedroom. Mira headed straight for Jake and the baby and put her arms around the two while Doc Meyer delivered the news. "It's a beautiful, healthy girl," he said.

Toke fell to the floor... and didn't move.

"He'll be okay," the Doctor added. The Doc clutched his bag and headed for the door. "When Toke wakes up tell him to come get me in a week and I'll come back and check on everybody. Come on Jake," he added, "take me home."

The week passed and Doc Meyer rode to the Island with Toke and declared everything okay. After visiting with Laura and the baby he said he had more people to check and headed out of the house. The Doctor spent most of the day on the Island, had lunch with Bess and Peter before visiting a few more people, followed by a quick drink at Willy's, and then back to Toke's before heading to the Shell Banks.

The calm waters of the bay seemed fitting for a boat ride home, and Meyer looked to the sky and smiled. There wasn't a single cloud overhead and the sun breathed with beauty and warmth. "Beautiful day," he yelled at Toke. Toke gave an understanding nod, his hand clutching the throttle on the high-pitched motor. "Make's one happy to be alive," he added.

Toke didn't nod this time, instead he slowed the motor to an idle and listened. "Gunfire," he said to Meyer. "And it's coming from the Bayou." It was now Meyer's turn to nod as Toke revved the engine and streaked north.

By the time Toke killed the engine, shooting was rampant in the Bayou. "Bout' time they figured out who the bad guys were," Toke said. Doc Meyer didn't like the comment, his life was about healing, so he hurried off the skiff and he began running as best he could for a seventy-two-year-old. Toke followed suite and soon they were in downtown Bayou La Batre.

It looked like Mardi Gras had come early. Men, women and children filled the streets, kissing and hugging. Gunshots echoed from all directions and people drank liquor and acted like fools on the open roads. Meyer grabbed hold of a passerby. "What's going on," he asked the man.

"Are you kidding Doc," the man replied. "You haven't heard? The war is over, Japan surrendered! They surrendered!"

It was August 15, 1945.

Chapter 64

When you're itching for a fight, 1941 to 1947 is a long time to wait. But the wait finally ended as the ballgame between the Island and the Bayou resumed. "You ain't dressed," Toke said to Laura.

"Because I ain't going," Laura responded. Laura laid two-year-old Diane on the couch. She stared at her baby as the child drifted off to sleep.

"But you gotta go. We always go," Toke pleaded.

Laura shrugged her shoulders. "No, I ain't gotta go, so I'm not..."

Toke rubbed the back of his neck, slid his cap onto his head, and headed out the door. Laura knew he'd make it back in a day or two and that he'd have a black eye or busted nose and be so stove-up that he won't be able to move for a week.

Toke only stayed one night and was home by dark the next day. Laura had been mostly right as he had a busted nose and lip and could hardly move. But Toke was Toke, and his irrepressible mood rejuvenated the kitchen as he walked in and tossed his hat across the table. "Didn't win, but didn't lose either," he said with a smile.

Laura bathed the baby and only grunted in reply.

"What's for dinner," Toke asked as he made his way to Laura and the baby.

Laura finished with the bath and lifted Diane from the basin of water. She wrapped a towel around the baby and held her tight. "You can have what's left in the bowl," Laura replied.

Toke wrinkled his nose as he looked at the pan of murky water. "No, I think I'll pass on that," he said.

"Your call," Laura added. She handed the baby to Toke and Toke's smile grew.

"You're a pretty baby," Toke said in baby dialect, his voice high and animated. "Yes you are. And I bet you're hungry, aren't you? Yes you are." Toke looked up and to Laura. "She said she's hungry."

Laura suppressed a smile. "Well she can eat at any time," she said.

Toke gave a wry expression. He looked at the baby then back to Laura. "Then I'll have what she's having."

Laura smiled and let out a laugh, she never could stay mad at Toke. She then went to the stove and began to scramble eggs.

Chapter 65

"They're robbing us blind," Saul exclaimed. Willy's bar overflowed with men, angry men.

"We gotta do something," Peter added. The truth was they had to do something but no one knew what that something was. Dauphin Island was changing, and the 1950's saw an unprecedented shift. It seems everyone had a vision of what the Island should be, the only problem being that the ones with the visions weren't from the Island. They were business men and elected officials, and Dauphin Island was going to be sold so it could become a mecca for travelers.

The Islanders' met with officials several times but it seems their voice meant little as survey crews, heavy equipment and a concrete plant were barged to the Island. As work began, hemming the Island in with seawalls, lines were drawn in the sand which meant it was no longer community property. Cattle and goats and most all other livestock were banned because developers knew that no one would spend money where animals could traipse through yards. Above that, a bridge, a roadway that connected the Island to the mainland was on the horizon as was electricity.

Quartered off.... that's why most of the Islanders' complained. Almost everyone lived in the 'village', and along with their houses they were sold the smallest plots on the Island, just fifty-feet wide. Few Islanders ever cared about property or the lines that defined those properties, allowing goats and cattle to roam free just as yard hens scratched and pecked anywhere they chose, but that changed on this day as parcels needed to be sold in order to pave-the-way for prosperity.

"Well what we gonna do," someone asked.

Men continued with the bitching and someone finally said, "Well I'm gonna take my land back. I've had my boat anchored in the same spot since I was a kid and I aim to keep the land that fronts that water." Other men shouted in agreement as the man continued. "I'm gonna go down there and build me a fence out of whatever I can find and make sure my boat is anchored for all to see." Men cheered in agreement as several of them marched out of the bar.

Driftwood, tree stumps, limbs and pine saplings formed a makeshift fence while several skiffs were brought around to the north side of the Island and anchored just off shore. It may not have been the best or fanciest of plans, but at least they were doing something and staking their claims. The men put the final pieces in place and looked at the barrier they had built. They hoped it would be enough.

As daylight broke, the men who'd built the fence and moored their skiffs returned, and the shadows of early morning were unable to hide their pain. The fence had been bulldozed into fragments and their skiffs sunk. All of these men needed their boats just to make ends meet and few had more than a dollar or two to their names let alone enough money to repair their skiffs. The bottoms of the skiffs were smashed and gutted with large chunks of concrete, the boats sent to the bottom of the bay.

There would be other days and other battles but for the native families that had lived here for generations, Dauphin Island was lost.

Chapter 66

In September of 1963 Toke Cullen fell ill. After many visits to many doctors and eventually a specialist, Toke's diagnoses proved unbearable. He had pancreatic cancer. Treatments were prescribed and Toke endured what he could, but by December he'd lost nearly eighty-pounds and a decision was made. There would be no further attempts at finding a cure.

In late-December Willy stopped in to see Toke. Toke lay in his bed and Willy took a chair next to him. The two talked, as they always had, Toke's pain the sole interruption. Exhausted, Toke eventually fell asleep. Willy sat in the chair a bit longer, the struggles of his own life, the years of pain and loss a hard reminder of how he'd reached this point. There's no denying that Toke saved Willy in the months following Will's death, and now, well now the last glimmer of sunlight faded into the dark recesses of his best friend's bedroom. Willy waited a bit longer before reaching into his pocket and retrieving some dollar bills. He tucked them into the fold of Toke's blanket and said his final goodbye. Everyone knew that Laura hadn't worked since Toke became ill and Jake and Diane earned little more than enough to take care of their own families. So everyone who stopped by these days gave what they could, leaving dollars and change and food so the Cullen's could make ends meet.

Toke called out and Diane rushed into the room. Toke tried to smile but it vanished behind his pain. "I want to get up," Toke said to his daughter. Diane was about to remove the blanket and swing his legs around to the edge of the bed but Toke held tight. The cold on this chilly day made him ache that much more.

Diane nodded in understanding. "Still want to get up," she asked.

"Yes," Toke whispered.

Diane brought Toke's legs around and helped him to his feet. Wobbly, Toke and his Daughter held tight. "Want to take a few steps," Diane asked.

Toke nodded, and as he stepped forward the wad of dollars Willy left behind rolled out from the blanket and drifted to the floor. The two of them stared at the money that lay on the wooden boards. "Damn, Diane," Toke muttered, "I'm shittin' greenbacks." The two laughed for a long time before Diane moved him back to his bed.

Toke's decline was swift...his days coming full circle, life to death. Children, grandchildren, brothers and sisters stopped in to say their final goodbyes. Toke could still talk, though it took most of his strength, and he finally asked that they all leave. He didn't want them to remember him this way. With the exception of Laura, the room became void, the lamp on the dresser the lone companion.

It was the evening of January 3, 1964 and Toke and Laura held hands. Toke turned to look at Laura, his face as calm as the waters of Dauphin Island Bay on a windless night, his only concern the wellbeing of his wife. "Tell you what," he whispered and then smiled. "When I get better we'll go fishing. If you pole the skiff then I'll throw the net."

Chapter 67

"Umm, is everything okay?"

Laura's eyes were fixed on something distant, her glare moving past the window pane and fruit trees just outside her kitchen window.

"Mom," Jake added.

Laura turned and looked at her son, a peculiar expression on her face.

"It's okay," Jake said assuredly.

The nod that came from Laura was slight, almost imperceptible. "Yea," she whispered. "Have you seen your Dad," she asked. "He's been fishing and should have been home by now. I'm so worried."

Jake frowned. There were plenty of days were Laura was unable to piece together the fragments of her life. Toke passed away more than twenty years ago and some days Laura believed he'd walk through the door at any minute while other days brought mourning as if he'd just died. Laura's mind believed what it believed and she spent most days crying and worrying. Through trial and error, Jake and his sister eventually discovered that the best answer was to change the subject, to give their Mom a reprieve from the ghost that haunted her soul. "Come on Mom, let's get you taken care of and we'll fix lunch," Jake replied.

Laura never protested, never complained, and never asked why her son was helping her remove two of the three pair of pants she was wearing. The decline had been painful and unimaginable, a desperate struggle for a Mother.

"Now let's get to that lunch," Jake said as he folded the pants and put them in a Chester draw.

"I can do it," Laura protested.

Jake smiled. "Well let me help then."

Laura returned the smile and the two headed to the kitchen. As they fixed lunch and then sat at the table and ate, Laura talked about Toke and her Mom and Dad, and more about Toke, and then she cried. "We're all born," Laura said with near clarity, "and then we die. And along the way we do our best to endure the pain." Those profound words came from somewhere, and until his final days Jake never knew where.

Not so much the physical, but certainly in her mind, life became painful for Laura. She only knew the things that were no longer a part of her life, those moments that had vanished with the sunsets. She could recall sitting in a skiff as Toke poled them across the water before baiting her hook so she could catch a fish. She remembered nights where the breeze filled their bedroom, softening the struggles of a long day and giving her reason to snuggle against the man she so dearly loved. She remembered all the laughter...... and even that added to her sadness. Her life had become memories that Jake couldn't see, and it made him want to cry.

Laura passed in July 1988, before the Alzheimer completely robbed her of the person she'd once been...and perhaps that wasn't all bad. She had lived and loved, married the man of her dreams, had children and grandchildren and spent a lifetime on an island that always seemed to take her breath away. She'd shown compassion and been given the same, enjoyed friends and Church and God and never doubted the kindness of strangers. She had seen beautiful days and taken breaths on warm summer nights. She had walked along the water's edge, her toes sinking into the cool sand, the moments easing her troubles. Life had been precious and meaningful for Laura, and Jake believed that God had shown considerable mercy in her greatest time of need.

The years following Laura's passing seemed to vanish with the morning dew. Islanders came and went, time marching forward as a generation closed their eyes... the call of gulls and lap of waves along the shore but a gentle reminder of their time here. Jimmy married a girl from the Bayou and along with their four kids they lived and loved and shared a life on the Island. He and Jake remained good friends, and when both had time they often spent it together. Jake and Jimmy made trips to

Arkansas to see their dear friend, and not a year went by that the three didn't share a week together or celebrate a marriage or birth of a child. And that leads us to Luther. Luther never married Ruth, Horace saw to that. Soon after Luther's return he uprooted his family and moved them to Houston Texas. But Luther was okay as he met the love of his life while receiving treatments at a VA in New Hope Arkansas. Luther's courage stole a young lady's heart and the two married, had children, and became best friends.

As for Jake and Mira, well their story ends here as well and it ends just as it should...... with two smiling faces and a love that blossomed beneath the warm summer sun.

This is the final book in the Dauphin Island Series... I hope you enjoyed them.

Vaile

For me, this had always been Toke and Laura's story (My Grandparents Charlie and Ora Lee) and a testament to the life they shared.

As for Ora Lee, she loved God and family, and in life she chose to become a Registered Nurse... devoting herself to the Mobile County Board of Health. She delivered countless babies in the rural part of the county and quite a few on the Island. She spent her days driving to those that needed her, and she always brought along more than just medical attention. Whether it was groceries or a few kind words, she always took care of those who had little.... As for Charlie, well he was a lot like the book, happy and joking and mostly carefree. He worked when able, delivering mail to the Island by boat or fishing or tonging oysters, and even spent a few afternoons at Willy's bar, but for the most part his job was simple.... he only had to love the woman he so dearly cherished.

Charlie and Ora Lee spent a lifetime on the Island, much like their parents before them, and to this day they remain side-by-side at the Catholic cemetery.... they wouldn't have had it any other way. As I said, this was their story and their love and their journey that I needed to share. I'm just glad I was given the chance to tell it.

As for Dauphin Island, I hope that story never ends.

Tempered by the water, the seasons are usually mild, often requiring a person to look hard for the signs of change. Citrus and fig trees are common, flourishing in their ideal conditions. Birds migrate through twice a year, making their layover a vibrant spectacle of color and variety. Nowhere on earth are the sights and sounds of so many different birds amplified by the changing of seasons.

During the day the wind sweeps off the crashing surf, filling the air with the unmistakable scent of salt. You can feel it in your hair and on your skin, and when you breathe it deep into your lungs it becomes a part of you. The sun rises and sets with daily magnificence while the moon makes every ripple on the bay dance to a tune so fascinating that it leaves you breathless.

Dauphin Island is graceful and vivid, and has a kindness that never fades. Its history is like a soft breeze that hadn't yet decided its direction, filled with colorful stories that change ever so subtly over time.

Those who have ever been a part of the Island have witnessed its strength, beholding knotted pines that stretch to the sky and centuries old oaks that sprawl in every direction, their roots snaking along the top of the ground and clutching at the sand that is so precious. Natural sand dunes rise swiftly to the south, buffering the harshest winds the gulf can offer while warm sunny days nurture the dense and plush habitation of palmettos and crape myrtles that underlay the inland sanctum.

Waters about the Island's gulf side run deep, with hurriedly paced currents rising and falling with the daily tides, carving and reshaping the land's form. The western point jets to a thin-spiny tip, which over time whips about like a viper's tail. There are vast salt water marshes, submerged sand bars, and of course... endless white-sandy beaches. Turtles and pipers nest as they have for eons on the shoreline while infant shrimp and crab thrive with undeniable ease in the tidal marshes. Here, the cycle of life works quietly, in both beauty and grandeur.

These days Dauphin Island is mostly quiet, circled by good friends...... and a wonderful place to call home.

www.ingramcontent.com/pod-product-compliance
Lightning Source LLC
Chambersburg PA
CBHW051323250626
47155CB00007B/2422